THE LAUGHTER OF DARK GODS

A compilation of stories from Ignorant Armies, Wolf Riders and Red Thirst

THERE WAS A tiny voice of warning within her, which tried to cry 'Daemon!' in such a way as to make her afraid, but the voice seemed to Adalia to be no more than a tiny echo, feeble and forlorn – and if it was the last vestige of that love and adoration which she had once given freely to Shallya, then its insignificance now was clear testimony of the transfer of her loyalty to another power. – *from* **The Light of Transfiguration** *by Brian Craig*

THE BUILDING WAS well lit, but filthy, hissing torches hanging from brackets in the walls. Strange designs had been daubed on the woodwork in brownish red paint, and an intricately carved wooden chest stood on a raised dais at the far end. At first he thought the stringy things hanging from the beams were ropes of some kind; then he got a good look at them, realized the paint wasn't paint, and this time his last meal won the race to escape before he could catch it. – *from* **The Tilean Rat** *by Sandy Mitchell*

SATURATED BY THE *fell magic of Chaos, the Warhammer world is a dark and dangerous place, where dead things walk, and nothing and no one is ever quite what they appear. First published in the early 1980s, these classic tales of action and adventure have been brought together in a new, revised edition which should appeal to all lovers of fantasy fiction.*

More Warhammer from the Black Library

· WARHAMMER FANTASY SHORT STORIES ·

REALM OF CHAOS
eds. Marc Gascoigne & Andy Jones
LORDS OF VALOUR
eds. Marc Gascoigne & Christian Dunn

· GOTREK & FELIX ·

TROLLSLAYER by William King
SKAVENSLAYER by William King
DAEMONSLAYER by William King
DRAGONSLAYER by William King
BEASTSLAYER by William King
VAMPIRESLAYER by William King

· THE VAMPIRE GENEVIEVE ·

DRACHENFELS by Jack Yeovil
GENEVIEVE UNDEAD by Jack Yeovil
BEASTS IN VELVET by Jack Yeovil

· THE KONRAD TRILOGY ·

KONRAD by David Ferring
SHADOWBREED by David Ferring
WARBLADE by David Ferring

· WARHAMMER NOVELS ·

ZAVANT by Gordon Rennie
ZARAGOZ by Brian Craig
THE WINE OF DREAMS by Brian Craig
HAMMERS OF ULRIC by Dan Abnett,
Nik Vincent & James Wallis
GILEAD'S BLOOD by Dan Abnett & Nik Vincent

WARHAMMER FANTASY STORIES

THE LAUGHTER OF DARK GODS

Edited by David Pringle

A BLACK LIBRARY PUBLICATION

Published by the Black Library,
an imprint of Games Workshop Ltd.,
Willow Road, Lenton, Nottingham, NG7 2WS, UK

The Laughter of Dark Gods, The Reavers and the Dead, The Other,
Apprentice Luck and A Gardener in Parravon first published in *Ignorant Armies*,
copyright © GW Books Ltd 1989

The Phantom of Yremy, Cry of the Beast and The Tilean Rat
first published in *Wolf Riders*, copyright © GW Books Ltd 1990

The Song, The Light of Transfiguration and The Spells Below
first published in *Red Thirst*, copyright © GW Books Ltd 1990

First US edition, July 2002

10 9 8 7 6 5 4 3 2 1

Distributed by Simon & Schuster
1230 Avenue of the Americas
New York, NY 10020

Cover illustration by Clint Langley

ISBN 0-7434-4309-8

Set in ITC Giovanni

Printed and bound in Great Britain by
Cox & Wyman Ltd, Cardiff Rd, Reading, Berkshire RG1 8EX, UK

See the Black Library on the Internet at
www.blacklibrary.co.uk

Find out more about Games Workshop
and the world of Warhammer at
www.games-workshop.com

CONTENTS

THE LAUGHTER OF DARK GODS
by William King

FROM THE BACK of his dark horse, Kurt von Diehl stared into the Chaos Wastes. A strange red haze hung over rainbow-coloured ground and the outline of the land seemed to shift like sand-dunes in a breeze.

He turned to look down at Oleg Zaharoff, the last survivor of his original gang. The rat-like little man had followed him all the way from the Empire through the steppes of Kislev to these poisoned lands at the edge of the world. Now their path led clearly out into the desert.

'It's been a long road,' said Zaharoff, 'but we're here.'

Kurt raised his hand and shielded his eyes with one black-gauntleted hand. He drank in the scene. Visions of this place had haunted his dreams ever since he had slain the Chaos warrior and claimed his baroque black armour and his runesword. He rubbed the inlaid skull on his chest-plate thoughtfully.

'Aye. Here hell has touched the earth and men may aspire to godhood. Here we can become masters of our own destiny. I have dreamed about making my way to the uttermost north, to the Black Gate. I will stand before great Khorne and he will grant me power. We will return and claim my inheritance from the brothers who ousted me.'

He spoke as a man speaks when he has a vision in which he does not fully believe, as much to convince himself as to convince any listener. He had his doubts but he pushed them aside. Had not the armour already granted him a measure of the strength of Chaos?

He made himself savour thoughts of his coming revenge. Soon he would reclaim his ancestral lands from the treacherous kinsmen who had banished him to the life of an outlaw.

Guided by the call that had lured him across a hundred leagues, Kurt nudged his steed on down the path. With a last look back towards the lands of men, Oleg Zaharoff followed him.

NIGHT CAME, A darkening of the haze that surrounded them, a flickering of fearful stars in the sky. Far, far to the north a dark aurora danced, staining the sky a deeper, emptier black. They made camp for the night within a ruined building, surrounded by grasping, fungus-covered trees.

'This must have been a farm once, before the last incursion of Chaos,' said Zaharoff. Kurt slumped down against a blackened wall and gazed over at him interestedly. Zaharoff was a Kislevite and knew many tales about the Wastes that bordered his native land, none of them reassuring.

'Two hundred years ago, when the sky last darkened and the hordes of Chaos came, they say that most of northern Kislev was overrun. Magnus the Pious came to my people's aid and the host was driven back. But Chaos did not give up all the ground it had conquered. This must have been part of the overrun land.'

He picked up something, a small doll that had lain where it had been thrown aside. Some freak of this strange land must have preserved it, Kurt decided. Sadly he found himself wondering what had become of its owner.

Shocked by his own weakness, he tried to push the thought aside.

'Soon the horde will march again,' he said. 'We will drown the world in blood.'

Kurt was startled. He had said the words but they were not his own. They seemed to have emerged from some hidden recess of his mind. He felt something lurking back there, had done since the day he put on the armour. He wondered if he was going mad.

Zaharoff gave him a strange look. 'How can you be so sure, Kurt? We don't really know that much about this place. Only what you have dreamed – and that your armour came from here. How can you be sure that we will find what we seek and not death?'

The words echoed too closely Kurt's own darker thoughts. 'I know I am right. Do you doubt me?'

Zaharoff threw the doll to one side. 'Of course not. If you are wrong we have lost everything.'

'Go to sleep, Oleg. Tomorrow you will need your strength. Doubt will only sap it.'

Kurt laid his sword and axe near at hand and closed his eyes. Almost at once he fell into blood-stained dreams. It seemed that he climbed towards some great reward over a mound of ripped and squirming bodies. No matter how fast he climbed he could not reach the top of the pile. A long way above him something huge, with baleful eyes, watched his struggles with amusement.

THE SOUND OF scuttling awoke Kurt. He snapped open his eyes and seized up his weapons. Looking across at Oleg he saw his companion was gazing around in fear.

'They come,' he said. Zaharoff nodded. Von Diehl arose and made towards the entrance. Before he reached it, he saw his way was barred by small bearded figures clad in dark-painted armour and clutching axes and hammers. Their skins were green or white as the bellies of fish from some underground pool. They were the height of children but as broad as a strong man.

Kurt knew they were dwarfs – but seduced to the path of Chaos.

'Khorne has provided us with a sacrifice,' said the leader in a voice as deep as a mine. Kurt beheaded him with one swift stroke, then he leapt among them, striking left and right with sword and axe.

'Blood for the Blood God!' he cried, bellowing out the warcry which echoed through his dreams. 'Skulls for the skull throne!'

He ploughed into the dwarfs like a ship through waves. Behind him he left a trail of red havoc. Small figures fell clutching at the stumps of arms, trying to hold in place jaws that had been sheared from their faces.

Kurt felt unholy joy surge through him, searing through his veins like sweetest poison. It seeped into him from his armour. With every death he felt a little stronger, a little happier. Mad mirth bubbled through him, insane laughter frothed from his lips. He had felt a pale foretaste of this madness in previous battles but here in the Chaos Wastes, under the eerie moons, it was like nectar. He was drunk on battle.

'Kurt, look out!' he heard Oleg cry. He twisted and took the stroke of a hammer on his armoured forearm. His sword fell from numb hands. He saw what Zaharoff had tried to warn him of. Two masked and goggled dwarfs were man-handling a long tube into position, bringing it to bear on him. He punched the hammer wielder in the face, feeling a nose break under the spiked knuckles of his gauntlet, then swung his axe back and threw it. The weapon went spinning through the air and buried itself in the head of the leading dwarf.

The warrior fell backwards, the tube lurched skyward and a gout of flame erupted from its tip. A white-hot sheet of flame blazed past Kurt's face. Something impacted on the structure behind him. The building exploded, the horses whinnied with terror.

He turned to look at the ruins of the old farm. Everyone else did the same for one brief moment. Kurt stooped and picked up his sword. The remaining dwarfs looked at him.

'Chosen of Khorne,' said the nearest one. 'There has been a mistake. We did not realize you were one of the Blood God's champions. Lead us and we will follow.'

He bowed his head to the ground. Kurt was tempted to hack it off, to continue the bloodletting, but he restrained himself. Such followers might be useful.

'Very well,' Kurt said. 'But any treachery and you all die.'

The dwarfs nodded solemnly. Kurt began to laugh until red tears ran down his face. His laughter died in his throat. He pulled off his helmet to check for cuts and he saw Zaharoff start, a look of pure terror crossing his face.

'What is it?' he asked. 'What do you see?'

'Your face, Kurt. It's beginning to change.'

KURT AND HIS warband pushed on further into the Wastes, seeking foes to slay and booty to plunder. Each day as they marched Kurt's face became more twisted, more like that of a beast. At first there was discomfort, then pain, then agony, but he endured it stoically. The dwarfs seemed pleased, taking it as a sign that their master was blessed by the Blood God. Kurt noticed that Oleg could no longer look him in the face.

'What is wrong?' asked Kurt. They were standing atop a butte of wind-sculpted ebony, looking down at a landscape where crystalline flowers bloomed.

In the distance, far to the north, Kurt could see dark clouds gathering.

'Nothing, Kurt. I am uneasy. We have encountered no one for days and a storm is coming from the north. By the look of those clouds it will be no natural tempest.'

'Come, Oleg, you can be honest with me. We have known each other long enough. That is not what worries you.'

Zaharoff looked at him sidelong. Behind them the dwarfs were stowing their gear, pitching small black tents with frames made from carved bone. Zaharoff licked his lips.

'I am troubled. I do not like this place. It is so vast and strange and empty. It could swallow a man and no one would notice he was gone.'

Kurt laughed. 'Having second thoughts? Do you wish to turn back? If you want to return I will not stop you. Go, if you wish to.'

Zaharoff looked back the way they had come. Kurt could tell what he was thinking. He was measuring the length of the way against his chances of survival on his own. To the south something large and black flapped across the red-tinted sky. Zaharoff shook his head, his shoulders slumped.

'I am committed. For good or ill, I will follow you.' His voice was soft and resigned.

Yorri, the dwarf chief, approached. 'Bad storm coming, boss. Best be prepared.'

'I'm going to stay and watch,' said Kurt. The dwarf shrugged and turned to walk away.

OVERHEAD BLACK CLOUDS boiled. The wind roared past, tugging at the fur of his face. Pink lightning lashed down from the sky. He watched the horses buck and leap with fear. They could not break free from the iron pins to which the dwarfs had tethered them. He could see foam on their lips.

Thunder rumbled like the laughter of dark gods. Another bolt of lightning split the sky. The crystal flowers pulsed and flared with many-coloured lights as the bolts landed in the grove. For a moment the after-image of the flash blinded him. When he looked back the grove was transformed. Pale witchfire surrounded the blossoms so that there seemed to be two sets of flowers, of solid crystal and shimmering light. It was a scene of weird, alien beauty.

Among the mesas of the tortured land dark clouds prowled forward like giant monsters. He watched as the dust-clouds swept over the crystal flowers, obscuring their light. Flecks of dust drifted up over the edge of the outcrop on which he stood.

He watched rainbows of dust particles dance and spiral in the air before him. They seemed to trap the energy of the lightning and glittered like fairy lights. Where the dust touched him his face tingled and his armour grew warm to the touch.

Once more the lightning flashed. Exultation filled him. He stood untouched and unafraid in the elemental landscape. It seemed that part of him had come home at last. He raised his sword to the sky. Its runes glowed red as blood. He laughed aloud and his voice was merged with the thunder.

'DAMN DUST GETS everywhere,' said Oleg Zaharoff. 'It's in my hair, my clothes. I think I even swallowed some.'

'The dust is powdered warpstone,' said Yorri. 'Ash from the gatefires that still burn at the northernmost pole, where the fires of hell spill over into the world. Soon changes will start.'

'You mean around here?' asked Oleg.

'The land. Our bodies. What does it matter?' The dwarf cackled.

Oleg smiled crazily. 'I do feel different.'

'Chaos will make us strong,' said Kurt, trying to reassure himself.

A dwarf scuttled closer. He came right up to Kurt. 'Master, we have sighted prey. Coming into the grove of flowers is a warband. By the colour of their armour and the lewdness of their banner I would say they are followers of thrice-accursed Slaanesh.'

At the mention of the name Kurt felt inchoate fury fill him. Visions of slaughter rose unbidden before his eyes. Sweet hate filled him. Ancient enmity lay between Khorne and Slaanesh.

'Prepare your weapons! We will attack them as they leave the grove.' The order had left his lips before he even had time to think.

The dwarf grinned evilly and nodded. Kurt wondered, was it just his imagination or were the slave-dwarfs' teeth growing sharper?

They waited at the edge of the grove where the path ran between two great mesas. The dwarfs grumbled happily in their own tongue. Zaharoff nervously sharpened his weapon until Kurt told him to stop. They crouched behind the shelter of some boulders. Nearby Yorri and his crewman had set up their fire-tube ready to blast the first target that came in sight.

The enemy came slowly into view. They were led by a woman clad in lime-green plate mail. Her yellow and orange hair streamed behind her in the breeze, and she smiled to herself as if in the throes of some secret rapture. Her mount was bipedal, bird-like, with a long snout and deep, human-seeming eyes. The woman carried a huge war banner. Spiked to its top was a child's head above the carven body of a beckoning woman.

A long chain of slender metal links bound a gross, bull-headed giant to the woman's saddle. The minotaur was half-again as tall as Kurt and muscled like a dwarf black-smith. It looked at the woman with adoring, worshipful eyes.

Behind it marched half a dozen beastmen. Each had one exposed female breast, although the rest of their naked bodies were obviously male. At the rear were two twisted elves, clad in thonged black leather and carrying crossbows. When the dwarfs saw them they gibbered excitedly to each other.

Kurt gestured for the dwarfs to be silent. The Slaaneshi moved ever closer, seemingly oblivious to their peril.

'Aazella Silkenthighs,' muttered Yorri. Kurt looked at him. 'She is favoured by the Lord of Pleasure. Beware her whip.'

Kurt nodded and drew his finger across his throat. The dwarf once more fell silent. Kurt gave Aazella his attention. He noticed that behind her the storm had affected the crystal flowers. They had grown to be higher than a man, and seemed thinner and more translucent, like blooms of glazed sugar. Bloated black insects moved over them, gnawing the leaves.

The enemy were no more than a dozen yards from them when the eyes of the impaled head above the banner opened. It licked its lips and spoke in a horrid, lascivious voice: 'Beware, mistress. Foes wait in ambush.'

Kurt leapt to his feet. 'Blood for the Blood God!' he shouted, gesturing his men forward with a motion of his axe.

With a roar, the dwarf tube spat forth its projectile. The missile buried itself in the chest of the man-bull, knocking it from its feet. It fell to the ground, its entrails pouring from its ruined abdomen.

His men raced forward to attack as Kurt charged the woman on her steed. The animal licked out at him with a flickering tongue, long as a rope, glistening stickily. It reminded him of the tongue of a toad. He chopped at it with his runesword, cutting it in two. The beast retracted its stump, whimpering in pain.

He closed and struck it with his axe. The blade failed to bite on the creature's resilient hide. Above him the child's head kept up a babbling stream of obscenities.

Aazella lifted the standard and smashed it into his chest. The blow landed with surprising force and knocked him from his feet. Above him the beast of Slaanesh skittered and danced. Despite the black spots floating before his eyes he managed to roll clear of its talons.

He lashed out with his blade, hamstringing the creature. It fell to one side as he pulled himself to his feet. The woman let go of the standard and rolled from her saddle. With amazing agility she performed a handspring and came to land in a fighting stance, pulling a long metallic whip from her belt.

She licked her red lips, revealing fanged incisors. Then she smiled at him. 'You seek a pleasurable death, warrior. I shall see you writhe in ecstasy before you die.'

'Die, spawn of Slaanesh!' Kurt bellowed, rushing at her. 'Die in the name of Khorne!'

As he invoked his dread lord's name he once more felt the strength of murderous bloodlust flow through him. He aimed a stroke which would have split her in two. She avoided it like a gazelle leaping from a lion's spring, then stuck out a foot, tripping him.

'Clumsy man,' she taunted. 'You'll have to do better.'

He growled like a wild animal and leapt to his feet. This time he advanced towards her more cautiously, feinting gently with his sword, preparing to swing his axe. Somewhere he could hear the voice of a child, taunting him.

He struck with the axe and once more she evaded it. This time she struck at him with her whip. It looped around his throat, blocking his breath. As it completed its last coil, he found himself glaring into serpentine eyes. The head of a snake tipped the lash. It hissed and bit into his cheek.

Knowing he was poisoned drove him to redoubled effort. Determined to at least sacrifice her in the name of his god, he dropped his weapons and with both hands grabbed the whip's metallic line. He jerked her towards him.

So sudden was his move that she did not let go of the weapon but was drawn towards him. He released the whip and grabbed her throat with his mailed hands. He began to tighten his grip.

They fell together like lovers. From the bite in his cheek waves of pure pleasure pulsed, mingling with his berserk hatred. He shut his eyes and squeezed ever harder as the pleasure mounted. It burst inside him as intense as pain and then he knew only darkness and cold.

'WHAT HAPPENED?' KURT heard a deep, gruff voice ask. The words were his own.

He raised thick fingers to his face to feel the fur of his forehead. His arms felt like treetrunks, thick and bloated. His chest felt broader. His voice seemed to rumble from a chasm deep within him.

From off in the distance he could hear an agonized scream which ended in mad, gibbering laughter and a moan of pleasure.

'I thought you were dead, Kurt,' said Oleg. His face drifted into view. It looked blotched and leprous. Two small growths had appeared on his forehead and his shoulder seemed to have a hump on it.

'You're not looking too well, Oleg,' growled Kurt.

'You have been... ill. After you killed the woman, you fell into a feverish swoon. You lay and gibbered for two long days.'

'What happened to her?'

'An unnatural thing. You both fell. Your hands were about her throat. I approached to give her the coup-de-grace but her armour rose from the ground and walked off into the wasteland. Her eyes were closed. I could have sworn she was dead.'

'We have seen the last of her,' boomed Kurt. 'What became of her men?'

'Yorri and the lads ate the beastmen. You can hear the screams of the elves.'

The little man shuddered. 'Truly, Kurt, we are in hell.'

'GREETINGS, BROTHER, WHITHER goest thou?' The speaker was garbed in rune-encrusted plate. A full helmet obscured his face except for reddish glowing eyes. He was tall and thin, predatory-looking as a mantis. Behind him was ranged a force of mangy beastmen. They loomed menacingly against a landscape of redly glowing craters.

Kurt studied the other warrior warily, suspecting treachery. 'I am bound for the deep lands near the Gates.'

'Truly thou art the chosen of Khorne,' said the other mockingly. 'A thousand years ago I spoke similarly. I am sure the Blood God will reward thee suitably.'

'Do not mock me, little man,' said Kurt dangerously.

'I do not mock thee. I envy thy determination. I had not the will to progress further in the service of our dark lord. I fear I was over-cautious. Now I wander these lands forlornly. 'Tis a drab existence.'

Zaharoff spoke. 'You do not seriously expect us to believe this tale? A thousand years!'

The slender warrior laughed. 'Ten years, a century, a millennium, what does it matter? Time flows strangely here at the world's edge. All who dwell within the Wastes learn that eventually.'

'Who are you?' asked Kurt.

'I am Prince Deiter the Unchanging.'

'Kurt von Diehl.'

'May I join thy quest, Sir Kurt? It may prove mildly amusing.'

'I'm not sure I believe in you, prince. A foppish, cowardly servant of Khorne.'

Once more the black prince laughed sweetly. 'You will find, Sir Kurt, that Chaos holds all possibilities. Here nothing is impossible.'

Zaharoff moved closer to Kurt. 'I do not trust this one. Perhaps it would be best to kill him.'

Kurt looked down at him. 'Later. For now he is useful.'

The beastmen fell into ranks beside the dwarfs. Dieter rode beside Kurt. Zaharoff limped along somewhat apart, keeping a cautious eye on their new companions.

THEY TRAVELLED ACROSS what once had been a battlefield. Here lay the bones of thousands of combatants. Rib-cages crunched under the hooves of Kurt's strangely mutating horse.

The dwarfs kicked a goat-horned skull between them, laughing and making coarse jokes.

Over the whole field arced an enormous skeleton. A spine as high as a hill was supported by ribs greater than Imperial oaks. Riding beneath it was like passing below the roof of an enormous hall. After a while even the dwarfs fell silent as the oppressiveness of the place grew.

'The Field of Grax,' remarked Prince Dieter conversationally. 'What a pretty fray that was. The massed hordes of Khorne faced the armies of Tzeentch, the Great Mutator. Sadly we fought near the lair of the dragon Grax. The clash of our arms disturbed his beauty sleep. He was a trifle annoyed when he was roused. I think our lords picked this place deliberately. It was their little joke.'

'I do not like the way you speak of the Dark Powers, prince,' said Kurt. 'It smacks of blasphemy.'

The prince tittered. 'Blasphemy 'gainst the Lords of Chaos, the arch-blasphemers themselves? Thou art a wit, Sir Kurt.'

'I do not jest, prince.'

The prince fell silent and when he spoke again his tone was bleak and absolutely serious. 'Then thou art alone in that here. Even our dark masters enjoy a joke. All thou hast seen here, all the worlds even, exist only for their amusement. The Four Powers seek to while away eternity until even they sink back into the Void Absolute. We are nothing more than their playthings.'

Kurt stared at him, fighting down the urge to draw his sword and slay the strange Chaos warrior. Walking across the field of bones, underneath the spine of the gigantic dragon, he felt dwarfed into insignificance and very alone.

THE SCREAMS OF the dying echoed in his ears. By the light of two bloated moons Kurt fought and slew. He raised his sword and hacked through the dogman's shield. His blow sounded like a blacksmith hitting an anvil. It ended with a pulpy squelch.

They fought against other followers of Khorne, honing their skills, winnowing out the weak.

He looked up and saw the radiant dark aurora in the sky. He shrieked his warcry and drove on towards the remainder of his foes. Nearby he saw Zaharoff gnawing at the throat of one of the dead. Blood stained the downy fur of his face, his eyes were pink and his long hairless tail twitched.

Guiding his horned steed with his knees, Kurt charged towards the enemy banner, hewing down anyone who stood in his way. A great beast, long and hideously canine, snapped at his leg. He wheeled the horse round and brought its hooves thudding down on the creature's head. He leaned forward in the saddle and hacked at the thing with his rune-blade. With a whimper it died.

In the distance he saw Prince Dieter fighting his way through a group of dog-headed soldiers, a long silver blade gleaming in his hands. He showed a delicate skill that seemed out of place in a wearer of the dread black armour of Khorne.

A shock ran through him and he looked down to see another Chaos warrior, a tall helmetless man with the long hair and beard of a Norseman. He frothed at the mouth and gibbered berserkly. His huge hawk-beaked axe had opened a cut in Kurt's leg.

'Blood for the Blood God!' roared the Norseman.

'Only the strong survive,' bellowed Kurt, bringing his own axe down.

The berserker ignored the fact that Kurt had caved in the side of his face and continued to chop away. Kurt smiled in appreciation at the man's bloodlust before cleaving his head clean off. Even after this the Norseman continued to hack away mechanically, lashing around him blindly, chopping into the ranks of his own men.

Red rage mingled with pain as Kurt charged the enemy's standard. At that moment he felt a vast presence loom over him, leering approvingly as he butchered his opponents.

He looked up and briefly thought he saw a gigantic horn-helmed figure silhouetted against the sky. The figure radiated bloodlust and insane approval like a daemonic sun. The feeling of approval increased with every foe Kurt slew.

Invigorated and exalted, he rode down the last few who barred his way, threw his axe at the bearer and snatched up the enemy standard. He broke it one-handed, like a twig. The enemy broke and fled and he rode them down.

'The field is ours!' he cried.

Afterwards, when the killing-lust had gone, he surveyed the field. The tremendous feeling of divine approval had gone and he felt empty. The battlefield seemed meaningless, the triumph hollow. Bodies were strewn everywhere in random patterns, like incomprehensible runes written by an idiotic god. The whole scene was like a painting, two-dimensional and cold. He felt disconnected from it.

He gazed out with empty eyes and for the first time in months found himself thinking of home. To his horror, try as he might, he could not recall what it looked like. The names of the family who had dispossessed him would not come. It was as if he dimly remembered another life. He had to fight back the suspicion that he had died and been reborn in a hell of unending warfare.

Staring at the devolved figure of Zaharoff, ripping haunches of flesh from the dead, revulsion overcame him. He was sick. He heard the trotting of hooves coming ever closer.

Prince Dieter looked at him and surveyed the carnage he had wrought.

'Truly, Kurt, thou art the chosen of Khorne.'

His voice held a mixture of mockery, awe and pity.

'WILL WE NEVER get to the Gates?' asked Kurt, looking back at the warband balefully.

Yorri scratched his head with the claw of his third arm. Zaharoff looked at him and twitched his tail. Kurt noted the red ring that surrounded his mouth.

'We may never reach them,' said Prince Dieter. 'Some say the Gates stretch off into infinity and that a man could ride from now until Khorne's final horn-blast and not reach them.'

'You are a little late in telling us this, prince.'

'It may not be the case. There are many tales about the Chaos Wastes, often contradictory. Sometimes both are true.'

'You speak in riddles.'

Dieter shrugged. 'What one traveller meets, another may not. Distances can stretch and shrink. The stuff of reality itself becomes mutable around the Gates as the raw power of Chaos warps it.'

Kurt stared off across the lake of blood. On it he could see ships of bone. Perhaps their sails were flayed flesh, he mused.

'I have heard it said that around the Gates one enters the dreams of the old Dark Gods, that it is their thoughts that shape the land. And what the traveller meets depends on which Power is in the ascendant.'

'What are the Gates?' asked Zaharoff. Kurt looked at him in surprise. It had been a long time since the little man had shown any interest in their quest. He seemed to have withdrawn into himself.

'They are where the Lords of Chaos enter our world, a doorway from their realm to ours,' said Kurt.

Dieter coughed delicately. 'That may be true but that is not the whole story.'

'Of course thou knowest the whole story,' said Kurt sardonically.

'Some say that one of the mighty sorcerers of old tried to bring daemons here but he got more than he bargained for. Some say that the Gates were a mechanism of the Elder Race known as the Slann, used for their ungodly purposes. The mechanism ran wild and a hole was created through which Chaos came into the world.'

'It was all the fault of elves,' said Yorri.

'It doesn't matter,' said Kurt. 'We will not find our goal by standing here talking.'

'Why dost thou wish to reach them?' asked Dieter.

'It's why I came here,' said Kurt. The trek was the only purpose he could latch on to that made any sort of sense in this terrible realm.

He could see how easy it would be to become like the doomed prince and simply drift from place to place in search of battle. In the realm of the damned, purpose was more precious than jewels.

THEY FOUGHT MORE battles and with every battle Kurt's power grew, and as his power grew so did the number of his followers. To Kurt every day merged into a dream of bloodlust. His life became an endless battle. His ladder to power was made of the bones of fallen enemies.

At Caer Deral, among the burial mounds of long-dead kings, he fought against the followers of the renegade god Malal. Beneath the eyes of a huge stone head he slew the enemy leader, a man whose face was white as milk and whose eyes were red as blood. He tore the albino's heart out with his bare hands and raised it, still pulsing, as an offering to the Blood God. The mark of Khorne's pleasure were the twisted goat horns that sprouted from his head. A company of red-furred beastmen marched from the Wastes to join him.

By the banks of a river of filth he routed the fly-headed followers of Nurgle and would have slain their leader, a gaunt woman on whose skin crawled leeches, had not something vast and soft and deadly risen from the mire and driven him and his men off. Khorne was displeased and Kurt's face changed once more, features running until his nose was two slits over a leech mouth.

After the Siege of the Keep of Malamon, which warriors of Khorne had struggled to take for a century, he rode on his mighty steed through the courtyard to look on the body of the once-mighty sorcerer. Two Chaos marauders had raised the corpse on the end of a pike while the host revelled through the wreckage of the castle. In a pool of the wizard's blood, by the light of blazing torches, he caught sight of himself. He saw a huge and monstrous creature with an ape-like face and tired, lost eyes.

Along with his mind he seemed to be losing even the form of a man, as the corrosive influence of his surroundings worked to transform him.

After that night, he tried to re-dedicate himself to Khorne, to lose himself in the wine of battle and drown out thoughts of his fading humanity in gore.

The host left the Siege of Malamon and swept across the Wastes like fire through dry scrubland. Everything it met died, whether allied with Nurgle, Tzeentch, Slaanesh or Khorne.

Within the councils of its leaders Kurt rose by virtue of his desperate ferocity.

Even among these, most violent of the violent, he stood apart by virtue of his ruthlessness and insane courage. Khorne showered him with rewards and with each gift his humanity seemed to fade, his sick hopelessness to withdraw, to form a small solid kernel buried deep in his mind.

Memories of his homeland, friends and family had all but gone, like old paintings whose pigment has faded to the point of invisibility. He became only dimly aware of the beings about him, seeing them only as victims or slaves. When after one desperate struggle Zaharoff's chittering voice called him 'master' he never gave it a second thought but took his former friend's servitude as his natural due.

Under a blood-red sky he fought with bat-winged daemons until his axe chipped and broke. From the body of a dead knight of Khorne he snatched up a strange and potent weapon, a crossbow which fired bolts of light and whose beams caused the bat-things to shrivel and curl out of existence like leaves in flame.

In a blizzard of ash he struggled against creatures even further down the path of Chaos than himself, amoebic shapes from which protruded stalked eyes and questing orifices. After that his armour fused to his flesh like a second skin. Zaharoff and the dwarfs came ever more to resemble the creatures he had defeated.

The host's casualties mounted and Kurt continued his progression towards its leadership. And everywhere he went Prince Dieter the Unchanging was close behind, his permanent shadow, whispering advice and encouragement and words of ancient, evil wisdom.

Every day Kurt became more aware of the presence of the Blood God in his heart. Every death seemed to bring him closer to his dark deity, every foe vanquished seemed to extinguish some small spark of his humanity and mould him further towards Khorne's ideal.

All his dark passions seemed to fuse and come to the fore. He became unthinking and unrestrained, acting on whim rather than conscious thought.

He lived in a state of permanent barely-restrained frenzy. The slightest infraction of his command, the smallest thing which annoyed him, resulted in someone's death. A warrior only had to glance at him the wrong way to feel the sting of Kurt's weapons.

And yet during all this time a small part of his spirit stood apart and watched what was happening to him with growing horror. Sometimes he would be struck with doubt and feelings of terrible loneliness which all his triumphs could not assuage. Part of him was nauseated by the unending violence that was his life and felt sick guilt at the joy he took in slaughter. It was as if his mind had become host to some malevolent alien creature which he did not understand.

It seemed to him in his more lucid moments, away from the drug of combat, that he had become a divided man, that his soul had become a field over which an unequal battle was being fought between his lust for power and blood and what remained of his humanity. There were times when he found himself contemplating falling on his sword and ending his torment, but such was not the way of Khorne's champions.

Instead he was always first into every skirmish, accepted every challenge to personal combat and chose the mightiest opponents. Invariably he was successful and the gifts of changed body and warped soul that Khorne granted reinforced the dark side of his nature.

THE END CAME swiftly. The host was progressing across a smooth plain towards mountains of glass. Its banners fluttered in a dry, throat-tightening breeze, it advanced in full panoply. Under a standard bearing the skull rune of the Blood God, the army's commanders rode and bickered.

'I say we ride north,' said Kurt, still obeying the command of some half-forgotten impulse. 'There we will find power and foes worthy of our blades.'

'I say we head south and harry the Slaaneshi,' replied Hargul Grimaxe, the army's general.

'I am with Kurt,' said Dieter. The rest of the warriors fell silent. They all sensed the coming conflict. Among the followers of Khorne there could be only one unquestioned leader and there was only one way to settle the issue.

'South,' said Kilgore the Ogre, glaring menacingly at Kurt. Tazelle and Avarone, the other great champions, kept silent. Their followers watched, quiet as huge black statues.

The part of Kurt's mind which still functioned tried to work out how many of the commanders would follow him and what proportion of the army would back him up. Not enough, he decided. Well, so be it.

'North,' bellowed Kurt, swinging up his alien weapon and blasting Hargul. The general's head melted and bubbled away.

'Treachery!' yelled Tazelle. All the warriors drew their weapons.

Battle began under the banner of the Blood God. It was a spark to dry kindling. Behind him Kurt heard the roar of the army's troops. Soon the screams of dying beastmen and mutating man-things reached his ears as the army fell on itself in an orgy of violence.

Old hatreds, made the more intense by being restrained by the discipline of the army, were suddenly unfettered.

Kurt smiled. Khorne would devour many souls this day.

He brought his weapon to bear on the rest of the commanders and pulled the trigger. Two more died under its withering beam before it was smashed from his hand by an axe.

'Blood for the Blood God!' roared Kurt, drawing his sword and hewing around two-handed. He hacked his way to the centre of the group of warriors and seized up the standard. He knew that by instinct the force would rally around its bearer.

Now, as never before, he felt the presence of Khorne. As he touched the banner the laughter of the Blood God seemed to ring in his ears, the shadow of his passing darkened the sky. He was giving his master mighty offerings. Not the weak twisted souls of stunted slaves or mewling men but the spirits of warriors, mighty champions who had much blood on their hands.

He could tell Khorne was pleased.

The sweep of his sword cut down any who came within its arc. He was tireless. Energy seemed to flood into him through the standard, amplifying his strength a hundredfold. He became an engine of destruction driven by daemonic rage. Bodies piled up around him as he destroyed all opposition.

He laughed and the sound of his mirth bubbled out over the battlefield. All who heard it became infected by its madness. In frenzy, they fought anyone near, throwing away shields, ignoring incoming blows in their lust to slay.

Kurt bounded over the pile of bodies and found himself face to face with the four remaining champions, the mightiest warriors of the host: Dieter, Avarone Bloodhawk, Kilgore and Tazelle She-Devil.

With a single blow he beheaded the ogre. He saw the look of astonishment freeze on its face even as it died. Tazelle and Avarone came at him, one from each side. He clubbed Avarone down with the standard, as the woman's blow chopped into the armoured plate of his arm. He felt no pain. It was transmuted into raw energy, a fire that burned in the core of his being. He felt as if his insides were fusing in the heat, that he was being purified in the crucible of battle.

The return sweep of the standard sent Tazelle flying through the air like a broken doll. Within Kurt's chest the searing power seemed to be reforming into something tangible and heavy. He felt himself slowing.

He rushed towards Dieter, seeking to impale him on the horned skull on top of the standard. Dieter stepped aside and let the momentum of Kurt's rush carry him onto his blade. Sparks flew as Dieter's long slender sword bored through Kurt's armour and into his heart.

Kurt stopped and looked down, astonished, at the blade protruding from his chest. Lancing pain passed through him, then he reached out, with a reflex as instinctive as the sting of a dying wasp, and with one twist broke the Unchanging Prince's neck.

'Truly thou art the chosen of Khorne,' he heard Dieter say before he fell to the ground.

Agony lanced through Kurt, pulsing outwards from his chest. It seemed as if molten lead boiled through his veins. Even the energy flowing from the standard was not enough to sustain him. Black spots danced before his eyes and he staggered, holding onto the banner for support.

The sounds of battle receded into the distance and Dieter's words echoed within his head until it seemed that they were echoed by a chanting chorus of bestial voices. At least it was ending, thought the submerged part of him that was still human.

For a moment everything seemed clear and the red fury that had clouded his mind lifted. He looked with fading sight on a battlefield where nothing human stood. Men who had reduced themselves to beasts fought on a plain running with rivers of blood.

Overhead in the sky loomed a titanic figure, larger than mountains, which looked down with a hunger no mortal could comprehend, drinking in the spectacle of its play-things at war, feeding on it, becoming strong.

The chorus of voices in his head became one. It was a voice which held a vast weariness and a vast lust; a voice older than the stars.

'Truly, Kurt, you are the chosen of Khorne,' it said. Blackness flowed over him and a wave of elemental fury drowned his mind. He felt the change begin in his body. The black alien being that had nestled within him, like a wasp's larvae within a caterpillar, was emerging, entering the world through the husk of his body.

The black armour creaked and split asunder. His chest and skull exploded. Wings emerged from the remains of his body like those of a butterfly emerging from a chrysalis. Shaking the blood and filth from itself, the new-born dae-mon gazed adoringly up at its master and pledged itself to an eternity of carnage.

With a mighty leap it soared into the sky. Beneath it, small clusters of warriors still battled on. It drank in the delicious scent of their souls as it rose. Soon it looked down on tiny figures lost in the vast panorama of a landscape laid waste by war and Chaos. It turned north towards the Gates, beyond which lay its new home.

Somewhere in the furthest recesses of its mind, the thing that had once been Kurt von Diehl screamed, knowing that he was truly damned. He was as much a part of the daemon as it had been part of him. He was trapped in the prison of its being, forever.

In the sky the dark god laughed.

THE REAVERS
AND THE DEAD
by Charles Davidson

HELMUT KERZER REALIZED that he was going to die when he saw the ship. He'd seen the sail long before the ship itself was visible, but somehow it had lacked immediacy; it was an abstract warning, not the reality itself. *Here be reavers.* But now the ship itself was visible, a dark hull slicing through the waves less than a mile offshore. The day's catch was still in the nets of the fishing boats, and the village was five scant minutes inland. Helmut felt his guts turn to water as he saw what was about to happen.

The worst element of the situation was the most obvious. Helmut couldn't cover the short distance to the village to warn them, couldn't sound the alarm, and buy time to disperse the young and the ancient into the forest. Because – he gritted his teeth – if he did warn them they would only ask what he had been doing up on Wreckers' Point. And when they found out they would kill him.

The practice of necromancy was not popular in these parts.

Not that Helmut was anything like a full-blown corpse raiser – oh no. He grinned humourlessly at the thought, as he watched the black sail of the pirates draw closer. Dead mice and bats! It was the unhealthy hobby of a youth who would have better spent his time mending nets, not the studied malevolence of a follower of dark knowledge. He looked down and saw, between his feet, the little contraption of skin and ivory that paraded there. The creature had died days ago; it seemed so unfair that it might cost Helmut his home or his life. His cheek twitched in annoyance and the vole fell over, slack and lifeless as any other corpse.

Death. Here on the edge of the Sea of Claws they knew about death. It stared his father in the face every time he put out to sea to snare a living by the whim of Manann; it had taken his grandfather and uncles in a single gulp, to cough them up again, bloated and putrid on the beach three days later.

He'd been a child at the time, too young for the nets and ropes; he'd hidden behind his mother's skirts as she and his father stood stony-faced in the graveyard when they laid three-quarters of the family's menfolk in the ground. It had been then that he'd wondered, for the first time: what if death was like sleep? What if it was possible to return from it, as if awakening to another grey, sea-spumed dawn? But he already knew that they had a word for such thoughts, and he stayed silent.

Wreckers' Point was thickly wooded; shrouded by a dense tangle of trees and dark undergrowth that stretched south towards the great forest.

It was a place of ill omen. In times gone by the wreckers had worked here, lighting beacons to guide rich traders onto the rocks of the headland. They were long departed, hounded by the baron and his men of yesteryear, but the spirit remained; a tight-minded malaise that seemed to turn the day into a washout of greyness, waiting for the night and the lighting of deadly fires. Rumour now had it that the hill was haunted – and the worse for any child who might wander up there.

Helmut gritted his teeth in frustration as he thought about it. His dilemma. That Father Wolfgang might wonder what he was doing, and summon the witch hunters. That some lad might follow him, to see what he did alone and unseen in the undergrowth. That if such a thing happened he might never learn… Fingernails dug into his palms. The anger of denial.

The ship was plainly visible now, rounding the headland and turning towards the beach where the boats lay. Any advantage had been squandered by the beating of his heart. Suddenly he realized that he was terrified; a cold sweat glued his shirt to his back as he thought about red-stained swords glinting in the light of the burning buildings. Reavers! If one of them should look up… could he see me? Feeling exposed, Helmut turned and pushed his way back into the tree-line.

Where was it? Ah yes. The path. A run, really, perhaps the work of a wild boar some time since – there was no spoor, or else Helmut's surreptitious use had scared the animals away.

The path led downhill, at an angle that would miss the village clearing and the highway by more than a bowshot. Helmut trotted, trying to duck and brush beneath the branches in silence. Afraid of betrayal. If anyone sees me… he reminded himself. Warning ritual, a prayer to whatever nameless god watched over him. Going to live forever. Which meant not getting caught.

Another fear gripped him: sick anticipation. That he should not warn the village, that the raiders might catch them all unawares and kill them. He would see his mother and father and young sisters gutted, wall-eyed, flies crawling over black-sticky blood. His family he might spare, but some of the others…

A memory rose to haunt him: Heinrich. Heinrich was a year older than he, and had marched off to join the baron's guard two summers past. Heinrich and two nameless youths tormenting him. Bright light of spring in a meadow back of the inn. Face pointed to the midden as they held his hands behind him. Childish chanting: 'Helmut, Helmut, weakling no-man, eating flies and telling lies, sell his soul to Nurgle's hole.'

Did they mean it? No more than children ever did. But they'd made his life a misery.

The other two meant nothing; but Heinrich had persisted, had appointed himself the dark messenger from the gods, sent to torment Helmut for sins unremembered.

Then he arrived at the far end of the path, and slowed, panting slightly, to look carefully around for intruders. No one else would normally visit this place... but it did no harm to check. He looked around.

No, the graveyard was deserted.

To call it a graveyard was to call the village shrine a cathedral; overstating the facts a little. Tilted, crudely-hacked slabs of slate bore mute witness to the cost of life on the edge of the sea. Moss-grown, age-cracked stones abutted new chunks hacked from the cliff face. *Wee remember Ras Bormann and hys crew, lost these ten days at see.* Canted away from its neighbour by subsidence and the gulf of decades. There was a small, decrepit shrine at one end, and a low wall around it, but nobody came here except for a funeral. Nobody wanted to be reminded. Other than Helmut.

He glanced round swiftly, furtively, then made a dash for the shrine. It was little more than a hovel, with an altar and a rough table on which to lay the coffin; such vestments as the village possessed were kept by Father Wolfgang. But beneath the altar – which now, wheezing slightly, he struggled to move – Helmut had made covert alterations. He'd been twelve when he discovered the ancient priest's hole and found it to his liking. Since then...

RAGNAR ONE-EYE glared more effectively than many a whole-sighted man, even with his patch in place. When he chose to remove it, the contrast – livid wound and burning eye – rooted strong warriors in their boots like grass before a scythe. He was not known as Ten-Slayer for nothing among his followers. He leaned on his axe-haft and waited, knowing where the Rage would take him; red and fast and furious, a tunnel running from his ship to the village of the fisher-folk by way of severed necks and gutted peasants and blood everywhere.

Where Ragnar trod, his bondsmen shivered, the whites of their eyes showing beneath the shadows of their helmets. Wolf-fur cloak and an axe that had shed rivers of gore, and a tread that had made many a foeman's blood turn to water. He stood in the bows as the fast, clinker-built raider ran for the shore, and turned to face his men.

He raised his axe. 'Listen!'

The rays of the twilight sun caught the edge of his blade, flashing feverish highlights in their eyes. 'We go to war, as ever. We will fight, we will loot, we will take honour and booty home when we leave, and the wailing of their women will be nothing in our ears. But this time is not the same.'

He paused. Before him, the shaman was readying his infusion, oblivious to the tension in the warriors around him. The cauldron bubbled as he stirred a handful of ground warpstone into the brew of battle. Ragnar felt a great hollowness in his chest, a lightness in his head as he inhaled the fumes.

'Listen!' he shouted hoarsely. 'The fisher-rats have gone too far. Their desecration offends the gods. Their dark magic has brought famine to our coasts; the fish rot in our nets and the enemies of Ulric walk in the lands of man. This time is different! Let our swords be red and our arms strong as we punish them for their evil!'

A roar answered him. If any of the soldiers had reservations they kept them well concealed. And soon, as soon as the shaman was finished, they would have none.

Ragnar looked down with his one eye, and the shaman looked up. Black eyes glittered in the man's thin, pinched face; he opened his mouth and spoke impassively. 'The sacred brew is ready, lord and master. Will you officiate?'

Ragnar grunted impatiently. 'Yes, by Ulric's blood. Now!'

The priest wordlessly held up the bowl, and a long, small spoon. Ragnar took both, and holding them, intoned: 'Blessed are they who drink the brew of Ulric, for they shall reign supreme in the field of battle, and dying shall experience the delights of heaven. Banish fear and doubt from our hearts and inner reins; make strong our hands to smite the enemy. Let us commence. Wulf!'

Wulf, a hulking lieutenant, stepped forwards. Ragnar raised the spoon to his face; wordlessly Wulf sipped from it, and turned away. A queue formed, in rigid order of rank. Presently, all had drunk from the bowl, and the ship was running through the breakers. Ragnar raised the pot to his face and, glaring out towards the beach, drained the mouthful remaining in it.

The slaughter was about to begin.

MARIA KERZER WAS not a happy woman. She was not old, but time had attacked her savagely. Married young, she had given her husband only one son before the sea stripped his family from him; and that one had grown up sickly and introverted. And her husband's lot had sunk, for when the ship bearing his father and brothers was lost, so was much of their fortune. So he drank, and brooded, and Maria raised chickens and geese and vegetables and prayed that she might yet bear him another son; and meanwhile the years stole up on her with the harsh, scouring winds of the coast.

That evening he returned from the beach early, stern-faced and angry. 'Where's that layabout son of yours?' he demanded, seating himself heavily on the stool by the fireplace where Maria did her spinning.

She shrugged. 'He does as he will, that lad. What's he done now?'

Klaus cast a black look at the door. 'He was to have mended the trawls, but I've not seen hide nor hair of him since noon. Doubtless the dolt's in hiding somewhere. If the net's not sewn he'll not eat, I promise you.'

Maria cast a critical eye at the hearth and poked it with an iron. 'Needs more wood,' she observed.

'Then fetch it yourself. I'll not be trifled with by the whelp!' His indignation vast, he settled down on the stool until it creaked.

Maria wordlessly opened the door and went outside. A few moments later she returned, bearing an armload of branches from the store.

'I smell smoke,' she said. 'Can you believe some man be burning wood outdoors at this time of year?' Her shoulders hunched in disapproval, she bent to place a length of kindling on the fire.

Klaus sighed. 'Woman,' he said, in an altogether softer tone of voice than he had used previously, 'how long have we been married?'

She answered without turning round, 'Twill be a score years next summer.' Still bent, she stirred the kettle of fish soup that hung on chains above the range.

'Tis long enough that I forget the oath that bound me to thee. The boy casts a long shadow.' Maria turned, to see a distraught look cross her husband's face. It gave her pause to wonder. Gloom she saw there often – but sorrow?

He stood up and reached out to take her hands. 'Forgive me,' he said roughly, 'I should not blame you. But the boy…'

'The boy,' she said, 'worries me as well. Not the scribin' stuff he had from Father Wolfgang, but the other.' She shivered. 'Wanderings at night and never there when you call. That fever the other year. And then,' she paused in recollection, 'when we laid the stone for your father. His face itself might have been rock.' She looked up to meet her husband's gaze. 'Good sir, I might rather he'd been some other's than mine.'

Klaus hugged her gently. 'Be that as it may, there might be others yet. And – what's that?'

They stood apart. Carried plainly on the wind was the noise of one bell tolling. There was only one bell in the village; and it only tolled for one reason. *Danger*.

HELMUT FUMBLED THE flint but caught it before it hit the damp floor. A scrape, a spark, and there was a brief flare of light from the tinder that settled down into the thin, yellow glow of a candle. It smoked in the damp air of the crypt. The halo of light caught Helmut's face, casting stark shadows on the walls. He reached up and pulled the altar back into place with a tug; now there was no sign to betray his presence. Gingerly he ducked forwards, then inched down the time-worn steps that led into the bowels of the earth.

Once there had been terror and evil in this crypt, but now there was only the oppressive weight of time, the press of centuries. Helmut knew about the liche. Long ago, decades before some mendicant priest had consecrated this altar to Morr, it had seen sacrifice to another, darker deity. Perhaps time had withered the liche away to dry bones and whispering dust, but in those long-gone days it had struck terror into the hearts of all who passed this isolated headland.

Strange fruit rotted among the branches of the oak trees, and when the flesh of living things had perished the naked bones walked the moonlit earth once more. The sacrifices were not of blood, but of something altogether less innocent. And this was the burial crypt of that source of ancient evil.

Impelled by some sense of urgency he only half comprehended, Helmut headed for the nether reaches of the dark tunnel. It led downwards, dropping a step every yard or so; narrow enough that men might walk in single file only, low enough that their heads must be bowed. Ten yards inside the musty entrance, Helmut passed a pair of niches in either wall. Within them, pathetic and crumbled by time, lay two skeletons wrapped in cerements that had long ago assumed the texture of mummified skin.

The tunnel was now far from the graveyard. Passing the guardian niches, he held the candle before him. The stones had resisted the grinding of roots and the infiltration of damp; the air was dry and musty, the floor thick with dust. As if in a trance he paced out the steps of the mausoleum, descending towards a doorway which suddenly loomed in front of him, oppressive and dark. Pillars to either side were carved into the semblance of twisted mummies, their mouths open in an eternal shriek. With a strange thrill Helmut realized that they might well be real, petrified in their dying terror by the ancient monster within.

This is it, he thought. He'd been here once before, but no further. The closed door with the human jawbone, yellowing with age, that served as a handle. Inviting him in. Is it worth it? He felt a hot flush. Yes! He reached out and grasped the bone, seeing in his mind's eye the battle that rolled chaotically up the beach, already shedding limbs and lives like the skin of some strange and bloody serpent. It was not for him; nothing of the kind. He had a destiny, and it was greater by far than that.

The oak door opened with a screech of dry hinges, and Helmut pushed through. The sight that greeted him held him paralyzed like a rat before a snake, or a priest facing a god. The liche held his eyes with a burning vision, grinning from empty eye sockets above a throne as shapeless as black fire. *Welcome*, it seemed to say in his head; *I've been waiting a long time for you*. Helplessly, he felt himself drawn forward by the deathless bony gaze. And the door closed behind him.

KLAUS KERZER'S FIRST reaction was to protect hearth and home. As Maria stood immobile, hearing the brassy clangour of the bell, he was already reaching for the heirloom which hung in oilcloth above the lintel. He swept it down from its pegs, swiftly unrolling the swaddling of greasy rags that protected the blade from damp. He looked at his wife grimly.

'Smoke you smelt,' he said; 'at high tide, and the bell tolling.' He breathed deeply and pulled the door open. 'Quick woman, rouse out your neighbours! Goodwife Schlagen, the Bissels. Everyone. Get them to the temple and take sanctuary there, or else wherever the rest go. But hide – I fear the reavers are coming.'

Her freeze broke. She embraced him swiftly, tears forming in her eyes. 'Come back to me,' she whispered.

'Go,' he grunted, turning his head away. The sword lay naked on the rough table, edge gleaming and sharp. His throat was dry. Despite his bulk and his brooding temper, Klaus Kerzer was no warrior. The sword merely emphasized how his family's fortunes had sunk over the years. He grunted again, in the back of his throat, then inexpertly took the weapon in both hands. It was long and heavy, and he hoped that he remembered what his father had taught him of its use. Behind him, Maria slipped into the darkness of the night. The bell still clanged mournfully, but now there was no mistaking the noises that carried from the beach on the chill night breeze.

He stepped outside just as the first of Ragnar One-Eye's soldiers reached the village.

OBLIVION'S SWEET AND sickly sea floated Helmut away. It was dark in the crypt, and he knew he slept – no one could, waking, face the liche and not flee screaming – for he sat on a stool that crackled beneath his weight and paid attention to the ancient monster.

Long ago, it seemed to say, *things were not as they are now. The people of this land were not poor fisherfolk and peasants, oppressed by the Imperial nobility and the ravages of war and piracy. Things were better – far better. They had me.* Whether it was truly dead or only half so remained a mystery. But there was no sign of malevolence, nor arrogant disdain; it talked to him quietly, like a friendly uncle or a visiting scholar. As if it sensed an affinity in him, and wished to enlarge upon it.

As he gazed upon the candle-lit skull of the robed and bejewelled corpse that sat, enthroned, against the wall opposite him, Helmut seemed to see visions of that far-gone time. It had been a bright age, golden in colour. The Nameless One had ruled mercifully for centuries from his fastness on the headland, exacting a tax of corpses and little else from his domain. Those who lived there closed their minds and their souls, leaving their mortal remnants to the high one; only foreigners chose to dispute his supremacy.

There had been endless days and endless nights of splendour in his fastness. The elixir of life, served from a golden bowl beneath a chandelier of fingerbones; the butler a black-robed skeleton. The dark studies of the eternal overlord who sought to extend his knowledge into every niche, temporal and spiritual, from pole to pole. The searing light of dawn, seen by eyes grown too sensitive for daylight but which yet anticipated a billion tomorrows. His Nameless splendour had ruled for five hundred years while all around him were little more than barbarians.

There came a time, the undead thing seemed to say, *when the burden became tiresome. When night alone was sufficient for me, and I chose to sleep, and meditate, for I had much to think upon. I had lived a hundred lifespans, and it happened so that I barely noticed the decline of my powers.* It grinned at him from the shadows. Helmut grinned back, lips curled in a rictus of fear and longing. Shapes speared out of the darkness to either side of the liche's throne; edges of boxes, a lectern, great leather-bound books clasped shut with bony locks. *I have been waiting a long time for my heir,* the skeleton stated in a silent voice which seemed as dry as the desert sands of Araby.

'Yes.' Helmut was surprised to hear his own voice, itself as dull as the rocks around him. 'Yes,' he repeated. How did you know? he asked. How did you know what I wanted? What I was afraid of? It seemed so right, to him, that he should be chosen. Heir to, to…?

The dominion. The dominion of Helmut Kerzer, necromancer. Yes, that was it.

'I accept,' he said, and although the corpse stayed seated in frozen splendour, a wind seemed to blow through the chamber. His candle guttered and died, but he didn't need it any more; Helmut saw with a clarity he had never known before. Behind the throne lay a flight of steps leading down, down to the rooms and abode and workshops of the Nameless One. Down to his new home. It had been waiting patiently for him, or for someone like him, for many centuries.

A feverish exaltation coursed through Helmut's blood; there was much for him to do, much that would need preparing afresh. Knowledge to be gained, books to be read, unspecified tasks to be carried out. As he pushed eagerly past the throne, its skeletal ruler slumped with a brittle crackle of time: dust rose in final release. It would be years before Helmut came to understand the nature of the spell he had succumbed to, and by then it would be far too late to escape. For now he was blinded by the promise of dark things.

FIRST THEY CAME ashore; then they burned the fisherfolk's boats as they found them. Horst the Hairless was still there, bundling his nets for the morrow, and he remained there afterwards, albeit with half his brains in his lap and the flies buzzing huge and hungry around him. Ragnar One-Eye voiced a wordless, ululating battle-cry; hefting his axe, he led a stream of soldiers up the trail towards the village.

'Forward and kill them!' he roared. 'Take what you want and torch the rest. Leave none behind!' Succinct; and, more to the point, exactly what the men wanted to hear. The fury of the battle brew was upon them, and they were in no mood for restraint. They charged towards the village in a stream of iron.

Ahead of them, Klaus Kerzer heard Horst's death-cry and Ragnar's deep voice. Shocked into a slow run, he made for the village hall. 'Foe! Fire! Murder!' he shouted raucously at the top of his lungs.

As Klaus staggered up the track, one of the foemen hit him with a thrown dagger. Shock and pain seared through him, and he fell heavily. As he lay groaning in the dirt, the raider paused to finish him off; but, unexpectedly, Klaus caught the reaver in the hamstrings with a desperate sweep of the heirloom sword, and the man fell cursing to the ground. With a gasp, Klaus raised the aged sword again, but this time the younger and more experienced fighter was far too quick for him: the reaver stabbed the older man in the throat, and Klaus's life began to bubble away. The sword fell at his side.

Klaus's yells, added to the mournful tolling of the bell, had brought the angry, frightened fisherfolk swarming out of their hovels. Some of them bore scythes and other farm implements of dubious vintage; one or two of the richer ones possessed genuine weapons, but none were armoured or trained, and collectively they were a pathetic match for the raiders.

The villagers milled around in front of the hall, incapable of forming any sort of battle order. The local priest had turned out, but there was no sign of real authority; no lord or knight to muster a defence around himself. The berserkers laid in with a will, hacking negligently at the terrified peasants. Ragnar snarled wordlessly, his axe-blade dripping; he was truly in his element. The ruddy glare of fire added a surreal element to the scene as one of the thatch-roofed cottages caught alight. Whether the blaze had been started deliberately or by accident was irrelevant – it spread rapidly, leaping from roof to roof like a ravenous beast on the prowl. The crackling roar thrummed through Ragnar's blood, heating his battle-fury to the boil.

Fleeing women and children fell victim to the raiders. A party led by one Snorri Red-Hair came upon a group of them from behind. Blood flew and screaming rent the air, as terrible as in any slaughterhouse.

Klaus Kerzer had been one of the first villagers to go down, his precious old sword in his hand. Thanks to that weapon, one at least of the berserkers limped whey-faced from the fray, blood pumping from severed veins. But Klaus never heard the screams of his wife, never saw the swinging axe-stroke that half-beheaded her. He died where he had fallen, wondering at the last why this had happened to him now – and where young Helmut had been when he should have been mending the nets.

Presently the fighting ceased for want of a living target for the berserkers' frenzied blows. Ragnar One-Eye looked down on the field of battle from a giant's perspective, his soul floating huge above his body. Corpses lay scattered like trees after a storm, and the steady crackle and snap of burning homesteads was the only constant sound. That and the quiet moaning of the few of his soldiers who had been lax enough to fall victim to fishermen and peasants.

At his feet, a body twitched and opened its eyes. Ragnar looked down incuriously, and saw that it was a priest. In the darkness his cassock was blacker than night, sticky with blood oozing from a deep gash in his belly. The putrid smell told him that the sacerdote would not live long.

The man was trying to speak. Ragnar payed little attention. He was trying to warn him...

'The curse...' Father Wolfgang gasped. His guts were cold now, and he knew what that meant. 'The evil of the headland. You'll release it, you fools!' The hulking barbarian showed no sign of interest, no indication that he understood. Wolfgang stopped trying. It was very cold, and in any case he wasn't sure that he should warn the raiders. A fate worse than death, perhaps, befitted them. Meanwhile, he could just relax a little. Shut his eyes. It would be all right; everything would...

Ragnar looked down. The priest was undoubtedly dying, if not dead already. A frown furrowed the Norseman's brows slightly. Had he tried to lay a curse on him with his dying breath?

Angered by the thought, he stomped away towards the blazing village hall. Heretics! Spawn of daemons! Worshippers of evil! These weak men of the Empire. Clean them out!

It was necessary, of course. Since the winter when the fish had been pulled rotting from the sea, netloads of grisly putrescence blighted by dark magic. The divinations of the shaman, oneiromancy and cheiromancy, had shown the source of the pollution to be this coastline. His town had starved out the winter, eating rats and drinking the blood of their horses to survive. Practitioners of evil lived hereabouts and must be wiped out. It was as simple as that.

Ragnar vacantly relieved himself against the charred remnants of what had once been the house of the Bissels, as inoffensive a family as could be conceived of. Then, feeling more himself, he looked round. Yes, it would do. Back at the beach they could camp for the night, bind such wounds as they had and prepare for the voyage home. He nodded gloomily.

Home...

HOME. HELMUT KERZER in his new home. A study and a laboratory, and the library of a necromancer who had been vast in his power and great in his terrible majesty. A bedchamber – or a crypt – fit for a dead prince. A robing room where the heavy robes of the mage hung in dusty rows. A dark exultation took hold of Helmut. It was as if he was returning to himself, after a childhood of darkness and ignorance. Somehow he knew where everything was, knew what the rooms were, as if he had lived here before in some past incarnation.

Nobody had ever told him of the dread life-in-death of the great necromantic wizards, much less of the whispered, rumoured ability some had to take possession from beyond the grave. In accepting the domain of a liche, Helmut had accepted far more than the old monster's possessions. Already he felt a power in himself that was new: a confidence and a knowledge dark in its intensity and external in its origins.

First Helmut lit the lanterns that, scattered through the mausoleum, shed a gloomy light upon the ancient dwelling-place. In the robing-room he paused for thought. Surely...? He shook his head. He had never possessed a garment that was not much-patched, handed down from some previous owner. Rags!

A black robe hung waiting. It crackled with age as he pulled it over his head, but it fitted well. The hood came

over his head and he laughed grimly, satisfied. The very
image of a wizard.

Next he proceeded to the library. Shelves that bowed
under the weight of mighty codices stretched to the ceiling
on two sides. There was no reading desk, but there was a
lectern in the shape of a hunchbacked, screaming skeleton.
A tome was already positioned on it, open to one leathery
page. Helmut walked round it, admiring the binding
which was of a curiously light, fine leather that could only
have come from one source. Then he looked at the first
page.

It was in a script and a language with neither of which he
was familiar. But he could read it, or something in him
could; it made perfect sense. He laughed again. Voles and
mice and dead squeaky bone-things in the forest! Such toys
seemed ludicrous now. Then he frowned, remembering the
reaver ship. It had been heading for the beach, a landing at
high-tide twilight, full of warriors dreaming of the mystery
of the axe. Impersonally he realized that there would be
plenty of material on hand for his new-found-trade; plenty
of familiar faces in strange, twisted contexts...

He turned the page and heard the electrifying crackle of
trapped power. Runes glowed on the parchment, gold-
encrusted shapes that sizzled with potential. Illustrations of
death and the unstill life beyond it, hermetic monsters and
people of the twilight. On the raising of corpses and the
ghastly perfection of skeletons. On the touch that brings
pain and death, and the touch that restores a semblance of
life. On the nature and treatment of vampires, ghouls and
the like. The elixir of life, and of death-in-life. His fingertips
glided from page to page, subtly memorizing the more useful items.

Then a thought struck him. A thought or a vision. His
spine chilled as sweat stood forth on his brow – cold sweat.
In his mind's eye he saw a picture of burning houses and villagers butchered, the priest's body gibbeted by the wayside.
Barbarous raiders retreating to the beach to feast and cele-
brate their victory. His parents lying unnoticed among the
dead, until the worms and beetles and small furry things
came out to feed on human flesh.

The book shut with a crack, dust flying from the spine at either end. Helmut stood with head bowed, a terrible tension in his shoulders. They would test me, would they, he thought with massive, terrible indignation? I, the heir! He still lacked the actuality of power, but nightmarish vistas were opening up to his dark imagination. With what he had here he could rule the headland for miles around. Poison the fish in swarms so that those who failed to fear him would starve, learning their lesson as their bellies bloated and ate the flesh from their bones. Did you do this, master? he asked silently. Did you prepare them for my arrival? Did you?

There was no reply, but somehow he was sure he heard a chuckle from beyond the grave.

Shaking his head, Helmut took the tome and placed it on one of the shelves; by instinct slotting them into the correct location. Pausing to consider, he selected another. The lectern creaked with a noise like a man racked by torture, as the codex settled onto it. The candles that lit this room smoked eerily with a smell like bacon; the fat of which they were made was wholly appropriate and readily available to any necromancer. He barely noticed the passage of time as he studied, feverishly trying to cram comprehension into his inexperienced skull. Spells and incantations normally beyond one of his experience seemed to be just barely accessible, falling into place with a curious, demented logic of their own. As if he already knew them, as if he had used them before.

Hours passed. Oblivious to time, Helmut slaked his thirst for forbidden knowledge at a well polluted by a subtle foulness. The power grew in him until he felt that his head would burst if he committed to memory another incantation. It was a monstrous feeling. Presently he shut the cover of the book, this time with delicacy and an almost lascivious feel for the well-tooled human leather of the covers. He looked about, then blinked and rubbed his eyes. Yes, it was time.

There was another exit from the hidden suite of the nameless master, and Helmut found it without difficulty. He himself had entered by the back door, so to speak; since when had a necromancer not desired easy access to the nearest graveyard? Deep within the forest he found himself climbing a short flight of steps to a trapdoor. It had been buried beneath soil for years, but the bearings were so well-balanced that, despite a small flurry of dirt, it opened effortlessly in the darkness.

Finding himself in darkness, Helmut clapped his hands softly, and muttered a cantrip he had known even before his accession to power. A soft, lambent light began to glow from an amulet that he swung on a chain before him. Let there be light, he thought. Enough to see by, at any rate. Tangled roots wove like ghastly tentacles across the ground, and the trees rose into the gloom of the forest like the legs of giants waiting to step on and crush mortals.

Helmut instinctively made his way towards the graveyard path that led to the village beyond. He never questioned how he knew where the path was – nor even why it had remained in the same place from century to century, down through the ages – but he found it all the same. He made his way towards the settlement quietly, pausing to sniff the air from time to time. The scent of woodsmoke and charred meat told its own story to his sensitive nostrils, a story of despair and suffering and pointless cruelty. The raiders didn't know – could not have known – that their target was not at large in the village when they struck. That their target had nothing to do with the village. That their ashes would be dust on the wind before the night was out. A cold anger grew in Helmut's breast as he drew near to the scene of the massacre. And a ghastly anticipation.

The first victim he saw was a child. Julia Schmidt, the baker's daughter. Blood on her dress, dark in the moonlight. Her mother lay nearby. He walked on. There were more corpses now; the reavers had fallen upon a fleeing band of women and children, slaughtering them like sheep. In the gloom they might have been sleeping, in cruel, uncomfortable postures forced upon them by the positioning of strange breaks in their limbs.

Helmut kept a rein on his anger. These were his people: firstly the people he had lived among – and latterly the people destined to be his subjects. Then he came to the village.

It was a scene of utter carnage. There were bodies everywhere; twisted and hunched peasants with their weapons still in their hands, oddly pathetic heaps of cloth containing mortal remnants. The wreckage of the houses still smouldered under the moonlight, ashes glowing red around paper-grey cores of charred wood. There was blood in the street.

He slowly turned around, until his eyes had taken in the entirety of the ghastly scene. No one was left alive; any survivors had fled. He felt no guilt, though. Guilt towards such as these was beneath him. But it wasn't always so, something nagged deep inside. He stilled the dissenting inner voice, and steeled himself for the final act.

No good. Tension and anger curled into knots around his spine. Straightening, he surveyed the corpses. Not one of the reavers had died here! The sight stiffened his resolve. Slowly he stretched out an arm, heavy beneath the sleeve of his black robe, and began to chant a soulless, evil rhyme.

Among the trees a strange rustling could be heard. A shuffling of ragged clothing, a sound like the sighing of the breeze that swung the felon on the gallows. Stick-figures were beginning to twitch and stir. Helmut continued remorselessly. Perhaps a minute passed, and then one of the bodies which was stretched lengthwise along the ground sat up. Moving slowly and arthritically, Hans-Martin Schmidt – the baker – crawled to his feet. He stared vacantly about with a face out of nightmare: mashed-in nose, a jaw that hung below his face by a tatter of drying meat. Seeing a scythe at his feet he bent and laboriously picked it up.

Helmut continued his spiritless, mournful chant. Julius Fleischer rolled over twice in the dust before he too sat up, clutching at the stump of a leg. The leg twitched towards him slowly, forced towards unnatural reunification with its master. The energy pouring into Helmut from the will of the dead Nameless One engorged him with a dark sense of evil; he was one with the night and the magic, as his servants crawled to their feet and, vacant-eyed, shambled towards him.

Finally the incantation was complete; the spell of summoning in place. Zombies were still staggering in, but already a hard core surrounded him. He looked about. The eyes that met his gaze were lifeless: some were merely gouged sockets, while others were hazed and dulled by the flies' feeding. For the most part these were the menfolk of the village, armed in death as in life. His eyes continued their search, until he saw his father. It might have been his father; its neck and head were too badly damaged for him to be sure in the darkness.

'Follow me,' he commanded in an ancient tongue, the learning of which was not possible in a night – not without enchantment. 'The enemy lies sleeping. In death ye shall reap your revenge for the afflictions of life; whereafter ye shall seek peace through my ministrations. Forward!'

He pointed down the path towards the beach and, slowly at first but gradually gathering speed, the horde of zombies plodded towards the reavers.

Ragnar One-Eye and his men were no amateurs. They had not forgotten to place a watch, nor to light fires on the beach. But a single guard was no match for the horror that swarmed out of the darkness in total silence save for the slithering of rank, battle-scarred flesh and the clanking of metallic death.

The guard stood transfixed for two fatal seconds, mouth agape, then he screamed, 'Attackers!' He was too late. The horde of death was already scrabbling and clawing its way over the sleepers, knives flickering in deadly arcs.

Helmut stood watching, controlling the attack by force of will alone. Something within him was crying out: if you hadn't dabbled, hadn't experimented with corruption, hadn't wakened the thing under the graveyard… No matter. He pushed the thought aside. Some of the reavers retreated to the boats, making to cast off and push them into the sea and escape.

A couple of his zombies followed, but he recalled them with a peremptory tug of willpower. Let the survivors bear warning to whoever had sent them! A cold smile that was most certainly not Helmut's own played about his lips as the last of the sleepers died beneath a struggling mound of noisome flesh. The first light of dawn was already beginning to show along the horizon: he turned and, ignoring the destruction around him, walked back towards the crypt.

It was as he had left it. The fighting hadn't reached the graveyard; a few poppies bobbed fitfully in the morning breeze as he pushed aside the altar stone and again descended into the musty darkness. But this time when he reached the inner chamber he paused before the throne and genuflected. 'Thank you, father. I am most grateful for your assistance,' he murmured as he contemplated the heap of bones piled there. The skull grinned at him.

It might almost have been his imagination that as he re-entered the apartment a bone-dry whisp of a voice behind him said: *Think nothing of it, my son.*

But then again, it might not.

THE PHANTOM OF YREMY
by Brian Craig

NOW, SAID THE story-teller, I will tell you a tale of Bretonnia, the country of the marvellous King Charles, who set himself further above his people than any other lord in all the Old World, and who had so many governors under him that he did not know their number, let alone their names.

This story tells of a town named Yremy, which was not so very far from the damned city of Moussillon – not far enough, in the opinion of its citizens. The great earthquake which had destroyed the heart of Moussillon had barely stirred the foundations of Yremy, and none of the houses of its gentle folk had fallen. Nevertheless, the tremors had left their mark upon the town, for once the rich and the mighty have felt turbulence in the ground on which they tread, they always walk in fear of losing their position.

This anxiety led the noblemen of Yremy to be especially stern and severe in their administration of the law. Whenever the governor had cause to speak to the good and honest men who had put him in his office he was proud to tell them that there was no other town in Bretonnia whose thieves were so fearful of the rewards of judgment, or where

49

the scaffolds were so frequently hung with the broken bodies of those who dared offend the law and its upholders.

With such an advantage as this, Yremy might have been a happy city, but the people of Bretonnia were always a discontented folk. There were among the ungrateful poor a more than tiny number who were embittered by the firmness of their masters, and resentful of the way in which its force inhibited their spirit of adventure.

'How should we live if we cannot steal?' they said to one another when they met in their secret dens and dirty inns. 'Must we go back to the land, to spoil our hands and break our backs planting and reaping? And for what? The best grain goes to the rich, who neither dig nor pick, and we are left with the turnips and the beets. We cannot seek honest work as watchmen, for we are the ones for whom watchmen must watch, and our masters would soon perceive that we had nothing to do. We must do what we can to reclaim the night for those who have stealthy business to conduct. We must discover among our ranks a robber of great daring, who can thumb his nose at the governor and his magistrates, and defy every effort of the guardsmen and the secret police to bring him to his reckoning.'

Alas, there was a long hard time when they looked among themselves for this paragon of cleverness, and could not find him. Yremy's thieves grew lean in the winter, and less capable in their trade as each of them in turn was caught about his business and returned to his family lightened by a hand.

THERE CAME A day, however, when there began a series of robberies which restored hope to the poorest homes in Yremy – not petty thefts of food and trinkets from the marketplace, nor even a skilful cutting of purses, but burglaries of the boldest kind.

These crimes were the work of a daring housebreaker who could climb high walls and break strong locks. Again and again he carried away fine jewels, virtuous amulets and gold coins, and sometimes weapons.

Only a handful of the people who were robbed in the early days of his career caught glimpses of this robber, and

they could say little about him save that he went about his
business clad all in black leather, wearing a mask to hide his
face.

ONLY ONE MAN came near to laying hands upon him in those
early days, but that was a fat merchant, who was at the time
clad only in a linen nightshirt, and he lost all enthusiasm for
a tussle when he saw that the thief was armed with a stab-
bing sword of the kind which is called an *épée a l'estoc*.

'He stole the bag of coins which was my worldly wealth,'
wailed this unlucky man, when he told his anxious friends
of his terrible ordeal, 'and did not hesitate to add insult to
injury, for he took my powdered wig as well when I cursed
him as a truffle-digging pig, and impaled it on a spike upon
my gate.'

In another realm, his hearers might have laughed about
the wig, but in Bretonnia a merchant who apes the gentry
by playing the fop is not reckoned a figure of fun, at least by
his own kind. The fact that the robber carried a sword was
taken more seriously still, for it was held to be proof of
murderous intent, and rich men began to quiver in their
beds for fear that when their turn came to attract the attention of the thief, he might puncture their bellies as well as
their wigs.

Within a matter of weeks every man of quality in the town
was howling for protection or revenge.

'We would expect such things to happen in Brionne,' they
cried, 'but this is Yremy where the law is firm and the peace
is sternly kept. Is this a phantom which robs us, that he cannot be captured and held? Is it some black magician who
evades our every precaution with his spells? Then let us call
upon our wizards and our priests to use their powers of div-
ination! Let us call upon the gods to reveal this miscreant
and deliver him to punishment!'

These anguished cries were heard even in the houses of the
poor, where they caused a certain merriment, and the name
of the Phantom was thenceforth on everyone's lips, whether
they hailed him as a hero or damned him as a villain.

The only comfort that the wealthy could find in the midst
of their distress was to say to one another: 'In the end he will

surely be caught, and then let us see what Jean Malchance and Monsieur Voltigeur will make of him!'

JEAN MALCHANCE AND Monsieur Voltigeur are two of the central characters of our story, and the only two who can be properly introduced – for the identity of the Phantom must remain a mystery until its climax.

Malchance and Voltigeur were names invariably coupled, for they had been friends since boyhood, schooling together, courting the same woman (and when Voltigeur married her Malchance swore to remain a bachelor for life!), and in the fullness of time performing their public functions in harness, as senior clerk and senior magistrate of the high court of Yremy. Voltigeur, who was ever the more glorious of the two, if only by a fraction, was the magistrate, while Malchance was the clerk.

Yremy was a large enough town to boast four magistrates in all, and an equal number of clerks, but whenever a man had cause to think of the high court of Yremy it was Malchance and Voltigeur who sprang first and foremost to mind. They were different from their fellows, because they had a lightness of touch in conducting their affairs which was born of long friendship. They were witty and clever, and their exchanges frequently evoked wild laughter in the public gallery of the court, even when the said gallery was packed with the friends of the accused.

To say that there was a lightness about their manner is not at all to say that there was any lightness about M. Voltigeur's sentencing. Even in that matter, though, the cleverness and wit of the great man shone through. Aided by Malchance, M. Voltigeur was most inventive in his choice of punishments, sometimes devising penalties which were previously unheard of in the whole of Bretonnia. Some said that he followed the spirit of the law more closely than the ordinary scheme of punishment, but it must be admitted that others assessed him differently. M. Voltigeur himself said only that he tried to make a punishment fit the crime by which it was earned.

It is of course true that many people believe the customary scheme of punishment to be already well-designed to serve the end of suiting the penalty to the crime. They hold that there is an abundance of natural justice in the common decree that a murderer should be hanged, a thief deprived of his offensive hand, and a petty traitor – which is to say, a woman who murders the man to whom she has been given in marriage – burned alive. But M. Voltigeur was not entirely satisfied with the beautiful simplicity of this ordinary scheme, and it was his invariable habit to attend to matters of finer detail, which led him to treat different thieves quite differently.

For example, a man who stole an amulet or a gold coin might be allowed by M. Voltigeur to keep his hand, but instead be branded upon the forehead with the imprint of that same amulet or gold coin, heated near to melting-point, so that he must ever bear upon his brow the image of that which he had unlawfully coveted. A man who stole a bolt of fine velvet cloth (an item of much value in civilized Bretonnia) might likewise be allowed to keep his hand – but only on condition that he went about thereafter clad in a shirt of prickly hair which tickled his skin most horribly.

By the same token, a poisoner would not usually be condemned by M. Voltigeur to be hanged upon the scaffold or (if of gentle birth) beheaded by the axe. Instead, he would be placed in the public pillory, and given a series of very noxious brews to drink, until his guts felt as though they were on fire, and the flesh upon his bones turned black and green as it rotted expeditiously away.

Even the poorer people of Yremy perceived a clever wit at work in these unusual punishments, and the loyal public which loved to see the executioner at work thought him a fine fellow for saving them from the ennui which might otherwise claim them when the common business of hanging became overfamiliar. M. Voltigeur was therefore an extremely popular man, frequently called 'the great judge.'

THE SO-CALLED Phantom had not been long at his work when it became apparent that there was something most peculiar in the pattern of his crimes. For one thing, members of the family of M. Voltigeur appeared more often in the list of his targets than seemed likely. These burglaries stood out for a second reason too: instead of wholesale plunder of the accessible assets, the Phantom removed only a single item from each household, often leaving behind jewels and coin of considerable value. In every case involving a relative of the magistrate, the object removed was something the owner considered very precious, but each victim asserted that the value was chiefly sentimental.

The close relatives of M. Voltigeur at this time numbered five. He was a widower, but had three surviving sons and two daughters. When the houses of all five had been invaded it became abundantly clear that some special of malice was at work.

The fifth incident, involving the younger daughter, left no other interpretation possible, for this daughter had been unwise enough to marry for love, and she possessed nothing that was authentically valuable. She did, however, have a carved wooden heart which was marked by a patch of red dye in the shape of a teardrop, which she treasured greatly, not so much because of its significance as an emblem of the goddess Shallya, but because it had been given to her by the mother she had lost in infancy. This object was of no worth to any other, yet the clever robber went to some pains to remove it from her.

When the news of this particular crime spread through the town the possibility was widely discussed that the Phantom was engaged in exacting some perverse revenge upon those near and dear to the city's favourite judge. All Yremy waited to see how M. Voltigeur would respond.

Now M. Voltigeur was a very dutiful man, though even his faithful friend Jean Malchance would never have said that he was unduly loving. He had been cool with his wife in the latter years of their marriage and he had always been cool with his sons. He was perhaps a little fonder of his daughters, but the fact that the younger had married for love had understandably annoyed him more than a little. But he who attacks a man's family also attacks the man, and when M. Voltigeur heard of the theft of the wooden heart he was moved to very considerable anger. He let it be known through the town that he would personally guarantee to double the price which had already been placed on the robber's head, so that the man who caught him would win a thousand silver coins.

No reward of that dimension had ever been offered in Yremy for the apprehension of a felon, and in the meaner streets the sum was much discussed.

Every petty robber in the town began to watch his friends with avaricious care, and every unhappy child yearned to discover proof that one or other of his parents might prove to be the robber, and exchangeable for ready money.

And when none of the poor could find the Phantom among his acquaintances, the rumour began to be put about that the robber must himself be a gentleman!

THIS OPINION WAS given further credence when the Phantom was very nearly apprehended in the garden of an impoverished marquis whose dwindling family fortune he had recently reduced by a further half. This time, the man who tried to stop him was no nightshirted milksop but a stout nightwatchman named Helinand, armed with a partisan which is a kind of spear, as those of you who know Bretonnian weapons will already be aware?

Helinand engaged the masked thief with alacrity, the pressure of his duty reinforced by greed, thrusting at him with his weapon as cunningly as he knew how. But his opponent was equal to his every challenge, parrying every blow with his own much tinier weapon.

'Three times I drove him to the wall,' Helinand declared, when he gave an acount of his adventure to M. Voltigeur, 'and thrice he slipped away, as delicately as if he were dancing. I could not see his face, but I know now that he is a well-schooled fencer, who fights as only a light-footed sportsman fights, and very cleverly. Though he dressed himself in the plainest leather last night, I would wager everything I have that he is used to calfskin and lace!'

'And did the wretch speak to you at all?' demanded M. Voltigeur, who found this ration of information far too meagre to assuage his hunger for news.

'Why yes,' said the unfortunate watchman. 'When he finally tripped me up and took my partisan away, he said that he was sorry to have put me to the inconvenience of chasing him, but that he could not be caught until he had settled his account with you, which he hoped to do within the week. I did not recognize his voice, alas!'

When M. Voltigeur heard of this amazing insolence his hands so shook with wrath that he was forced to ask Jean Malchance (who was well-used to taking dictation from him) to write down a proclamation for him, which he then gave to the First Crier of Yremy, demanding that it be loudly read in every quarter of the town.

The message which the criers gave out was this:

'I, M. Voltigeur, magistrate of Yremy, am sorely annoyed by the miseries inflicted upon my friends and my children by that low felon which the silly common folk have named the Phantom. I declare that this so-called Phantom is in reality worthy of no name save that of Rascal and Coward, and I say to him that if he bears any grudge against me, then he ought now to direct his attentions to my own house, and to no other. Should he answer this challenge, I promise him that he will be caught, exposed for the shabby trickster which he is, and delivered to the kind of justice which his horrible crimes deserve.'

This was an unprecedented event. Never before had a magistrate of the town sent such a message in such a fashion. Whether the man for whom it was intended heard it cried, none could tell, but wherever it was broadcast there were hundreds of interested ears to catch it and thousands of clucking tongues to pass it on, with the result that when the curfew tolled that day there was no one in Yremy who had not heard it repeated. It had been told to ancients so deaf they could hardly hear it, and youngsters so small they could barely understand it, and there was no doubt at all that if the Phantom was within the walls of the town, then the challenge must have been delivered. The citizens waited, thrilled by excitement, to see what would happen next.

IN THE MEANTIME, M. Voltigeur had not been idle. As a magistrate of the town he had in the normal course of affairs a guardsman to stand outside his front door, and now he obtained three more from the governor, so that the guard at the front might be doubled and one of equal strength placed at the back of the house.

Inside the house he normally had a staff of thirteen servants, including six men. Not one of the six was frail and three – the coachman, the groom and his personal valet – were powerful fellows none would be eager to fight. M. Voltigeur ordered that from the day of his decree no more than two of his men should be asleep at any time, and that the others should all go armed; to those who were practiced he gave short swords, while those who were unskilled were instructed to carry cudgels.

Naturally, there came also to his aid the valiant Malchance, who loyally promised that he would sleep on a couch outside M. Voltigeur's bedroom door, and would see to it that the six servants were distributed about the house most carefully, so that each and every landing might be kept under perpetual surveillance.

Nor did Malchance stop at such precautions as these. Mindful of the possibility that the Phantom's elusiveness might be laid to the account of magic, he brought into his friend's house the most talented of the town's licensed wizards, a man named Odo. Odo, declaring that the thief had not yet been born who could steal goods which had been placed under his protection, set magical alarms upon the doorways, which made the entire house into a cunning trap.

Malchance suggested then that M. Voltigeur's valuables should be gathered together into three strong chests, and he sat up all evening, closeted with his friend, compiling an inventory as the things were put away. When that was done, he sent for Odo again, beseeching him to set sealing spells upon the locks of three chests, and also the lock of the room in which they were placed. Though these spells were but petty ones Odo, full of the confidence which wizards always have when their work has not yet been tested, assured M. Voltigeur that in combination with the other precautions they would surely suffice to ward off any vulgar servant of the thief-god Ranald.

THAT NIGHT, M. Voltigeur went to his bed determined to sleep as soundly as he normally did, in order to demonstrate his contempt for the Phantom and his faith in the precautions which he had taken. Unfortunately, his composure was not quite adequate to this intention, and he lay tossing and turning for many a long hour. Whenever he dozed off he found himself beset by horrid nightmares in which men he had sentenced to unusual deaths rose from their paupers' graves to march through the empty streets, heading for an appointed rendezvous with him, which he felt that he would somehow be obliged to keep.

The fourth or fifth time that a bad dream sent him urgently back to wakefulness he felt such an overwhelming impression of dread that he reached for the firecord which he had laid beside the bed, ready for an emergency. Having blown vigorously upon it to make it grow bright he applied it to the tallow nightlight which was nearby.

When the flame caught he took up the nightlight, holding it before him so that its faint radiance spread as far as it could into the four corners of the room. He did this to reassure himself that he was still alone and safe, but the plan misfired.

He was not alone.

Nor, he felt, as his heart seemed to sink into his belly, was he safe.

Seated at the foot of the bed was a very curious person. M. Voltigeur could not tell whether it was man or woman, because a dark hood concealed the cut of its hair, and a leather mask hid its face. Its slimness suggested womanhood, but there was no hint of a breast beneath the black silken shirt which he could see through the gap where a dark cloak was imperfectly gathered about its torso.

There was no doubt in his mind that he was confronted by the infamous Phantom of Yremy.

M. Voltigeur opened his mouth to shout for help, but the figure put a slender finger to the lips of its unsmiling mask. The gesture seemed more conspiratorial than threatening, and the magistrate was very well aware of the absurdity of keeping silent, but he nevertheless stifled his call.

'How did you come here?' he asked, instead – his voice hardly above a whisper.

'Did you really think that you could keep me out?' asked the visitor. The voice was light, but had an odd throaty quality. He could not tell whether it was man's or woman's – and for all he knew for certain, it might have been an elf's.

The Phantom continued: 'Did not Helinand tell you that I would come to you within the week, great judge? Did you doubt that I meant what I said? Was it not, therefore, a silly thing you did when you issued so public an invitation?'

'What do you want with me?' asked M. Voltigeur, his own voice grating a little because his mouth was so dry.

'Only justice,' said the other, 'and a punishment to fit your many crimes. I come tonight only to pass sentence upon you – you must wait, as I have waited, for the sentence to be carried out. I will return again tomorrow to hear your plea for mercy... and on the third night, the sentence will take effect.'

'What sentence?' whispered M. Voltigeur, feeling an urgent wish to know what the Phantom planned.

'No ordinary fate,' said the voice from behind the mask. 'Like yourself, I am not so lenient.'

Then, and only then, did the magistrate recover sufficient presence of mind to cry for help – and cry he did, letting loose a scream whose clamorous panic surprised all those who heard it. As he screamed, some reflex made him put up his arm before his face, as though to ward off an anticipated attack. But no attack came, and when he dropped his arm again to see what was happening, there was no one to be seen. The room was quite empty.

The door burst open then, and Jean Malchance rushed in, brandishing a full three feet of polished blade, all ready to cut and slash. At exactly that moment the sound of the wizard's voice could be heard from another room, crying: 'The alarm! The alarm! The door is breached!' Within minutes the footman and the coachman arrived, and then the other servants one after another, cudgels at the ready.

But there was nothing for them to do. There was only M. Voltigeur, devoid of powder and paint, sitting up in his bed, looking foolish.

THE SCENES WHICH followed can easily be imagined. The room, which had no hiding places to offer, was searched with absurd thoroughness. Odo swore by all the gods that no one could have passed through the door until the alarm was raised. The guardsmen at the back of the house were summoned, and stoutly testified that no one had passed them, and that no one could have climbed to the shuttered window (whose shutters were still closed tight) without their seeing him.

On considering these facts, everyone save M. Voltigeur came quickly to the conclusion that no one had entered the room at all, and that he must have dreamed his encounter with the Phantom – but in order to save the magistrate's feelings they assured him that he must have been the victim of an illusionist's magic, which had compelled him to see that which was not there.

Though he was half-inclined to believe them, the magistrate did not like to think that such fear had been aroused in him by a mere illusionist, and he muttered darkly about the possible involvement of necromancy, as evidenced by the evil dream which had disturbed him – but in Yremy as in other cities of the Old World, necromancy was far more often talked about than actually encountered, and even M. Voltigeur could not bring himself to place much credence in that theory.

Unfortunately, the conclusion that M. Voltigeur had only dreamed his encounter with the Phantom seemed slightly weaker in the morning, when he and Malchance went to inspect the room where the three chests of valuables had been so carefully placed.

Though the magically-sealed door was apparently undisturbed the chests were not. One had been opened, apparently by sheer brute force, and its various contents had been scattered haphazardly around the room. Closer inspection revealed that though the wizard's spell had saved the lock from damage, its protection had not extended to the rusted iron hinges, which had been torn apart.

The magistrate and his friend sat down with the inventory, and after two hours of meticulous counting concluded that one object and one only was missing: a silver comb, which the late Madame Voltigeur had often used to put up her lovely hair.

M. Voltigeur swore all those involved in the affair to the utmost secrecy – with the inevitable result that the story was all around the town by noon, its every detail earnestly discussed by roadwardens and ragamuffins alike.

THERE IS ONLY one thing that the poor people of a town love more than a heroic villain, and that is a mystery. They swapped questions with one another with avid interest. Who could the Phantom possibly be? What magic or trickery had allowed him to enter the magistrate's house and escape again undetected? Why had he taken the silver comb? All these puzzles received careful consideration, but none of course could compare in fascination with the most intriguing question of all, which was: what sentence had been passed on Yremy's great judge? What punishment, to fit what crime?

The people racked their memories to recall every criminal on whom M. Voltigeur had ever passed sentence, whether living or dead (for those who are executed rarely die childless, and even in Bretonnia – though it is not the Empire – sons are expected to avenge fatal wrongs done to their fathers). The rumour spread that some unlucky person singled out by the great judge for a particularly nasty punishment must in fact have been innocent of his crime, and that the bloody libel of his false conviction was now to be wiped out, and the penalty repaid in full measure.

M. Voltigeur did not stir from his house that day, but this did not prevent him from hearing the cries and cheers of the ragged, hungry children of the street, who informed him with delighted squeals that he was doomed, and that the second morrow would be the most miserable of his whole existence.

The humble people of Yremy were not the only ones who were struggling to recall some particular case which might give a clue to the Phantom's identity. M. Voltigeur himself was as determined as anyone to find that clue, and had called upon loyal Malchance to jog his memory by reading from the scrupulously-compiled lists of indictments kept by the court all the names of those who had had the misfortune to come before him.

The clerk did as he was asked. He recalled to M. Voltigeur's mind the three highway thieves whose feet he had ordered flayed, so that they might never walk the roads again. He listed the prostitutes convicted of picking their clients' pockets, whose own 'pockets' the magistrate had ordered to be sewn up tightly with catgut. He suggested the names of a couple of tax-evaders who had been castrated in order to remind them of the condition which the town would be in if adequate provision were not to be made for its defence against marauders.

But all these were trivial matters, and M. Voltigeur opined that when all things were carefully considered the only kind of case likely to have evoked such an extraordinary response as the Phantom's would be a case of murder.

Malchance then read out the list of murderers condemned to death by M. Voltigeur, which turned out to number fifty-two, but in the main it was a dull enough list, enlivened only by the occasional cleverness by which the deaths of the accused had been contrived. There seemed to be no one on the list who had not fully merited death.

M. Voltigeur then decided that they must concentrate their attention on those who had committed crimes involving magic – for he was sure that magic of some sort had been involved in the remarkable events of the night.

Alas, Malchance did not need to consult the records closely in order to remind M. Voltigeur that he had never had occasion to pass sentence on an authentic wizard. If such a one had ever committed crimes in Yremy, he had not been apprehended – a fact which, on reflection, could hardly be deemed surprising. In the last thirty years, in fact, the ever-vigilant guardsmen of the town – aided and abetted by licensed wizards and the priests attached to its miscellaneous shrines – had only managed to arrest four petty spellcasters. This tiny group consisted of three illusionists and one apprentice elementalist.

The last-named, who had been turned in by his own master after trying to penetrate the mysteries of his calling ahead of the appointed schedule, and also committing various other misdemeanours, was immediately rejected as an exceedingly unlikely Phantom. In any case, his punishment had been relatively mild and not particularly unusual – he had been buried in the earth up to his neck and slaughtered by a shower of stones hurled in an entirely unmagical fashion by a troop of guardsmen.

The illusionists seemed for a moment or two to be more promising suspects. Because illusionists were by nature deceptive, it was always difficult to determine exactly what had happened before, during and after their capture, and there was always a possibility that the responsible persons might be deluded into thinking they had executed an illusionist when they had in fact allowed him to walk free, or executed a double in his stead. The three in question had all seemed relatively incompetent – they would not otherwise have been captured and tried – but it is one of the best-loved tricks of the master illusionist to disguise himself as an incompetent illusionist, thus to persuade his enemies that they have seen through his impostures when in fact they have merely torn away the first of many veils.

M. Voltigeur, however, had been the presiding magistrate in only one of these three cases, and that a rather sordid case of fraud and petty theft. The case was rendered less interesting still by the fact that in a rare fit of orthodoxy the magistrate had ordered that the thief suffer the commonplace penalty of losing a hand. The only exceptional item on the record was that M. Voltigeur had decided that as there were two counts, the man should also lose the least two fingers from his other hand. It was difficult in the extreme to believe that the Phantom could have achieved his feats with one hand lacking and the other mutilated, so this suspect too was set aside.

His failure to find any inspiration in the court lists redoubled M. Voltigeur's determination to protect himself from the second promised visit of the Phantom. The guard outside the house was increased to eight. All six of the servants were issued with blades, and Jean Malchance acquired from the governor's own armoury a flintlock pistol with gunpowder and shot, which he gave to his friend with the instruction that it must be saved as a last resort.

Odo was asked to spread his alarm spells more liberally, with the aid of a wand of jade borrowed from Verena's temple. He was also asked to occupy the room to the right hand side of M. Voltigeur's. One of the minor shrines of

the town, dedicated to the veneration of Morr, responded
to the unique situation by sending a priest to assist in matters of magical defence – an unusual step, given that priests
usually considered their magic too noble to be wasted in
petty secular affairs.

This priest was a skilled diviner named Hordubal, who
was lodged in the room to the left hand side of M.
Voltigeur's.

Jean Malchance again elected to place himself outside the
bedroom door, as the final line of external defence. He further suggested that as a new precaution he and M. Voltigeur
should bring the three chests containing the magistrate's
valuables to his bedroom. He helped his friend pack them
most carefully, and when they were locked he summoned
Odo again, instructing him to place alarm spells as well as
magical seals upon the locks. Then he put them away
beneath the bed – where, he said, they would surely be safe
from any interference.

WHEN DARKNESS CAME M. Voltigeur made no attempt to go to
sleep, having resolved this time to remain awake. He kept no
less than five stout candles burning in his room. Alas, as the
night wore on, his determination to stay alert was put to an
increasingly severe test by a seductive drowsiness which con-
tinually crept up on him.

Four or five times the magistrate drifted off to sleep, only
to dream each time that all the men he had ever condemned
to death were rising from their graves and marching through
the streets of Yremy, calling to him to meet them at a place
assigned by destiny, to which he knew that he would in time
be drawn.

No sooner had he lost count of the occasions on which
this happened than he opened his eyes with a sudden start,
and saw a figure standing at the foot of the bed, wrapped all
around by a dark cloak. Shadowed eyes were staring at him
through two holes cut in a leathern mask.

'It will do no good to strive against your fate, Monsieur
Magistrate,' said the voice, which sounded like the rustling
of fallen leaves stirred by a cold north wind. 'Sentence is
passed, and only remains to be carried out.'

This time, M. Voltigeur did not pause to debate matters with the Phantom. Nor did he bother to cry out to rouse his friends, but clumsily brought the pistol from beneath his sheet, and fired it.

The effect of what he did was not quite what he had expected. Instead of an instant explosion there was a sinister hiss and a great gout of white smoke which stung his eyes horribly. When the explosion came, after several seconds had passed, he had ceased to expect it and it made him jump with alarm. The recoil – which also came as a great surprise – wrenched the weapon from his hand. To the cloud of white smoke which had already blinded him there was added a much thicker cloud of black, and when he was finally able to see again he was not at all surprised to find that the visitor was no longer standing by his bed.

As the door burst inwards to admit the sword-wielding Malchance, M. Voltigeur leapt to the foot of the bed, fully expecting – or, at least, desperately hoping – to see a corpse stretched upon the rug. But all that was on the floor were the wide-scattered contents of one of the treasure-chests. The lid had been wrenched away by sheer brute force which had burst the hinges asunder.

Next door, the voice of Odo could be heard crying: 'The alarms! The alarms! The door is breached, and so is the chest!'

One by one the servants arrived – but it appeared that they already suspected what they might find, for their blades were not held aloft, and when they found that the Phantom was nowhere to be seen they did not seem at all surprised.

Through the rest of the night the magistrate and his friend worked methodically through their inventory, in order to discover what had been taken from the second chest. By the early morning they were certain that one thing and one thing only was gone: a fine embroidered chemise trimmed with the fur of a rare white hare, which the late Mme. Voltigeur had used as her favourite nightshirt.

M. Voltigeur did not trouble to swear the company to secrecy, for he knew by now how futile such a gesture would be. The whole town seemed to know what had happened almost before the rising sun was clear of the horizon, and by high noon there was not a single detail of the night's events which had escaped the scrupulous attention of the gossips.

WHEN HE HAD eaten a far-from-hearty breakfast the magistrate summoned Jean Malchance, Odo and Hordubal to a conference, and implored all three to help him make some sense out of what had happened. He begged Odo to tell him what kind of magic had been worked to bring the Phantom into his room despite all possible precautions, and to leave it again so cleverly.

'Monsieur,' said Odo, who had been racking his brains for some time in the hope of excusing the apparent failure of his magical alarms, 'it seems to me we can only conclude that the so-called Phantom is indeed a phantom, in a perfectly literal sense. This is no illusionist protected by a spell or potion of invisibility, for he does not come through the door or the window at all. It can only be a ghost, and if it appears in this house, it is surely the ghost of one who died in this house.'

'Ghost!' exclaimed M. Voltigeur, who had not thought of such a possibility, and was loath to consider it now.

'Whose ghost?'

Odo hesitated, but felt obliged to say what was in his mind. 'I am reluctant, monsieur, to say what will probably seem a shocking thing, but I think we must consider your late wife the most likely candidate, for the things which the Phantom has taken from you and from your younger daughter are certainly things which your wife once owned. Can you remember, perchance, whether it was your wife who gave to your other children the things which were subsequently removed from their possession?'

While the wizard was speaking a deep frown came upon the magistrate's face, but M. Voltigeur did not react angrily. He was a man used to weighing evidence and drawing scrupulous conclusions, and when he considered the question which Odo had posed he realized that although he had not seen the connection before, all the objects removed from the houses of his sons had indeed been given to them by their mother, and that the trinket stolen from his elder daughter had likewise been a gift from her.

'But what possible reason could my late wife have for haunting me?' complained the magistrate. 'I was ever as just and fair in my dealings with her as with the world at large. She lived and died in comfort, with all that a woman could desire, and had the privilege of bearing seven fine children, only two of whom died in infancy. I cannot believe that she might want to hurt me.'

'And yet,' said Hordubal, who seemed enthused by the possibility of finding an explanation of events which had utterly mystified him, 'perhaps there is other evidence to incline us in the direction of an explanation of this kind. My lord Morr is the god of death and the god of dreams, and I felt his nearness when I slept last night in your house. You have admitted that each time you have seen the Phantom you have awakened momentarily from a dream in which graves seemed to open to yield up their dead, and that you have had a sense of being drawn to some fateful rendezvous. Perhaps your encounters with the Phantom were the meetings of which your dreams spoke.'

'No doubt it was kind of Morr to send me an illuminating vision,' said M. Voltigeur, with a sharpness born of disbelief, 'but I might wish that he had made it clearer.'

At this, Hordubal shook his head sorrowfully, and said: 'It is we who are the servants of the gods – they are not ours. We should be grateful for what they send, not resentful that they do not tell us more.'

'Most certainly,' agreed Odo, in a pious way.

But M. Voltigeur only scowled, and turned to his friend. 'This is nonsense, Jean, is it not?' he said. 'Assure me, please, that there is another way of interpreting this case, which these silly men have overlooked.'

'Well,' said Jean Malchance, smoothly, 'it certainly seems to me that there are several facts which are difficult to explain within this theory. The Phantom has certainly not been restricted to the bounds of this house, as true phantoms usually are. He has not even confined his attentions to the houses of M. Voltigeur's kin. He has carried out raids all over Yremy, and he was solid enough to engage the watchman Helinand in a very substantial duel. And if the Phantom were in truth a ghost, how could he break the hinges of the chests? I must remind you that when I burst into M. Voltigeur's room last night the contents of the chest were already strewn across the floor, and it seemed that Odo's magical alarm had proved no more effective than his magical seal.'

'Quite so!' cried the magistrate. 'What have you to say to that, Master Spellcaster? And since the alarm on the chest proved to be ineffective, how can we be sure that the alarms on the door and window of my room were not defective also? It is my belief that this Phantom is as solid as you or I, but that he is so clever a magician that your frail spells have been utterly impotent to keep him at bay!'

'Well,' replied Odo, in the offended tone which all wizards adopt when their competence is questioned, 'you may believe that if you like, but I must agree with my friend the good servant of Morr, that you have too haughty an attitude to man and god alike. My magic is a good and humble magic entirely appropriate to the needs of Yremy's people, and if it is not enough to protect you in this case I can only conclude that you do not enjoy as much favour with the goddess Verena as your calling has led you to suppose.'

'Peace!' said Jean Malchance, in a soothing fashion. 'It will not help us to become annoyed with one another. Nor will it help us to blame the gods for what they have or have not done, for I cannot believe that they are behind what is happening here. Let us think about this logically, and see where reason might lead us.'

'Oh, certainly,' replied Odo, unmollified. 'Let us do that, and let us discover what feeble creatures we are, who hope to reach the bottom of such mysteries. If my magic has failed, then more powerful magic must be at work, and that is all there is to it.'

'Perhaps so,' said Malchance, evenly, 'but I think that there is another way to interpret what has happened here, and with your permission, M. Voltigeur, I will describe it – though I must warn you that you may not like it any better than what these men have said.'

'I am a magistrate,' replied his friend, stoutly, 'and I am eager to hear all evidence and argument, wherever it may lead.'

'Well then,' said Malchance, 'let us consider the possibility that Odo's precautions were not so easily evaded. We packed the chests together, you will recall, and locked them all. Then I left the room in search of Odo, did I not, returning some minutes later so that the alarm spells could be set?'

'That is so,' said the magistrate. 'But I did not leave the room. No one could have removed the objects from the chest before the spell was set.'

'But it is possible so far as I can tell,' said Malchance, 'that the objects we later found strewn around the room were not in the chest when the alarm was set, and could have been distributed before the lock was broken. Assessing the evidence purely from my own point of view, I cannot help but ask myself whether it might have been the case that the chest was broken open at exactly the same moment as the lock on the door, when I burst into M. Voltigeur's room. If that were true, there might have been no failure of the alarms.'

'But that is absurd!' exclaimed the magistrate. 'I tell you, Jean, that the objects were not removed while you were out of the room. Who could have done it, save for me? Who could have secreted them, and later have strewn them around the room, except myself? And who, except myself, could have broken the lock on the chest at precisely the time that you burst through my door?'

Jean Malchance spread his arms wide, and said: 'There you have it, in a nutshell. Who has seen the Phantom in this house, except yourself? No one. Who could possibly have done any of these mysterious things, except yourself? No one. Ergo, I must ask that we take seriously the proposition that you are the one who has done them!'

Here Malchance was forced to pause, because M. Voltigeur appeared likely to suffer a fit of apoplexy.

The clerk put a reassuring hand on his friend's shoulder, and said to him in a kindly tone: 'Of course, I do not say that you have done these things knowingly, but only that you must have done them. You could have conjured up this ghost. You could have taken these relics of your dead wife from your children's houses. You could be the Phantom, and it is hard to see that anyone else can have done what the Phantom has done. What other explanation is as probable?

That you have been bewitched or accursed is certainly possible, but I must in all conscience say that we cannot seriously doubt that yours are the hands which have actually carried out these actions.'

M. Voltigeur was of a different opinion. 'This is absurd!' he howled. 'It is monstrous! I have been your firmest friend for forty years, Jean Malchance, and now you accuse me of this! I am a victim of robbery and evil haunting, and the only conclusion which my friend can reach is that I have robbed myself and haunted myself! It is no wonder, you serpent of ingratitude, that I had the wit and wisdom to become a great judge, while you remained my clerk. Logic be damned! Your contention is the vilest slander I have ever heard, and I only wish that I could find a punishment to fit such a crime, for I would surely exact it. Leave my house, and take your worthless spellcasters with you. Begone! I will face this vicious Phantom alone, and I will find out who he is for myself.'

It is doubtful that Odo or Hordubal would have been overanxious to agree with the curious hypothesis which Jean Malchance had advanced, but when M. Voltigeur exploded in this manner, and called them worthless, they were by no means inclined to dispute it. In fact, they each came quickly to the conclusion that M. Voltigeur was equally excessive in his ingratitude and his ungraciousness, and that Jean Malchance's charges, however unlikely they might seem, must have struck a spot made sore by conscience.

Jean Malchance, on the other hand, seemed to repent his reckless words, and begged to be allowed to remain – in order, as he put it, to help M. Voltigeur defend himself against himself – but this only roused M. Voltigeur's anger to a higher pitch, and he would not be content until his former friend was banished from his house.

The two spellcasters went with him, feeling very aggrieved by the way that their sincere attempts to help had not been better appreciated.

By NIGHTFALL, THE story of the quarrel was all around the town, and so was the rumour that the notorious Phantom had all along been none other than M. Voltigeur himself, turned to a life of crime by arrogance and impiety. Many people who had never imagined such a possibility soon began to say that they had expected it, having always been certain that a judge who handed down such unusual sentences could have no real respect for the law.

Thanks to the incautious suspicions of Jean Malchance, M. Voltigeur went to bed that night a much less admirable man, in the estimation of his neighbours, than he had been before. In his own mind, however, he was absolutely certain that he was not guilty of the perverse charges which Malchance had so unexpectedly levelled against him, and he was enthusiastic to prove it in whatever manner he could.

He distributed his servants about the house as before, and the guardsmen about the grounds, but he was not prepared to trouble himself with magical alarms and magical locks in whose efficacy he could no longer trust.

Before he went to bed he carefully searched through the one chest which had not been plundered, and removed from it a small oval portrait of his dead wife, which had been painted before their marriage, and presented to him as a token of her respect – for she had ever been a respectful woman, who had never taken advantage of their intimacy to excuse any lapse of politeness.

He could not be entirely certain that this portrait was the article most likely to be sought by the Phantom, but it seemed altogether likely. He placed the portrait beneath his pillow.

He had kept the pistol, having persuaded himself that he had missed his shot on the previous night only because he had not understood how the cursed thing was supposed to work, and had failed to hold the barrel straight when he was bewildered by the smoke and the recoil. He was determined that his hand should be steadier this time, if he had the opportunity to fire another shot.

The careful taking of these precautions calmed his anger somewhat, but they could not quiet his anxiety, and when he went to bed he felt as though an iron band had been drawn around his waist, squeezing his belly. His head was like a seething cauldron, his thoughts like bubbles bursting randomly upon his consciousness, so that he hardly needed to fall asleep in order to experience delirium.

Two images kept coming back to him while he waited: the image of the graveyard where the dead were rising from their tombs, bent on keeping their appointment with the man who had sentenced them to death; and the image of Jean Malchance, who had undergone in a single instant of time a dramatic transformation from friend to foe.

It was the latter image which possessed him more firmly. What had made Jean do it? Was he, too, the victim of some awful magic? Might he too be accursed?

Because these images kept rising into his mind despite the fact that he was wide awake he was forced to search for something solid to look at, for the purpose of distraction. He took the portrait from his pillow, and occupied himself in staring at the face of the young girl whose wise and careful father had done him the honour of accepting his most generous offer for her hand.

Remarkably, the sight of the picture calmed him more than anything else he had done. As he stared into the painted eyes he became convinced that if this really was the face of the fiend which haunted him, then the ghost had certainly not risen of its own volition, but had been torn from its rest by the foulest necromancy.

But that, he thought, can hardly be possible. A necromancer must hate his victim more than he loves his own life, for he who injures others with the aid of daemons or vile spells must also injure himself. No one could hate me thus, for in all that I have done I have only been the humble instrument of the law.

Having reached this conclusion, he began to think as a judge again, and as a man of reason, with his thoughts quite unclouded by wrath and barely upset by tremors of fear. And then, quite suddenly, he saw all that had happened in a different light, and guessed at last who the Phantom must be.

HE LOOKED UP then, and saw that the Phantom was with him, standing at the foot of the bed, just as he had on the previous night. Those shadowed eyes were watching him through the holes of his mask.

M. Voltigeur raised the pistol, and pointed it carefully at the mask.

'My hand is steady tonight, Jean Malchance,' he said. 'I promise that I will not miss again.'

Jean Malchance reached up without delay to remove the mask from his face, as though he had become tired of the masquerade in any case. He looked at his friend with eyes as hard as flints, and replied: 'You cannot kill me, monsieur. I have already seen to that.'

M. Voltigeur licked his lips, and stared into the naked face of the man who was most definitely not his friend, but must have been his enemy for longer than he cared to think.

'I believe that you have,' he whispered. 'Or that you think so. But whatever wicked spell you have used, or whatever daemon it may be to whom you have sold yourself, you cannot be entirely sure. Dark magic is ever treacherous, and is said to be very likely to misfire, destroying its user instead of his victim.'

'The same is said of pistols,' the other retorted, calmly.

'But pistols do not care what they may destroy,' said M. Voltigeur. 'I have always believed that even the instruments of the foulest magic must hesitate to harm the good. And whatever hatred you nurse against me, you must allow that I have ever been a good and honest man, always as fair as I knew how to be.'

'I believe that you underestimate the power of dark magic,' said Malchance, 'and I know full well that you overestimate your worth as a man. Fair as you knew how to be you always were, but your failing always lay in what you knew how to be.'

M. Voltigeur's finger tightened a little on the trigger of his weapon, but he did not press it yet. He was not so very frightened, now that he knew what it was that he had to face.

'I thought you were my friend, Jean,' he said, piteously. 'Why were you not my friend, when I was always friend to you?'

'You hold the answer in your hand,' replied Malchance. 'I could have forgiven you the rest. I could have forgiven you for winning every other contest in which we took part as boys or men. I could have forgiven you for becoming a magistrate while I remained a clerk. I could even have forgiven you for becoming famous for those cunning sentences you passed, though fully three in four were ideas which I put into your head. I am the man who fits punishments to crimes, Monsieur, and I am doing now what I have always done.'

M. Voltigeur looked at the portrait which he held in his hand.

'I remember that you liked her,' he said, quietly.

'Liked her!' said Malchance, stifling a cry of pain and showing for the first time that ire which he must have kept hidden for many long years. 'I loved her with all my heart, and she loved me. But she could see that there was a magistrate in you and a clerk in me, just as she could see that there was gold in your family coffers and only silver in mine. She loved me, but she would not marry for love. She would rather have a man without a heart, whose fine clothes and full pockets made up for the emptiness that was inside him. If you had loved her as I loved her, I would have understood, and forgiven, but I could not forgive you what you are, and what you made of her.'

'But men and women should not marry for love!' said the great judge, with the air of one stating the obvious. 'It is our reason which sets us above the beasts, and we must live by that reason and not by silly passion. It is passion which drives men to use dark magic, and to sell their souls, thus to hurt themselves more horribly than any penalty of the law ever could.'

'I have not used much magic,' Malchance told him. 'Far less than you think, I do believe. I had only to use a petty spell which would blind you to my actions unless I desired that you should see them. I was beside you while you packed your chests, and removed whatever I wished before you closed them and before Odo put his seals upon them. I slept within your door, not without, and could do what I wished, unnoticed, even while you kept your vigil. It was from within that I opened the door – and thus broke the magic seal – on each of the two occasions. I admit, though, that my arms were at full stretch the night I had to break the weakened chest as well, having earlier strewn its pilfered contents about the floor.'

'But you are only a clerk,' said M. Voltigeur, 'and as a clerk you surely have no skill in magic at all!'

'I can read,' replied Malchance, 'and that rare talent, which made me your servant because I could do it better than you, allowed me to search in forbidden books for that which men of my station are not supposed to have. You do not know what I can do, monsieur. You do not know me at all, for I am merely an appearance to you, about which you cannot truly care – just as she was.'

M. Voltigeur looked again at the portrait.

'Why did you steal her gifts to my children?' he asked.

'Because they should have been gifts to my children. It should have been my children that she bore, and not yours. You have no right to these things I have taken – you have no right to your own family, though I know you would not care if they were taken away, and so I have not sought to hurt them. I loved her. All her love-tokens are rightly mine, and all the things which she loved.'

'Oh Jean,' said the magistrate, with a sigh, 'you are a great fool. I was your friend, and you should have been mine. Instead you are a famous robber and a faithless betrayer. How will I find a punishment to fit such crimes?'

'We are not here to pass judgment on me,' said Malchance. 'I have been occupied in passing sentence on you. In the eyes of the people of Yremy you, not I, are the famous robber. My denunciation has carried to every covert and corner of the town, and because it came from your trusted friend it is believed! And in the morning, valuables stolen from many houses will be discovered in those chests beneath your bed, to add the final proof. Your confession, dictated to me in your final hour of life, and signed by your own hand, will also be offered in evidence – I have it in my pocket now, with your name already forged. Your loyal footman who admitted me tonight fully believes the story which I told him, that I was bitterly sorry about our quarrel, and came to make amends.

'When I swear that you died by your own hand, and that I was just too late to prevent it, I will shed such tears that no one would doubt me for a moment. Every detail is now in place.'

'Not quite,' said M. Voltigeur. 'I have not died by my own hand, and have no intention of obliging you in such a matter. In fact, I rather think that I might shoot you dead instead.'

'Alas,' said Jean Malchance, 'I think that you are wrong, and can only hope that you will not be too disappointed.'

'I must stand by my belief,' said the magistrate, 'that your evil magic will not work on a virtuous man, and that whatever daemon has given you your skill will come for your soul, not for mine.'

And so saying, he fired his weapon, determined this time that the smoke and the recoil would not affect his aim.

The powder in the pan sizzled madly for a moment, and then the pistol blew up in his hand.

The force of the explosion sent fragments of twisted metal into his eyes. One tiny sliver penetrated to a deeper level, and killed him on the instant.

Jean Malchance had thrown up his arms to shield himself from the explosion, but he quickly lowered them again.

Poor man! he thought. You were ever a poorer judge than you thought. It does not need magic to block up the barrel of such a stupid weapon as that, and only the pettiest of spells to accomplish it unobserved. If I have damned myself for such a little thing, so be it, but I do not think I have.

The coachman arrived then, followed by the footman and the valet, and all the other servants who had kept such fruitless watch.

'Alas,' said Jean Malchance, 'the poor man was so deluded and deranged that he thought his phantom had come back to haunt him again. But see! It is only a portrait of his dear late wife.'

So saying, he picked up the little picture – bloodstained now – which had fallen on the floor, and when the servants had looked at it, he put it in his own pocket, and took it away with him.

MALCHANCE WAS QUITE correct in his estimation that the people of Yremy would believe what he told them, and he had more than enough apparent proofs to convince them. He pretended to be so stricken by grief that he never served again as a clerk to the court of Yremy, but retired to live in solitude, alone with his memories and his secrets.

M. Voltigeur, who was famous while he lived as the great judge, became more famous still after his death, albeit briefly, as the Phantom who had haunted himself. It was said of him by many that he had devised the most fiendish of all his punishments for himself.

Whether Jean Malchance was damned for those petty magics which he had used to secure, as he saw it, a penalty uniquely fitted to his enemy's trespasses, no one knows. All that is certain is that he died but a few years after, and that just before he died he made a full confession of the whole affair – not to any eager priest of Verena or Morr, but to a wandering story-teller like myself, whom he first forced to swear that the tale should never be told within the walls of Yremy.

The inevitable result of that injunction, of course, was that everyone within those walls had heard the whole of it within a fortnight – and the lowest of the low were for once united with the highest of the high in thinking it the finest tale to which their humble town had ever given birth.

THE OTHER
by Nicola Griffiths

THE CITY OF Middenheim reared up on its fist of rock, blocking the glitter of weak autumn sunlight and throwing a shadow across the line moving patiently up the slope of the viaduct towards the east gate. The air creaked with harness; iron-rimmed wheels rang softly against stone. Stefan stood up in his stirrups to get a better look at the jam of carts and foot travellers.

'It's more than two weeks yet until Carnival.' He pulled at his reins in irritation; the horse snorted and curvetted.

'Stefan,' his father said mildly.

Stefan relaxed his grip a little, patted the horse on the neck. Herr Doktor Hochen nodded approval. Stefan's attention wandered.

He stared down at the back of a craftsman's neck. It was creased with dirt; the rough leather jerkin had rubbed a sore into the skin. It ought to be cleaned with good lye soap before it festered.

He imagined the edges of the sore swelling, glistening red and tight as the poisons accumulated; he could almost taste the thick sweet smell of decay.

His horse danced, sending a stone skittering. Stefan swallowed bile.

'It's going to take longer crawling up this viaduct than to ride from Hunxe.' He tried not to think of the man's neck, festering, swelling. 'We should have ridden on last night and not bothered staying at the inn.'

'The gates would have been closed at that hour.'

'They would have recognized you.'

'Perhaps. But the Watch might be a little overzealous about its duties at this time of year.'

Stefan looked at the sunlight gleaming on his father's soft-tanned boots and brown riding velvets, and wondered why a physician important enough to be summoned all the way to Grubentreich to minister to the son of Grand Duke Leopold would not be prepared to force the Watch to recognize him. Whatever the hour.

Privately, he suspected that it was because his father was getting too old to sit on his horse comfortably for any length of time.

'Perhaps we should have taken a coach from the inn at Hunxe.'

His father's shoulders hunched in anger but he spoke quietly, without looking up from his reins.

'You might be eighteen, Stefan, and old enough to have applied for your own physician's licence, but it seems you do not yet have sufficient manners to mind me to grant it.'

Stefan knew an apology would only make things worse. As it was, his father would probably delay the licence for a week or so. He stayed quiet and concentrated on trying to ignore the ache of two days' riding.

Ahead, the faint background noise grew louder. Stefan thought he could hear shouting.

'Sounds as though there's a fight in front.' He stood up in his stirrups but could not see what was happening.

The shouting got louder; a ripple of movement spread outward, reaching them in the form of a rustling of clothes as people shifted from foot to foot. Several scrambled up onto their carts to get a better look.

'Hoy!' Stefan called. 'Can you see what's happening?'

'Someone's had his wagon turned right over on its side.'

'Ask him if anyone's been hurt,' his father said.

'Can't tell,' the man shouted, 'but the Watch are coming out.' He paused. 'They're coming this way.'

'Tell them we're physicians.'

UNDER THE DIRECTION of two members of the Watch, the wagon had already been hauled upright by unwilling bystanders. A guardswoman led them through the crowd.

The air was sharp with the reek of wine which still poured from the shattered barrel. A man wearing the coarse clothes and leather gauntlets of a waggoner lay on his back in shadow. A woman knelt at his side, gently probing his shoulder.

Herr Hochen handed his bag to Stefan and looked around. He walked over to a flat-bedded cart.

'Lift him up here,' he said to the guardswoman.

The woman kneeling at the man's side stood up, shadow line slicing across her body diagonally from collarbone to hip. One knee of her pale green trousers was stained with wine, like a bruise. A cotton scarf, the same colour as the wine stain, was tied around her upper left arm. She was wearing a light cloak against the autumn chill but it was slung back over her shoulders, out of the way, and pinned with a wooden brooch. She was young, seventeen perhaps, but fatigue or something else made her seem older. Her hair, light brown and just long enough to be tied back, was dull with travel dust.

'He should not be moved until his leg is splinted,' she said.

'I need to get a good look at him, my dear.'

'His shoulder may be broken too.'

'He'll be taken good care of, don't worry. Are you his daughter?'

'No.'

'I see.' He turned to the guardswoman. 'Lift him up please.'

Stefan turned away from the injured man's pain as two guardsmen heaved him onto the cart. The woman stooped to pick up a leather satchel which she slung over her back. Stefan recognized it as the kind of thing travelling musicians carried and wondered how she knew about splinting bones. She saw Stefan watching her. He blushed, but walked over.

'You don't agree with my father's methods?'

'No.'

'Don't you know who my father is?'

'No.'

'Herr Doktor Franz Hochen.'

'So now I know his name, as well as the fact that he doesn't know his job.'

'He's the most well-respected physician in Middenheim. In fact, my father is the representative of the Guild of Physicians and advises the Emperor on health, education and welfare.'

'Then if he is not ignorant, he has caused that waggoner suffering wilfully.'

'That man was poor, you could tell by looking at him. If we treated him here, we'd get no fee. So that cart will take him to the Temple of Shallya where the initiates take charity cases. Later, if it turns out he has got funds, then my father would be pleased to treat him. As it is, my father is probably paying for the use of that cart out of his own pocket. He's too generous.'

'I see.'

It was the exact tone his father had used earlier.

'We could prosecute you for practising healing without a licence,' he said.

'You wouldn't.' It was a statement. 'Who authorizes these licences?'

'My father. He makes recommendations to the elector from the applications received by the guild. Why? Do you want to apply?'

She studied him a moment.

'Perhaps.'

And then she turned and forced her way into the crowd.

Stefan was left staring at the people she had pushed past. He felt foolish. He did not even know her name.

THE NIGHT WAS mild and damp. Stefan walked along the Garten Weg slowly, enjoying the smell of grass and wet leaves. He stopped and listened to the unusual quiet. When he set up his practice, he would buy a house somewhere in clean, orderly Nortgarten, overlooking Morrspark where it was always peaceful.

He smiled. Today, his father had handed him a parchment stamped in blue and fastened with the elector's seal; he could set up his practice whenever he liked. He walked north and then east along Ostgarten, leaving the quiet behind.

Burgen Bahn heaved with people. It was nearly midnight but with only a week to Carnival, hawkers and pleasure-seekers lit lamps against the dark and did business while they could.

Stefan stooped through the doorway of the Red Moon. A fire blazed at one end and torches sputtered around a stage at the other; the room was full of noise. His cloak steamed in the heat.

'Stefan!'

He waved and made his way over to his friends' table. They poured him wine while he took off his cloak.

'Welcome, Herr Doktor Stefan,' one of them said, handing him a leather cup.

Stefan grinned.

'Thank you, Josef.'

He sipped and leaned back in his chair to get a good look at the stage, letting the heavy wine slide over his tongue. Tonight was his night; he wanted to savour every moment. To one side of the stage, a heavy-set man was tuning his rebec while another sat cross-legged, running through some repetitive tune on the pipes.

Stefan missed the point at which the rebec began to thread the room with the counter melody; it was just there, weaving the audience in tight.

Two women began to dance. They moved easily, perfectly in time, ignoring the audience. To Stefan, it seemed that they danced for each other, swaying in and out of each other's reach but never touching. He watched, fascinated, as they stepped in close and silk skirts slid up the smooth muscle of their thighs at the same time. They held that position, close enough to feel the heat of each other's skin, for several heart-beats.

When the music finished, Stefan clapped as loudly as the rest. Several of his friends threw money onto the stage. Eva always hired the best entertainers in the city.

'And that was just the first act.' He filled his goblet and took a long swallow, waving the wineboy over for more.

'Look,' Josef nodded over to a tall woman in a cloak who had just arrived. 'Eberhauer's here.'

Janna Eberhauer, the deputy High Wizard, took her seat next to the owner of the Red Moon who smiled and stroked her arm, then stood, gesturing towards the stage.

'Looks like Eva's going to introduce the next one herself.'

'...for our next performer. She's young but very, very talented. Katya Raine.'

A young woman walked onto the stage carrying a pair of hand drums. Stefan leaned forward. It was the girl he had met by the east gate, the healer. Her loose trousers and sleeveless shirt were soft black. The scarf tied around her arm was black too. Her feet were bare. She sat down and settled the drums between her legs.

'Tonight, we sit well fed and snug, with the Carnival moons overhead and wine lying warm in our bellies.' There were a few cheers and shouts. 'But tonight I will sing of a different place, a village where hungry people sit in their houses roofed with straw while autumn hardens to winter.'

The audience was silent while Katya's hands moved over the drums, stroking and tapping, cupping the sounds, bringing them to life. They spoke of ground brittle with frost, of breath steaming in air bright as glass, of a deep and waiting cold. Power built under her fingers. Her eyes glittered with reflected torchlight and she swayed slightly, her head moving from side to side with the beat. Shadows caught and dissolved on the planes and ridges of her cheek and neck. Her fingers moved blindly, gently as moths. She sang...

...of a young woman kneeling on the floor of an old cow byre, feeding a fire with chips of goat dung. She was excited, impatient. Finally, satisfied with the height of the flames, she opened a small leather pouch and slid a stone onto her palm. It was dull and red. Using tongs, she held the stone over the flames. Now she would see if she was right: if it was heartsblood stone, it would glow in the heat and then, cooled in wine, it would be a treasure beyond price. The wine could be used in many healing tinctures, drop by precious drop. Or so she had been told by her great grandmother.

With a flat crack, the stone exploded; she coughed in the smoke. Her left arm was stinging and when her eyes stopped running, she saw that it was smeared with blood. A sliver of stone must have caught her. She examined the charred dust on the end of the tongs: whatever the stone had been, it was not heartsblood.

That night, she woke in pain. Her arm was hot and swollen. Careful not to wake her sister who shared her pallet, she slid from under the sleeping furs and went outside into the moonlight. Around the puncture hole, her arm was puffy and tender. There was still something in there. It would have to come out.

The next day, the arm was sore where she had cut into the flesh but it no longer felt unnaturally heavy and hot. The woman wondered what the stone could have been. That night, she woke up again. She unwound the bandage; the arm was healing well but she felt strange, lightheaded. Outside, she did not feel the cold, it seemed that voices and hot breath whispered over her skin. Her body sang with excitement. She ran, laughing and mad, through the freezing night. It was dawn before she returned to her family's cottage, exhausted and bewildered, with blood on her hands and lips. Frightened as she was, she had the wit to wash herself before she lay down to get what rest she could.

The young woman tried everything, all her healing arts, to fight the madness growing inside her. But her efforts were useless; the stone which had shattered into slivers had been warpstone, and one speck of warpstone dust could wrench away sanity and mutate a body into something not human. Day after day, she fought the urges swelling up inside her. At night, when the dark influence pulled at her mind, she lost all memory of what she did. When she did sleep, her dreams were full of killing and tearing. Under the scarf tied about her left arm, her skin healed in a scale pattern, like a snake.

And then the morning came when she woke from her madness to find her whole arm covered in green scales and her nails hooked into claws. Inside the cottage, her entire family lay with their throats ripped out, stiffening in their own blood. She felt no doubt: she had done this thing. She was no longer human.

By noon, she had laid a huge fire in the centre of the cottage. She fastened the shutters from the outside, then she went inside and locked the heavy door. Using a twig, she pushed the key under the door out of reach. Now there was no way out. She lit the fire and burned herself to death.

KATYA SAT SILENTLY on the stage, her drums beside her. The glitter was gone from her eyes. Janna Eberhauer, the deputy High Wizard, watched her intently. The whole room was still. She had made them look into the face of a fear they lived with day by day, the horror that was warpstone – its power to pervert healthy daughters and well-loved sons into mutated forms who, shunned by law-abiding people, lost their sanity and turned to the worship of unspeakable gods. In silence, Katya picked up her drums and left the stage.

The audience stirred, then began to applaud. Coins showered the stage. Wineboys scraped the money into a pile for her to collect later. Stefan drained his cup, filled it and drank again.

'Hoy!' He called a wineboy over. 'Parchment and quill, quickly.'

When he had finished he folded it, scrawled Katya's name on the front and gave it to the waiting boy along with a copper coin.

The boy smirked but threaded his way past the crowded tables and through a curtain at the back. A few moments later, she stood by his table, holding the note.

'Did you write this?' She tossed it onto the table. 'I can't read.'

'It says... uh, it asks would you like to join me for some wine?'

She sat down.

'I enjoyed your performance.'

'Thank you.'

'Yes. Though I've never heard of heartsblood stone.'

'Before she died, my grandmother's mind wandered. She talked about strange red stones and how good spirits would reward hard work with pots of gold all in the same breath. When you're young you believe anything. Especially if you want to believe it.'

'I could almost believe that you sang from knowledge.'

'Only almost?' she asked.

Stefan's friend Josef looked at the scarf tied around Katya's left arm.

'Clever. Nice bit of deception, that. But maybe it's not deception,' he said boldly, 'maybe you really are a mutant.' He was drunk.

She looked amused, not shocked.

'Have I sung my song so convincingly that I must take off my scarf to prove I'm not some creature of the night?' She turned to Stefan. 'I'd like that wine now.'

He beckoned another wineboy.

'Bring a bottle of wine and a cup for the lady. Make it one of your best and there'll be some coppers in it for you.' He handed the boy five gold crowns, then felt embarrassed at his extravagance.

'I'm celebrating,' he told her. 'I got my licence today.'

'I have applied for mine,' she said.

The wine came before he had to reply. He poured for all of them.

'Where will you practise?'

'No idea yet,' he said.

'You have no real vocation for healing, have you, Stefan?' she said quietly. Close up, he saw that her eyes were dull with fatigue and ringed with blue. She seemed thinner.

He shrugged.

'I wouldn't call mixing potions to aid the overtaxed digestions of rich people a holy duty, if that's what you mean.'

'The rich are not the only ones who need care.' She looked at him steadily.

His nostrils filled with the stench of people lying in their own filth, rotting from inside with disease, and the sound of their thin cries deafened him. His stomach rippled; he did not see the wineboy approach the table.

'Fraulein Katya? The deputy High Wizard wishes to speak with you.'

Without a word, she stood and followed him.

Stefan's hand shook as he reached for his wine. A few tables away, Janna Eberhauer leaned close to Katya, talking softly.

Josef followed his gaze. 'Don't take it too hard, Stefan. She's probably happier with her own kind.' He laughed. 'I wonder how Eva's feeling about this.'

Stefan turned to look at him, full of revulsion. Who for, he was not sure.

OVER THE NEXT few days, images of Katya haunted Stefan. He saw her as he had that first time, by the gate, stained with wine, sure of her skill; he heard her singing, remembered the glitter of her eyes. But he dreamed of a different Katya, a Katya who slipped her arms around him from behind and kissed him until he moaned. And when he turned to reach for her, the arms she held out to him were scaled and taloned.

'STEFAN, WHAT CATCHES your interest in here?'

His father sounded pleased to find him in the room which doubled as library and record repository. Stefan turned round, a scroll pushed through his belt.

'I was just looking through a few records to see if I could find an exact definition of a mutant.' The lie came easily.

His father looked interested.

'Exact definition? Can't say I've ever really thought about it.'

He went over to a cupboard and rummaged around. 'There might be something in the... ah, here we are.' He dragged a volume from an orderly pile and laid it on the table. 'Now, let's see...'

'Perhaps I should look. You've always found references for me. Now that I have my licence, I ought to do my own reading too.'

His father looked so pleased that Stefan was ashamed of his deception.

'Well then, I'll just take what I came for and leave you to it.' He gathered up the pile of scrolls on the table; Stefan held the door for him. 'There have been times when I've doubted you would ever make a physician, Stefan, but perhaps I have been wrong, perhaps after all you will be sorting through this pile of licence applications one day. I'm proud of you.'

Stefan pulled the parchment from his belt and sat down. *Application for Licence, Physician's Guild: Katya Raine*, he read. She must have hired a scribe.

He scanned the contents. She came from Schoninghagen, almost a hundred miles to the south and west. What had made her travel all the way to Middenheim? He tucked the scroll back into his belt and left.

IT WAS ONE of those rare autumn afternoons when the sun streamed clear and warm into the city. Stefan had not bothered with a cloak. He shouldered his way through the crowds along Burgen Bahn. With only three days to go until Carnival, he was thankful that the Red Moon was not in the middle of the Altmarkt where it was certain to be even more crowded.

The closer he came to the Red Moon, the slower he walked. Katya's application rubbed against his skin where it lay hidden beneath his shirt. He did not know what he wanted of her. To talk to her, maybe. Or maybe not. She attracted him but made him uneasy. By the time he saw the distinctive brick of the Red Moon, warm against the grey stone of the other buildings, he was considering abandoning the whole idea and walking straight past.

The door of the Red Moon opened and Katya slipped out, carrying her satchel. She turned down Zauber Strasse. Stefan peered around the corner after her; she had not seen him.

He followed.

Two thirds of the way along the street, she turned into an alleyway. She walked swiftly between houses without pausing to look around; she must have travelled this way several times before. She turned again, left then right, and Stefan almost lost her, just catching a flicker of blue as she went in the back entrance of a big house. He marked the colour of the paintwork and the style of roof tiles. It should be possible to recognize the right house if he worked his way back through the alleys to the front.

It was Janna Eberhauer's. He should have known.

Eberhauer, the deputy High Wizard. And Katya. He felt as though he could not breathe. It took him a few moments to realize that he was shaking with rage. And around and around in his head, like a temple chant, ran the thought: he should have known, he should have known.

He went round the back again and settled against a wall where he could see the door but where he would be out of sight of anyone leaving. No matter how long it took, he would wait. Then he would find out what was going on.

By the second hour, the sun was sinking, leaving the alleys in shadow. He stamped his feet to keep them warm and wished he had worn a cloak.

His legs began to ache and he was hungry. The wall he was leaning on was damp. Doubts gnawed at him: what if she had left by the front door? He pushed it to the back of his mind.

The stars were showing. The remains of his rage sat in his stomach like an undigested meal. He would not give up, but he was achieving nothing here.

STEFAN REACHED THE Red Moon just before midday. His muscles were stiff and aching, and he wore a cloak against the freezing mist. He hoped he would not have to wait long.

This time she did not carry the satchel with her drums but a different bag. Something a physician might carry. Instead of turning down Zauber Strasse, she walked south along Burgen Bahn. It was easy to follow her through the crowds without being seen. It became even busier as she led him along Ost Weg; by Markt Weg the crowds had become so dense that he had difficulty keeping her in sight. When they reached the Altmarkt, he moved to within three strides of her back, trusting to luck that she did not look round.

Luck almost abandoned him when she went into an apothecary's. Trying to duck out of sight, he crashed backwards into a barrow full of fruit alongside a stall. He panicked when the owner shouted at him then calmed as he realized Katya would not be able to pick out one noise from another in the din: fruit sellers hawked their wares; a mother pulled down her child's breeches and held him over the gutter while he shrieked in protest; a woman, passing the mother and child, got splashed and began to shout. Stefan helped the angry stall owner to pick up the fruit.

When Katya came out of the shop, she turned out of the Altmarkt towards the Old Quarter. Stefan's heart thumped. The Old Quarter was not a safe place to be, at any time. There were no crowds to hide behind there. He wished he was carrying a knife, even though he had never used one before, except to cut meat. He turned a corner. Alleys led off in all directions. He panicked; Katya was nowhere to be seen.

There was no warning; a kick caught him behind the knees and he went down, his arm twisted up his back and a knee on his spine. Stone scraped his jaw as his attacker pulled his head around to get a look at his face.

'It's you.' Katya made a sound of disgust and let him up.

Stefan stood up slowly. She had knocked the wind out of him.

'Are you hurt?'

'No,' he managed.

'Good. Explain why you're following me.'

He wanted to shout at her, tell her how much she had frightened him.

'Why are you practising without a licence?' he blurted instead.

'I have applied. It's only a matter of days before I receive the official stamp of approval. Then your orderly mind can rest from its worries about proper paperwork.'

He said nothing, remembering the parchment against his ribs.

'Come with me and see the people I treat. Then tell me I need a licence before I lift a finger to help them.'

He was so close that he could smell the damp wool of her cloak, her sandalwood perfume. Mist stung his scraped chin; she could have broken his neck while he lay on the ground. Unease knotted his belly.

They walked through the worst part of the old quarter.

'Those I treat are poor, sick, old. They are not gentle people. Prepare yourself for that.'

Splintered buildings gaped at him like broken teeth, waiting to swallow him, trap him in their rottenness and despair.

'This way.'

They climbed over rubble blocking a doorway. Her sandalwood was not strong enough to counter the smell of filth
and neglect. Inside, it was gloomy; many windows were
boarded up. Stefan jumped as a shadow moved nearby.

'They wonder who you are.' She put her bag on the floor
near the remains of a staircase and took off her cloak. She
gave it to him to hold. 'Wait here.'

She climbed the stairs and disappeared into the darkness.

Stefan tried to concentrate on the cloak in his hands. It felt
rough. When he was rich, he would buy her a cloak of fine,
heavy wool, lined with silk. A green cloak, the same colour
as the trousers she had been wearing by the east gate. Then
he remembered Eberhauer.

Something moved.

'Who is it?' Sweat wormed down his back. 'Anyone there?'
His voice was swallowed by the dark. Something was watching him.

A shadow inched its way across the floor towards the dim
light. It sat back on its haunches and tried to speak. Panic
leapt like lightning up Stefan's spine. He ran.

He did not look where he was going, he just ran, pursued
by visions of the mutant with lumpy and misshapen limbs
and running sores, whose elephantine skin grew too far
across its eyes and stretched over its mouth making speech
almost impossible.

WHEN KATYA FOUND him he had stopped retching. He pulled
himself into a ball.

'Leave me alone.'

She squatted down beside him and felt for fever.

'Keep away from me!' He pushed her hand away.

After a while, he asked, 'Why do you do this?'

'Because they need me.'

'Mutants don't need anyone.'

She was silent so long he thought she was ignoring him.

'The one who frightened you is called Siggy. He is not a
mutant. When he was two years old, his father spilled burning lamp oil on him. The burns were so bad that his arms
and legs healed all out of shape and his skin thickened and

grew back in all the wrong places. He can't stand properly
and it hurts for him to move around even a little. Without
proper attention, his skin dries out and cracks. I can help
him with that.'

Stefan tried to remember Siggy's face but the memory was
slippery. He did not know what to think. Burns might
explain the disfigurement.

'Are you telling me the truth?' His voice was hoarse.

'Siggy is not a mutant.'

He was uncertain.

'I could still report you for not having a licence.' It was like
a talisman, a ritual chant to dispel confusion.

'I can help some of them, Stefan. You could too.'

He wanted to believe her but his fear was real. She stood
up.

'Come on.'

She reached down to help him up. Her cloak slid back to
reveal the scarf tied around her arm. Fear slammed through
him again.

'Show me,' he licked his lips, 'show me what's under that
scarf. Then I'll help you.'

She went still. 'I won't bargain with you.'

'Why not? There will be things you need, certain ingredi-
ents you won't be able to buy without showing a licence. I
could get them for you.' He pushed himself upright. 'Show
me what's under the scarf.'

'You don't know what you're asking.'

'Show me.'

'When I sing, Stefan, I do more than mouth a few words
to a pretty tune. I give an audience mystery, myself an air of
otherness.' She touched the scarf gently. 'This is my mystery.'

'Show me. That's the price of my help.'

She was silent a moment.

'It may not be what you want to see.'

She unwound the scarf. Stefan's stomach curled in a tight
fist as the last twist of cloth fell free.

'Look.'

The arm was perfect and unblemished. Where the scarf
had been, the skin was pale. Stefan reached out to touch it
with his fingertips. It was warm and smooth.

There was no relief; the tension burrowed deeper into his stomach. He did not understand why. He wanted to walk away and never see Katya Raine again and could not; he had made a bargain.

'Make me a list of the things you need. I'll deliver them tomorrow.'

THE RED MOON looked smaller in daylight. It smelled of stale wine and ash: the remains of last night's fire lay in the grate. An elderly woman had gone to tell Katya he was here.

Stefan was tense and his head ached slightly; he had not slept well. He flinched when Katya entered the room. She was limping slightly.

'I tripped over my drums in the dark last night,' she said, gesturing at her leg. 'It's bruised, but nothing a bit of comfrey won't cure.'

Stefan could not imagine Katya being clumsy.

'I have everything you asked for.' He placed a small sack on the table between them.

'Thank you. How much do I owe?'

'I don't want your money.' Confusion made him abrupt. He did not want to touch anything which had been near her. But she was beautiful.

'Thank you again.' She paused. 'Would you like a drink while you're here?'

'No. I have to get out. I mean, I have to go.'

He retreated ungracefully.

He walked slowly along Burgen Bahn, not wanting to go home. On the Ostgarten Weg, dwarfs were building a huge wooden platform overlooking the park. Graf Boris and his family would sit there tomorrow and watch the Carnival fireworks. The hammering and hoarse shouts as pieces of timber were lifted into place and fastened together were muffled and unreal. He turned left off the Garten Weg and down Grun Allee which ran along the southern edge of the Altmarkt. Here, he found what he wanted: noise and bright colours to push the fear he did not understand from his mind. He wandered there for hours.

As the afternoon began to turn to evening, he found himself standing next to an old woman, watching a sleight-of-hand artist who had set up his table between a flower barrow and a beer seller. The man was pulling eggs and brightly coloured scarfs from his mouth and tossing them into the audience. There was scattered applause. He bowed, then took a cage from under his table. Inside, a snake hissed; its tongue flickered in and out. Stefan stirred uneasily.

The old woman poked him in a friendly fashion.

'All done with misdirection,' she said, nodding at the magician who was holding up the snake while displaying its empty cage, assuring the crowd that there was no hidden trapdoor or false base.

'What?' Stefan said. He was poised on the edge of realization.

'I said, it's all done with misdirection. While we're looking at that empty cage, he's…'

Misdirection. Now he knew why there had been no relief at the sight of that unblemished arm. Oh, gods, misdirection.

'Here, are you all right?' The woman's voice seemed miles away. 'You're white as a bedsheet.'

He had been fooled. She had fooled everyone. He had to do something, tell someone.

JANNA EBERHAUER STOOD silently by her fire, contemplating the flames. Her hair was loose and she was wearing her bed robe.

'What are you suggesting?' she asked mildly.

'That perhaps she is not all she seems,' Stefan said carefully.

'And you came to me.'

'I don't want anything to happen to her. But if she…' He swallowed. 'Mutants are an abomination. You're the deputy High Wizard.'

The curtain screening the room from the sleeping area drew back. Katya limped through, brushing her hair. She looked ill. Stefan stared, immobilized by shock. She had been there all the time. She limped towards him.

'Keep away from me.'

'Stefan, I'm not evil.'

'Why are you risking so much?' he asked Eberhauer. 'You can't help her. Nobody can.'

'Yet you came to me, to ask for help.'

Faced with the wizard's calm, he felt foolish and graceless. Katya lowered herself into a chair. He saw how carefully she moved.

'What's the matter with her?' he asked Eberhauer.

'I can still speak for myself,' Katya said. She reached for a cup of water and took a sip. 'The story I told, the song, is essentially true in one respect.' She put the cup down and began to roll up the bottom of her trousers. It was an obvious effort. Eberhauer moved to help her.

Fear flexed like a snake in Stefan's belly.

'No,' he croaked, 'I don't want to see.'

Eberhauer looked up from the bandage she was unrolling.

'You accuse and meddle without knowing anything,' she said calmly. 'Now you will learn.'

'No!' Horror lapped at his reason. 'I can't!'

'You can.'

Eberhauer rose and took his hand. He could not resist as she led him over to where Katya leaned back in the chair, her eyes closed in exhaustion. Her right trouser leg was rolled up past the knee. Bloody bandaging lay in a heap on the rug.

Stefan looked.

There was a slash across the back of her calf, the sort an inexperienced swordsman might make trying to hamstring an opponent. It was a recent injury, beginning to scab over. He frowned.

'I don't understand.'

'Examine it closely.'

Around the healing gash, almost too faint to be seen, was a tracery of cracks. In a scale pattern.

'We tried to excise the speck of warpstone that must still be in there,' Eberhauer said, impossibly calm.

'It's evil,' he whispered.

'Listen to me. Katya is not evil. Warpstone acts on her flesh and its madness pulls at her mind. But that is not evil. As to the madness, she is strong. She resists still.'

'But her skin...'

'I am not evil,' Katya said from the chair. 'I am not mad.'
Stefan refused to hear her, he spoke to Eberhauer.

'But she will be, in the end.'

'Without help, yes.'

They were both looking at him. The air was thick and
sticky, difficult to breathe.

'Oh gods, you want me to do it. You want me to hack at it
again, slice into the muscle, bone deep, and cut, and cut.
No.' He backed towards the door. 'It won't work, it just won't
work. Even if I cut the whole leg off.'

Eberhauer was silent a moment, watching the flames.
'Warpstone dust is materialization of Chaos-matter into
solid form. Magic is the manipulation of energies inherent
in Chaos.' She looked at him directly. 'I am a wizard. This
thing is possible.'

THEY HELPED KATYA onto the bed; Eberhauer stroked her hair
and began to hum while Stefan gathered what they would
need. He rolled up the rug and laid the gloves, bowl, ban-
dages and other things on the floor. The wizard stood,
letting the sound build as she raised her arms over her head
and down again in a slow circle. She nodded to Stefan: Katya
slept. He wiped the leg down and poured raw alcohol over
his knife.

Though he had never cut into living tissue before, he used
the knife easily, like a quill, marking the edges of the exci-
sion then sliding the blade in sideways to part skin from
muscle. He mopped at the blood. The muscle was red and
plump beneath his fingers. He cut into it. Around him, the
humming became more insistent, singing through his
hands.

He stopped at a tight knot of tissue. The vibration in his
hands became an angry jangle. This was what he was looking for. He probed at it, eased what looked like a fleck of
dirt onto the tip of his knife. This was the focus of all his
nightmares; so small. It was glowing. He lifted it out into
the air.

Eberhauer's humming swelled into a sound thick enough
to stand on; Stefan could feel the force of it flowing down
his arm, recoiling from the malignancy poised at the end of

his knife. His fear became anger, a refusal of the torment of Chaos, for his sake, for Katya's sake. He joined his negation to Eberhauer's. The warpstone dimmed and began to smoke, curling smaller and smaller until there was nothing left.

STEFAN SAT BY the bed and watched her breathe. There were still hollows under her cheekbones but the dark circles under her eyes were fading. Outside, the first fireworks of Carnival stained the sky.

Janna Eberhauer came and stood behind him.

'She'll leave us, won't she?' he said.

'Yes.'

'Where? Back to Schoninghagen?'

'She told me she's always wanted to see the north. She will go there, I think, to the snow and ice.'

'You want her to stay.' He knew how much the wizard had risked, and perhaps why.

'I want whatever is right for her. And she has found all she came here for.'

'Not quite.' He reached inside his shirt. The scroll of parchment was stamped with Katya's name and sealed with the blue of the elector. He laid it on the coverlet near Katya's hand, stood up.

'Tell her it might be useful if she ever comes back. And tell her,' he looked down at the woman sleeping on the bed, 'tell her I plan to work at the Temple of Shallya a while, until I know what I want.'

He closed the door quietly behind him and stepped out into the splash of light and colour which was Carnival.

THE SONG
by Steve Baxter

'NICE RING, SAM. What's the sparkly stuff – glass, or some-thing less expensive?'

Buttermere Warble, known to his friends as Sam, looked up with a start. On the other side of his table was a small fig-ure with a grinning face and a thatch of brown hair. 'Oh. Tarquin. It's you. Your boat's in, then. Oh, good.'

Now more halflings came crowding into the tavern after Tarquin. Jasper, the barman of Esmeralda's Apron, pot-belly wobbling, growled at them to shut the damn door. Even here, deep in Marienburg on the murky rim of the Elven Quarter, the winds off the Sea of Claws had power.

The halflings pulled up stools and began settling around Sam's table. Soon he was ringed by a jostling rabble. 'Join me, why don't you,' Sam said drily. In his line of work it was useful to have contacts at all levels of society – but you could have too much of a good thing…

'Aw, Sam, aren't you glad to see us?' A skinny young halfling called Maximilian dug a worn pack of cards out of his woollen coat and began shuffling them.

'Oh, sure. I was getting so sick of calm, peace and quiet.'

Tarquin sat opposite Sam. 'So what's the story with the ring?'

Sam's ring was a fat band of gold; shards of crystal caught the light. Another young sailor bent over to see. 'Broken glass must be in this year.'

Sam covered the ring with the palm of his hand. 'It's personal.'

Tarquin shook his head in mock disapproval. 'Oh, come on,' he said. 'We're just off the boat. Tell us while we're still sober.'

'I told you, it's personal.'

'How personal?'

'A tankard of ale.'

Maximilian laughed. 'Ah, keep it.' He slapped cards on the rough tabletop. 'Three Card Pegasus. That's what I want to spend my sober time on...'

But Sam pushed back the hand he'd been dealt. 'Sorry, lads. Deal me out.'

Tarquin sat back, mouth wide. 'You're kidding. Dragon High Sam refusing a game?'

'What is it?' Maximilian asked. 'Funds low? No juicy cases recently?'

Sam shook his head. 'No. I'm sworn off Pegasus, that's what.'

'Why?'

'Well, it's kind of connected to the ring. But it's basically because of what happened last time I played...'

The circle of faces were fixed on him now. 'Come on, Sam. Tell us.'

Sam looked significantly at his tankard.

Tarquin picked it up. 'Don't tell me. That's personal too, right? Well, you win, Sam. I'll get your ale. But it had better be worth it...'

Sam leaned forward and folded his arms theatrically. 'Right. Picture the scene,' he began. 'It was in the Apron; in this very bar. This table, I think. I can't remember too clearly.' Briefly the halfling's face grew dark, belying his jocular tone. 'I'd... had a bad day. I'd taken it out on one or two tankards–'

'So tell us something new.'

'I was playing Pegasus. And losing. I couldn't even cover the pot. But there were only two of us left in the hand.' He paused.

'And?'

'And I held three Dragons.'

A collective sigh rippled around the table.

MY ONLY OPPONENT was called Eladriel (Sam went on). An elf. Tall, with a streak of gold in the silver of his hair; quite distinguished looking, like a lord almost, even with his knees crammed under the halfling-sized tables. Slumming it a bit down here in the Apron, obviously.

(Jasper growled in warning.)

I remember his eyes. Black as a bird's, they were; they pinned me as I tried to decide what to do.

'Well, Sam?' Eladriel said. 'Do you fold?'

I took another pull at my tankard and tried to think straight. Only three Unicorns can beat three Dragons; we all know that. But I'd lost too much.

'No,' I said. 'I don't fold.'

'Then cover the pot.'

'You know I can't,' I said a little bitterly.

Eladriel smiled, showing even teeth. 'Fold or cover,' he said.

I stared at my three-Dragon hand. 'I'll use a marker.'

Eladriel ran a delicate finger over the edge of his three cards.

'Now, come,' he said slily. 'Markers in a place like this? I think not. You don't have anything of value?'

I knew without looking. 'Nothing.'

Eladriel tutted. 'Everyone owns something, no matter how low they sink.'

'Thanks a lot.'

I stared at those black eyes.

'Fold or cover,' he snapped.

'Name it,' I said thickly. 'Name the stake you want.'

His voice was low. 'Are you serious?'

'Name it.'

'Your mind,' he said rapidly. 'Your very being. Your last asset. Gamble your mind, my friend.'

Another player reached out of the darkness and touched my arm. 'No, Sam. Fold.'

'I know you, Warble,' Eladriel hissed. 'You are... an investigator, are you not? And one of some repute. Your mind is good – for a halfling...'

Now anger mixed in with the booze and the fatigue – just as the elf wanted, I suppose now – and I decided I was going to teach him a lesson.

The coal eyes glowed. Three Dragons leapt at the edge of my vision.

'I'm in,' I said.

'Sam, this is crazy–'

'I'm in. And I'll see your hand.'

Eladriel smiled. And he laid his cards on the table.

You know what they were.

'I know a little battlefield magic,' said Eladriel briskly, and he drew a small, wasp-waisted bottle from his coat. 'I'm an old soldier, you see. This won't hurt, Sam.'

He passed his fingers before my face, once, twice–

I stared at his three grinning Unicorns and the world fell away.

I FELT WARM, but numb. As if I'd lain in a bath for too long, but my head was still working. So I was alive.

Or was I? Could this be the afterlife? I tried opening my eyes. I saw a fat face, round ears, a huge pot belly.

It was Jasper, bending over me.

'I'm finding the afterlife a little disappointing so far, I have to say.' My voice was thick, my mouth dry, but it all worked.

Jasper straightened up and snarled in disgust. 'Eight days out flat haven't dulled your tongue, then.'

'How long?' I tried to sit up.

My back – and backside – were stiff and cold. I'd been lying on rough sacks in what seemed to be the cellar of the Apron.

Jasper began shifting crates around the cold brick floor. My view of him was oddly washed-out, as if I was looking through a thin mist.

'It was like you were asleep. Kept you clean and fed, though,' he added gruffly.

I stood shakily, legs tingling. 'Yes, but by the fields of the Moot, Jasper, couldn't you have moved me around a bit? Haven't you ever heard of bedsores? The blood pools, you see–'

Jasper grunted. 'You're lucky to be able to give cheek, after that damn fool bet. Remember?'

I nodded, rubbing my neck. 'But, Jasper. I held three Dragons. What could I do?'

'Not risked your life. I didn't expect you to wake up.'

I thought it over. 'To be honest, neither did I. People who have their minds taken normally don't, do they?'

He hoisted a barrel over each broad shoulder. 'And by the way. You had a visitor.'

'What? Who?'

'While you were asleep. A messenger from an elf lord, he said. Go to the large house at the north end of Lotharn Street. You'll find something of value. That's what he said.'

'What lord? What thing? What?'

'What? What? I preferred you when you were asleep… You're the investigator; you work it out.' Jasper trudged up the cellar stairs. He called back without turning, 'There's food in the kitchen. And your gambling companion kindly left you the pack of cards. I put it in your pocket.'

'Thanks. Ah… Jasper,' I said, following him. 'I owe you.'

Jasper grunted. 'Just leave money for the food.'

'Lotharn Street, eh?'

I CLIMBED OUT of that cellar into an early morning. A thick mist lay over Marienburg. The mist glowed with sunlight. I walked north through the Elven Quarter, breathing deep.

Now, you know Lotharn Street. You climb gradually until, at the northern end, you reach a fine view of the city as it sprawls over the islands in the mouth of the Reik. That morning the Hoogbrug Bridge seemed to arch into the sky and I could see the sails of a Kislevite frigate jutting out of the mist around the feet of the bridge–

(Yes, all right, Tarquin; I am getting on with it.) The point I'm making is that it was a great-to-be-alive morning, a morning when your skin tingles and your blood runs so fast you feel like doing handstands…

Except I didn't feel like that. I felt as if I was hardly there at all.

To me the colours of the city were pale, as if I was standing in a faded painting. I strained to hear the fog bells of that Kislevite freighter, but my ears seemed stuffed with wool.

Earlier I'd walked past a Tilean street trader, a fat, swarthy human who sold broiled meat on sticks. I couldn't smell the hot meat. And when I bought a piece it tasted like soft wood.

I didn't feel ill, you understand, despite my days unconscious. Just – absent. Not complete.

For the first time I began to feel frightened. After all, I'd had my mind, my very self, taken away – and given back.

Or had I? What if I was no longer complete? How would I feel? And why would anyone play such a trick?

I had a feeling this mysterious elf would have the answer. And I wasn't sure I'd like what I'd hear.

At the northern end of the street a house stood alone. It was surrounded by a head-high wall topped with iron spikes. The spikes were barbed. Cute, I thought.

There was a thick wooden gate, standing open; I walked through into a courtyard of cobbles. The house itself sat like a huge toad in the middle of the courtyard, a box of dreary stone with tight window slits.

The door was a slab of weathered wood with a brass knocker in the shape of a war dog's head. I thought it would bite me when I lifted it.

The door creaked open and out of the darkness thrust a face like a melted mask.

I jumped back. I couldn't help it. A scar like a strip of cloth ran from the scalp right down one side of the face. The chest on that side was crumpled like a crushed egg, and one arm was a lump of gristle.

That wreck of a face twisted into a half-grin.

I managed to say, 'My name is–'

'Sss-ammm.' The lips would barely close, and spittle sprayed over a distorted chin. 'I know. He'shh ex-pecting you.'

'Who?'

But the creature just turned slightly and, with the good arm, gestured me in. The door was barely open. I had to squeeze past, and the wrecked arm brushed against me, cold as old meat. I thought I'd throw up. The old cripple grinned wider.

The house was built around a single large room. A little light leaked through the slit windows as if by accident.

The room contained a bottle.

The bottle was about the size of my fist and it had a wasp waist. It sat on a simple table at the centre of the stone floor.

Yes, Tarquin, there was more in that room than a bottle. In fact there was a whole lot of precious stuff. I'll come to that. But to me, you see, that bottle glowed like a pearl in mud. I walked up to it and stared, drawn, almost afraid to touch...

'Hands off.'

The voice was painfully familiar. A tall figure emerged from the shadows at the back of the room. I wrenched my gaze from the bottle long enough to take in a fine, inhumanly slender face, a golden streak in silver hair.

'Eladriel,' I said. 'The card player. Of course. So you really are a lord...'

Talking was an effort. My eyes dropped back to the bottle and I felt my hands rise, tugged to the glass as if by magnetism...

There was a growl at my neck, a breath that stank of sour milk.

'Down, Aloma!' Eladriel snapped.

Yes, Tarquin; he said Aloma, a girl's name. I was as surprised as you are.

'And you,' said Eladriel. 'Arms by your side.'

I did as he said. The foul breath moved away. Eladriel relaxed and walked closer. 'No need to be frightened of Aloma,' he said, smiling. 'As long as you behave yourself.'

'Aloma? He's a she? I mean... it? Er – you're kidding.'

'Not at all. Used to fight at my side in my younger days. Without her I doubt if I would have done half as well on all those campaigns. Mightn't have survived, even. With her help I got out with enough profit to buy my way into a Marienburg shipping concern and to settle into this–' he waved an arm '–comfortable retirement. Dear old Aloma–'

The Aloma-thing blushed. Yes, blushed. It was like watching a side of mutton go foul.

Eladriel went on, 'Her strength's extremely rare, of course.' He whispered behind a delicate hand, 'I suspect there's a little ogre blood in the mix there somewhere… Yes, dear Aloma,' he said more loudly. 'Getting a bit long in the tooth now, of course, but still as tough as any two warriors… and in case it should occur to you to try anything let me point out that her single good arm could crush your spine like a twig.'

'Uh-huh. I'm reconsidering the pass I was planning.'

'And she was quite a beauty before her injury.'

'Really?'

Eladriel's smile faltered. 'Well, no, not really. But she has her uses. Now then, gambler, no doubt you're wondering why I've asked you here.'

With a supreme effort I stepped back from the table. 'Get to the point, Eladriel. What's in the bottle?'

'Bottle?' he asked innocently. 'Which bottle? Do you know what he's talking about, Aloma?'

My hostess cackled like a blocked drain. 'What-t boss-tle?' she slurred.

'Oh, very funny,' I snapped. 'What a double act.'

Eladriel nodded calmly, still smiling. 'I think you already know what's in there, Sam. Can't you feel it? Aren't you drawn to it? Haven't you been feeling a little – not all there?'

Aloma sniggered. I held myself still, dreading his answer.

'You are in there, Sam,' he said in a matter-of-fact way. 'The rest of you. Now listen carefully. That bottle is sealed. And I've put another of my old battlefield spells on it, an aura of invulnerability. Do you know what that means? The glass can't be broken; it will resist any blow. Only I can open the bottle, release you and make you whole, you see. And any time I want I can do this.'

Blank.

I was lying on the floor. I must have hit the table on my way down; my forehead throbbed.

'Easy as snapping a finger,' Eladriel said softly. 'Neat, isn't it?'

I tried to keep my voice level. 'What do you want, Eladriel?'

'I can tell you what I don't want. And that's to waste my strength holding half a mind that was a bit lightweight to start with. Tell you what, why don't we trade?'

He turned and began to pace about the room, glancing over objects stacked around the walls on shelves and low tables. There was a painting of a bowl of flowers; Eladriel ran his finger around the edge of its frame. Then he moved to a sculpture of a girl's face, turned up to the sky; Eladriel cupped her cheek in the palm of his hand.

'See this stuff?' he asked. 'Human art, you know. It has an element of... vividness that's missing from elven work, I always feel. A rawness, perhaps. I'm a collector, you see.' He coughed modestly. 'I've gained a certain reputation in some circles as a connoisseur of early Tilean belt buckles. Perhaps you've seen my monograph on the subject–'

'Oh, of course,' I said. 'During a hard night in the Apron my mates and I talk about nothing else. Tilean bloody belt buckles.'

Eladriel raised a manicured eyebrow but otherwise ignored me. 'There is quite a little community of us, you know. Collectors of human art. And some of us,' he said in a conspiratorial whisper, 'go a little further.'

'Further?'

'Some go so far as to – ah... collect, shall we say – the artists as well. Do you understand? Poets, painters, dancers...'

I couldn't believe it. 'Elves running a market in humans? Eladriel, there are five hundred elves in this city... and about twenty thousand humans. If they ever find out there's a human slave market they'll kill you in your beds.'

He looked shocked. 'Slave? What a sordid word. These little creatures are well cared for and are free to practise their art before an appreciative audience. What more could they ask?'

I considered. 'Freedom? Choice?'

He ignored me. 'And of course, it makes economic sense. Why buy eggs if you can own the goose? Besides, those humans who do know about it will make sure the rest don't find out. Elven money means a lot to this city.

'As I was saying. There was one particular artist. A singer. A girl called Lora... quite lovely, apparently. Well, she came

up for auction one day, and there was quite a buzz in the circle. Even to hear her sing, just once… But there was a
pre-emptive bid. From Periel.' He spat the name.

'*The* Periel? The elf lord who owns the island close to High
Bridge?'

'He may.' Eladriel sniffed. 'Well-to-do, I understand.'

'Right,' I said. 'Probably as "well-to-do" as the rest of you
interlopers put together.'

Eladriel sniffed again, looking carefully indifferent. 'Well,
because of Periel, no other elf got to hear Lora sing.'

I laughed. 'And I bet that must have driven you wild.'

Eladriel sighed. 'Lora may be the finest singer of her gen-
eration. I really must hear her voice.'

'Oh, sure. Purely for aesthetic reasons. Tweaking Periel's
nose has nothing to do with it.'

'Even just once, a single song. Well, then. So sorry to see
you go.' He moved his arms in a brushing motion. The
hideous Aloma grunted and began to shuffle towards the
door. 'So is that clear?'

I was baffled. 'What?'

'Why, what I want you to do for me, of course. Arrange for
me to hear Lora sing.'

There was a lump of ice forming in my stomach; I heard
my breathing go shallow.

'Steal her from Periel? The most powerful elf in the city?
But… how?'

He looked elegantly surprised. 'Why are you asking me?
You're supposed to be the resourceful investigator. That's
your problem, isn't it? Here.' He handed me another bottle,
identical to the one containing a bit of me. 'This also has a
protective aura. Maybe you'll find it handy.'

I stared at the bottle. 'I suppose there's no point asking for
my usual thirty crowns a day plus expenses–'

Blank.

I was on the floor again. '–but in the circumstances I'll be
happy to waive the fee,' I said as I picked myself up and
pocketed the bottle. 'Don't bother, Aloma, I'll show myself
out. By the way, lay off the eyeshadow. Be subtle…'

* * *

IT WASN'T EASY getting to Periel. As one of the city's most successful sea lord merchants he's rich enough to have bought layers of privacy.

My first problem was that he doesn't even live in the Elven Quarter. So I chose a shapeless old coat and a red woollen hat, and set off into the lowlier human districts of Marienburg, working my way towards the mouth of the Reik.

It wasn't a pleasant experience. Not everyone welcomes strangers, even halflings. So I walked through stench-ridden streets with my shoulders hunched and my head down, enduring suspicious stares.

Second problem. Periel lives on one of the rocky river-mouth islands. He likes his privacy. The island's not the biggest piece of rock in the Reik – but it's all Periel's, it has a great view of the open sea, and there are no bridges to it. You wouldn't think that was possible in this city of bridges; but it is.

So I needed a boat.

I found a depressing little tavern on Riddra Island, at the west end of the Suiddock. There were rusty fishhooks and patches of damp on the walls; the tables were sticky with dirt and the ale was gritty. I never thought I'd miss the Apron, but this place was even worse.

(Joke, Jasper. Joke.)

There were three customers in there, sitting in gloomy silence at separate tables. I selected the cleanest-looking of them, bought two tankards of damp grit, and sat down.

The fisherman eyed me warily – he couldn't take his eyes off my red hat – but gradually, in grunts and half-sentences over more tankards, he began to talk.

His name was Kurt. He was a wiry man with a shock of black hair. He survived by scraping herring out of the Sea of Claws. His boat's timbers had a creeping fungus, the herring catch was down that year, and his wife was having it off with a cod-grader called Norbert.

Boys, he was the conversational equivalent of a case of piles.

But he was due to take his boat out at high tide that evening and – after a little encouragement – he agreed to carry a passenger on a small detour.

And so I found myself rowing – yes, rowing – Kurt's creaking boat through the straits of Marienburg. Kurt sat at the stern, picking at a net with black fingernails. The light was fading but it was still brighter than the inside of that tavern at midday. Kurt began to stare at me. I stared back.

'You've got a secret,' he said at length, 'and I know what it is.'

My heart thumped. 'Oh, yes?'

'Yes.' He eyed me shrewdly.

I sized up the situation. Kurt was not much taller than me but a lot broader – and, thanks to Eladriel, I wasn't all there. If Kurt had felt like it he wouldn't have had much trouble taking my purse and dumping me over the side.

'What are you going to do about it, then?' I asked, eyes locked with his.

Surprisingly he shrugged. 'Nothing. Don't worry. Your secret's safe with me.'

'It is?'

'Yes.' He turned his face away from the wind, spat out a chunk of green phlegm, and wiped his mouth with the back of his hand. 'I know why you're wearing that hat,' he grunted at length.

'Hat?' I put a hand to my red woollen cap.

He placed his hand on his scalp, grabbed a handful of hair, and pulled the whole black mass right off his head. The afternoon sunlight glinted off his skull. 'See?' he said, waggling his wig. 'You're as bald as an egg under that stupid hat, aren't you?'

I agreed enthusiastically and kept rowing.

PERIEL'S ISLAND WAS a stub of rock a few hundred paces across. A few scrubby trees clung to nooks in near-vertical cliffs. A tower, simple but well-built, stood to attention at the peak of the island.

We circled the cliffs until we came to a tiny harbour. There was a small, well-kept boathouse at the top of a beach of pebbles. The place was deserted.

His wig jammed back on his head, Kurt tied up against a jetty. He agreed to wait until dawn, winking and staring at my head.

I walked up the beach, footsteps crunching. There was a narrow staircase cut into the rock behind the boathouse and I climbed a hundred steps to the island's flat summit.

The wind off the sea scoured that plateau and made me pull my coat close. The last of the western light picked out the tower's clean lines, and I could see a door. It looked ajar.

I stared for a while, wondering. Could it be that easy? I took a few tentative steps forward–

I heard a snuffling breath, like a pig digging for truffles, a footstep thumping into the soft earth.

No, it wasn't that easy, I decided. I stood stock still, hands empty and at my side. And round the curve of the tower came the last barrier around Periel's privacy.

He was four times my height and about as broad – and that was just his chest. Stumpy legs thumped into the earth. A breechclout swaddled a thick waist. His head was small and pig-like, and little eyes peered at me with suspicion. He hefted a club from one huge hand to the other. The club was tipped with iron bolts. His skin was the colour of dung, and matted with sweat, like a horse's. Let me tell you, boys, his personal hygiene left a lot to be desired.

I smiled. Well, I tried to. 'How do you do?'

The creature hissed softly.

'You're an ogre, aren't you?'

His voice was like a wooden box full of gravel. 'And you are not invited.'

'I'm here to see the Lord Periel,' I said briskly.

The ogre ran a rope-like finger over the tip of his club. 'Shall I brain you,' he mused, 'before throwing you into the sea?' His shoulders moved in a grotesque shrug. 'Why make a mess?' And he laid his club delicately on the ground and advanced on me, hands spread.

ANYWAY AFTER I'D got the ogre's club off him and had knocked him unconscious, I made my way to the open door and–

What do you mean, you don't believe it? You really want the boring details? Oh, very well...

That ogre came closer, muscles working in his shoulders. Frantically I tried to concentrate, to think through the cobwebs Eladriel had left around my senses. I remember thinking that I'd finally run out of cards to play – and that gave me a clue.

Quick as a flash I dragged my battered pack of cards from my pocket. 'Wait!' I said.

The ogre kept coming, his feet leaving craters in the ground. I began shuffling the cards and working simple tricks. Gradually the boar-like eyes were attracted by the flashing colours.

The ogre slowed to a stop, staring at the cards; and those huge hands dropped reassuringly.

'Before you so justifiably throw me off the cliff,' I said smoothly, still working the cards, 'please let me make you a gift.'

The ogre looked at me, and at the cards. 'Thanks,' he said, and reached down for the pack with one hand and for my throat with the other.

'Hold on,' I cried, skipping back. 'I have to show you how to use them.'

The ogre studied me doubtfully, probing a mouth-sized navel with one finger. Rapidly I dealt out two hands of three cards. 'Let me show you a game. It's called Three Card Pegasus. It usually ends in a fight, and you'd enjoy that, wouldn't you? We both take three cards. Now then, I look at my hand... Not bad. What have I got to stake? How about this–' I took off my woollen hat and laid it on the ground between us.

The ogre ran a puzzled thumb over his cards.

'And what's your stake?' I asked brightly.

He growled menacingly.

'Well, let's make this a demonstration hand, shall we?' I went on rapidly. 'Now show me your cards... Oh,' I exclaimed happily, 'I only have Eagle high, but you have a pair of Dragons! You've won! Here.' I held out the hat. 'It's yours.'

The ogre took the hat, poked at it dubiously, and then jammed it over his skull.

'Yes, well, the red wool clashes a bit with your dominant pigshit brown,' I observed, 'but never mind. Now, another hand?'

The ogre nodded his great head. He hissed over the cards and stamped his thick feet in a kind of dance.

Well, it took about half an hour, I suppose. By the end of that time I'd not only got my hat back; I also owned the ogre's breechclout, his unique collection of giant bat droppings, the right of marriage to his first-born daughter... and his club.

The ogre sat on the damp ground staring miserably out to sea, picking at the breechclout I'd loaned him back. 'Never mind,' I said, feeling almost sorry for him, 'that's the way the cards run sometimes.' And, with all my strength, I smashed the club into the back of his neck.

All right? Can I get on with the story now?

As I was saying... I made my way to the tower's open door. Heart thumping a bit, I stepped out of the wind and into musty darkness.

Torches cast blobs of light over bare stone walls. I was in a corridor which led to a patch of brightness. I stopped to listen, let my eyes adjust to the gloom. Then I heard the song, drifting along the corridor:

The laughter of children can never be held
By silver box or golden band;
The bird's song dies in the ornate cage
And the snowflake melts in the palm of the hand...

It was the voice of a girl. I stood there, transfixed. How can I describe it? Well, perhaps I shouldn't try. I can only say that even in my misty state that song of trapped beauty reduced me to tears.

Blinking, I took silent steps along the corridor. At the end I stopped, still in shadow, and peered into the central chamber.

Torches high on the walls cast a gloomy radiance. A fire flickered in an iron grate. A table stood at the centre of the carpeted floor, and on it rested a half-empty pitcher of wine, a single glass goblet, the remains of what must have been a rich meal.

And in a large, leather-covered chair reclined the Lord Periel himself. He was taller than Eladriel, his hair perhaps a little thinner, but he was dressed rather more sumptuously in a cloak of soft leather. As he listened his fingers were steepled before his face and his eyes were closed. I thought I could see a single tear glinting on his eyelid, and my respect for him rose a little.

Half-hidden to me in my shadowed nook, the girl singer stood meekly before the lord's table. She entered the chorus of her song again–

...silver box or golden band...

And, fearful not only of detection by Periel but also – oddly – of confronting the source of all that beauty, I stepped forward.

She was human, but with an almost elven slimness. Her hair was night dark and plaited around a silver comb. She wore a dress of the purest white silk, and held her hands before her as she sang.

Her face was downcast... the face of a prisoner, I thought. She can't have been more than seventeen. Her beauty was of an inner, almost ethereal type, and I wanted to cherish her.

Now the song reached its climax and her voice soared:

And the snowflake melts in the palm of the hand...

She reached a high note that seemed almost beyond my hearing, and there was an odd ringing–

–and the goblet shattered into a thousand pieces. Periel opened his eyes with a start.

I stepped back quickly. The merchant lord toyed with the fragments on the table. 'Lora,' he said softly, 'your voice is perfect beyond the dreams of mortals.'

She bowed her head.

He stood, stretched, gathered his cloak tight around him. 'Well, I must retire. Another day haggling with the City Fathers over trade agreements tomorrow. If only I could spend more time at home with my treasures... of which the most exquisite is my Lora. Goodnight, my dear.' And he made his way up a staircase that led from the back of the chamber into darkness. I heard a door close softly, some-where above.

The girl Lora relaxed once her master had gone. She sat on a stool at the table and began picking at a bowl of fruit, humming softly to herself in that gorgeous voice. As her hands flickered over the fruit I saw how her fingers were encrusted with jewellery.

She made a delicate tableau in that gloomy place, a work of art as fine as any of Eladriel's. I just stood there for a while, hardly daring to breathe, drinking in that beauty (and no, Maximilian, I did not notice the sort of detail you're interested in).

At last I stepped into the light, fingers to my lips. She kicked over her stool and stumbled backwards, eyes wide. Grapes dropped from her fingers to the carpet. She crammed one tiny fist into her mouth.

I mimed hush. If she screamed I was finished. I took another step into the room, trying to smile. 'I won't harm you,' I whispered. 'I'm your friend. I'm here to help you.'

She seemed to relax a little. She dropped her hand from her face but kept her blue eyes fixed on mine.

My blood rushed like a waterfall; and the nearness of that beauty nearly overwhelmed me.

'Who... who are you?' she asked.

I sighed. Even her speech had a quality like... like the finest lyre which–

(All right, all right, I'll get on with it.)

'My name's Sam Warble,' I said. I raised my hat.

'What do you want?'

'Another lord called Eladriel knows that you're being kept here by Periel. And he sent me to you.' I sat on her stool, and kept smiling. I told her the tale of my recruitment by Eladriel, and gradually she came forward into the light.

'But that's awful,' she said at last. 'How could this Eladriel do such a thing to your mind?'

I shrugged, trying to look courageous. 'I'm not important. What matters now is you, my lady.'

'Are you here to free me?'

'Would you like that?' I asked gravely. 'Does Periel harm you?'

'Oh, no,' she said, with a flutter of manicured fingers. 'Far from it. He's a perfect gentleman. He feeds and clothes me well; I have everything I ask for. I don't even have to sing if I don't feel like it.' She touched her cheek, shaking her head gently. 'I have everything but my freedom.'

I nodded, tears filling my eyes again. "And the snowflake melts in the palm of the hand...' You were singing about yourself, weren't you? You, Lora, you are that snowflake.'

She covered her eyes delicately. 'I am a free spirit who is withering in captivity.'

'Where are you from?'

'A little village a few days' travel from Marienburg, on the edge of the Reikwald Forest. My family are poor but honest. My father raises pigs.'

'Pigs?'

'Pigs. One day emissaries of the Lord Periel came riding into the farm on their fine horses, waving their bags of gold at my father...' Fragile shoulders shook, and she wept softly.

Well, I'll tell you, boys, it was all too much for me.

I leapt up onto the stool and took her shoulders; her warmth flowed into my hands. 'Listen to me. Eladriel didn't send me to free you. He sent me to capture you, to return you to him. You'd exchange one gaoler for another. But I'm not going to do it.'

I took her hand and led her towards the corridor – towards freedom. But she pulled her hand from mine and backed into the centre of the room. 'What are you doing?'

'Come with me.' I felt my cheeks glow with passion. 'I'll free you from the clutches of Periel, but I will not give you to Eladriel. I'll hire horses and return you to your family... Trust me.'

She looked at me doubtfully, toying with a particularly large ring. 'You'll return me? What, to the pig farm? And all that dirt?'

I still didn't understand. 'Well, it might be a bit muddy, but it's freedom!'

Lora ran her hands over the exotic fruit, touched her silken gown. 'I was never very fond of pigs,' she said thoughtfully.

'But you're a free spirit who is withering in captivity. And so on.' I was getting confused.

'Oh, I am! I am! It's just...' She giggled. 'Well, look, perhaps it would be better if you came back another day. Would that be terribly inconvenient?'

I couldn't believe my ears. 'Come back another... My lady, I am not here to sell potatoes. This is not a routine visit. Do you have any idea what I've been through?'

She smiled nervously and pushed at stray strands of hair. 'It's just that there's so much to pack... Well, you know how it is.'

And then I saw it. 'Ah. Yes, Lora. I think I do know how it is.' A look of understanding passed between us. You see, lads, she was a songbird who had grown far too used to her comfortable cage. And who can blame her?

'Perhaps I should come back another day, then.'

She smiled eagerly. 'Oh, yes, I think that would be so much better. Thank you for your thoughtful visit – but wait.' Suddenly she sounded genuinely concerned. 'What about you?'

'Me?'

'If you go back to this Eladriel empty-handed, won't he hurt you?'

'That's a point,' I said, my common sense returning painfully. 'Yes, that certainly is a point. I seem to be stuck, don't I?...' And then I had an idea. 'Or maybe not. I wonder?'

I pulled out Eladriel's magic wasp-waisted bottle. 'Lora, would you mind singing your song again? I think I may be able to trap it in this bottle; there's a spell on it, you see. Perhaps that will be enough for Eladriel.'

A look of pretty doubt creased her oval face. 'Well, of course, if you think it will help. But won't my singing shatter the glass? You must have seen what I did to Periel's goblet.'

I scratched my head. 'I think you're right. Eladriel's invulnerability spell is designed to ward off impacts, not the effects of a song.' I wrapped the bottle in my woollen hat. 'Let's hope this will protect it.' And then, as I thought through all the possibilities of the situation, I felt a smile spread over my face. 'And if this works out, it could be the best solution of all...'

So, her voice barely a whisper, Lora sang for me.

Her words reached again into my heart. I clutched the bottle desperately, trying not to make a fool of myself. Once more she reached the final line. 'And the snowflake melts in the palm of the hand...' I felt the bottle quiver within its woollen cocoon.

But it held. The last echo died away, and I shoved the stopper into the bottle's neck.

'Thank you,' I said, wiping away tears. 'Lora... I will never forget you, and–'

There was a rumble, a heavy footstep on the stair. 'Lora? I heard your voice. Are you all right?'

Lora's eyes went wide. 'Periel!' she hissed. 'We've woken him. You must go.'

'Of course.' And – after one precious brush of my lips on her hand – I ran down the corridor.

ELADRIEL RAGED. I stood there in his boxy home on Lotharn Street, enduring it; it was like being at the eye of a storm. Beside me, licking her broken lips and cackling, stood the delicious Aloma.

I tried to concentrate on what Eladriel was saying, looking for an angle. But even now I could barely keep my eyes from a small bottle perched on a ledge behind Eladriel... a bottle that contained the rest of me.

'What,' Eladriel howled, his mouth inches from my face, 'is to stop me from snapping you in two right now?'

I took a deep breath and played my only card. 'This,' I said, and I held up my prize from Periel's island.

Eladriel snatched the bottle. 'Well?'

'I could not steal the girl,' I said, head hanging. 'After all, a clod like me could never hope to match the brilliance of a lord like you or Periel–'

Eladriel grunted. 'Don't state the obvious.'

'But,' I went on doggedly, 'I have brought, as a pitiful consolation, a single song.'

'A song?'

'Just remove the stopper, my lord.'

Eladriel, looking puzzled, did so. And Lora's perfect voice drifted into the room.

I forgot my peril, and tried to relish these last seconds of pleasure. Whatever happened, I would never hear that voice again. Eladriel shook his head, dabbing at his eyes with a handkerchief. And beside me Aloma blew her huge nose into her hand. Some people are just gross.

The song was nearly over now, and the voice began to climb.

…melts in the palm…

And the bottle shattered in Eladriel's hand. He jumped, startled, and let the fragments fall to the floor.

I felt a rush of blood and breathed deeply, exhilarated. Because – as I had hoped – there had been a second shattering, like an echo, from a shelf behind Eladriel; and I was whole again.

Eladriel turned on me with a growl. I fell to my knees and talked fast. 'My lord, I beg for mercy. I did all I could. You did say that a single song from Lora would be enough. And I've given you that…'

Eladriel towered over me, breathing hard, the lingering beauty of the song obviously wrestling with his basic meanness. Finally he stepped back. 'Very well, Sam. Get up. I'll spare you. This time.'

Surreptitiously, moved by an odd impulse, I scraped together a few fragments of the song bottle and pocketed them before I stood.

'At least I heard Lora once. And I'm sure I can find more uses for you.' Eladriel turned and made for the alcove within which he'd placed the second bottle. 'But you'd better improve your performance in the future. Remember I still hold your…'

He fell silent. He'd reached the alcove, and was running a baffled hand through bits of glass. Then he swivelled, his face a rich purple.

I stood there trying not to tremble, waiting to be struck down by Eladriel's renewed rage.

The moment stretched.

Then, beside me, there was a hideous wheezing sound. It was Aloma laughing. Eladriel and I turned and stared.

'The sh-song,' she spluttered. 'It broke the oth-th-ther bosh-ttle and sh-set him free. He'sh tricked you, my lord…'

She cackled on. And after a few seconds, wonder of wonders, Eladriel's face creased into a smile. 'She's right. You've got the better of me, haven't you? Go on. Get out.'

'What?'

'Get out!' he roared, laughing. 'Before I change my mind.'
I got.

'...AND THAT'S WHY,' Sam Warble finished, 'I'm off gambling.
Okay?' And he downed the last of his ale.

Tarquin was rubbing his chin. 'Not a bad yarn, I suppose,
but it doesn't quite tie up. What's it got to do with the ring?'

Sam looked surprised. 'Why, isn't it obvious? I took the
fragments of Lora's bottle and had them set in gold, as soon
as I could afford it. Just a little souvenir.' And he stroked the
ring tenderly.

Tarquin shook his head and stood up. 'No. That's too glib,
Sam. Good try. Listen, do you want to come for some food
down the Admiral's Galley?'

Sam smiled. 'Not tonight. Leave me with my memories.
I'll be all right.'

Tarquin laughed. 'Suit yourself.'

The others stood and pulled their coats closed.
Maximilian picked up his cards. 'Give you a tip, Sam.'

'What's that?'

'You kept me with you until you got to the ogre. I just
couldn't swallow that bit. I mean, who would stake something as unique as a collection of giant bat droppings on a
pathetic pair of Dragonkin? I ask you.' Shaking his head, he
followed the rest.

Sam, left alone, shrugged and studied his ring for a few
minutes. Then he blew gently over the inset glass. The shards
chimed as if with a hundred tiny voices, and fragments of
words could be heard: *...snowflake melts... laughter of children...*

Jasper came to the table to collect the discarded tankards.
'So no one believes your tall stories, eh, Sam?'

Sam smiled. 'They saw right through me, didn't they? I'll
just have to try harder. Oh, Jasper – listen, do you know anyone interested in a collection of giant bat droppings? Price
negotiable...'

APPRENTICE LUCK
by Sean Flynn

KARL SPIELBRUNNER HAD been apprenticed to Otto von Stumpf for six months now, more than long enough for him to realize how much he hated the antiquarian book trade. Karl had a fatal combination of vanity, ambition and intelligence, and he knew well enough that unless his luck changed all he had to look forward to was ending up with his own poky little shop, as bent and crabbily reclusive as von Stumpf. Of course, there were far worse fates in Middenheim, the great and terrible City of the White Wolf. If Karl's dead father – the only family Karl had, apart from some country cousins he had never seen – had not been a drinking companion of von Stumpf's, no doubt Karl would be just another orphan trying to scratch a living on the streets now, a likely victim for drug pushers, racketeers, pimps or cultists.

Far worse fates, yes, but not by much, Karl thought, as he stood at the dusty window and watched the shabby, narrow street and the occasional passer-by. It was summer, and stiflingly hot in the shop. A fat bluebottle buzzed in one corner of the window; the husks of others were scattered on the leatherbound tomes which leaned against each other in the window.

There was so much going on in the world, yet Karl was stuck here in charge of a lot of tattered dusty books. A wizard had moved into some rooms down the street, for instance, a tall mysterious foreigner. Some said he was a necromancer; everyone said he was up to no good. And something was rumoured to be stirring in the myriad tunnels that undercut the rock on which the city was founded. The Watch was on maximum alert, and only last night the body of a goat-headed man had been found near one of the main sewer inlets.

For a moment, Karl saw himself at the head of one of the elite patrols, a grim-faced Watch captain armed with a glittering sword, maybe a decorative scar on one cheek. Then the bluebottle buzzed loudly at the dusty window and Karl's daydream collapsed stillborn. Musty smell of crumbling paper, shadowy ranks of outdated books looming into shadow: this was his fate. His only consolation was that as usual his master was away at the Wolf's Grip, the grim little tavern which drained most of the shop's profits. Otherwise Karl would certainly have been put to some useless task or other, recataloguing stock or sweeping away the sticky cobwebs which festooned the crumbling plaster of the low ceiling – and no doubt von Stumpf would be giving him a lecture in that nagging, whiny voice of his, telling Karl how lucky he was, to be apprentice to the venerable firm of von Stumpf and Son (Karl didn't know what had happened to the Son, but he guessed that he had run away as soon as he could). And if von Stumpf had been there, Karl wouldn't have been able to take his chance when his luck suddenly changed.

It arrived in the unlikely form of Scabby Elsa, a bent, hook-nosed old crone who specialized in reselling rags stripped from the corpses thrown from the Cliff of Sighs. Just as Karl was settling to a forbidden snack of black bread and cheese, she pushed open the door and hobbled laboriously over the uneven floor with something clutched to her shapeless bosom. The bluebottle left off bumbling at the window and spiralled around the greasy shawl wrapped over her head, attracted by the sour, rank stench of her layers of rotting rags.

'A little something for you, young master,' Scabby Elsa said, and set what she had been carrying on the scarred rubbish-strewn table which served as a counter.

It was an old, old book, text handwritten in an upright clerkly style on octavo parchment, bound in fine-grained leather with gilt stamping on the spine, the front somewhat buckled and stained. Karl took only a moment to realize it had to be valuable; much as he hated the book trade, he had taken care to pick up the necessary knowledge and tricks. Now it looked as if that care might actually be about to pay off.

'I'll take a gold crown for this fellow,' Scabby Elsa said. Her smile revealed blackened gums, and the stench of her breath almost knocked Karl down. 'No less, now, but no more either. That's what I needs, and that's what I takes.'

'Ten shillings,' Karl said quickly. 'The cover is damaged; no one would offer more.'

'It fell a long way, like its owner. Lucky it fell on someone else, or it would look a lot worse. Fifteen, then.'

'Twelve, and that's my final offer.'

'Done,' Scabby Elsa said.

Karl kept what little money he had managed to save tied in a corner of his shirt. He undid the knot and counted out the price. Scabby Elsa scooped up the coins with a surprising deftness and hobbled out of the shop, pursued by the bluebottle, which had fallen in love with her – or at least, with her smell.

His heart beating quickly and lightly, Karl pulled down the window shades and locked the door.

With luck, von Stumpf wouldn't be back until at least the end of the afternoon. He had plenty of time to examine his prize.

The book was a grimorium, a handbook of magic, and written in old-fashioned but plain language, too, not some kind of code. From the style of binding and the yellowing of the edges of the parchment pages, it had to be at least three hundred years old, from the time of the Wizards' War perhaps, or even before.

Karl leafed through crackling pages. A spell of bafflement. A spell of binding. Hmmm. He would take it to the shop of Hieronymus Neugierde, the largest antiquarian shop in the city. He was bound to get the best price there... maybe enough to escape his apprenticeship.

Karl began to examine the book more closely. He would need to know as much as he could to get the right price. He realized with a start that the leather cover was not made of tanned animal hide, but human skin; he could make out the pores, even little hairs. It felt clammy to his fingertips, as if somehow still alive.

He opened the book again and laid it face down, peered down the spine; there were often clues about a book's origin and age to be found in the binding sheets. Sure enough, there was a scrap of paper inserted there. When Karl fished it out, an insect, a shiny-backed beetle, came with it, scurrying across the table and falling to the floor before Karl could crush it.

Some kind of map had been drawn on the scrap of paper, the ink fresh and no use in dating the book. All the same it was interesting, a carefully marked route snaked through intricately labyrinthine passages, avoiding all sorts of traps and deadfalls and pits, to a sealed chamber marked with a single word written in red. A treasure map, maybe, although there was no indication of what the treasure was.

Karl studied it for a long time before he realized that it must be a map of part of the system of tunnels which the dwarfs had long ago cut through the rock on which the city stood. When he had riddled all he could, he put it in his pocket, then went into the back room where he slept and hid the book under his pillow. He would examine it further tonight, and tomorrow sell it for the best price he could, then thumb his nose at von Stumpf and live the way he wanted, not at the old fool's beck and call. He might even be able to sell the treasure map to some gullible adventurer – and there was no shortage of such people in the city – foolish enough to venture into the dangerous tunnels beneath the city.

Karl was thinking of all he could do with a pocketful of gold crowns as he let up the blinds. And then he jumped back in shock. The foreign wizard was peering through the dusty glass, his face only inches away from Karl's own. When he saw Karl he straightened up and pushed at the door, and although Karl hadn't unlocked it, the door opened at once.

'I am looking for a book,' the wizard said.

'Well, we have all sorts of books, sire.' Karl's mouth was dry. The wizard was very tall, and despite the summer heat wore a sweeping black cloak, its red lining embroidered with all manner of weird signs of power. His face was long and white, framed by untidy black hair and a black beard. A pair of small round spectacles perched on the end of his long nose; they magnified the wizard's fierce blue eyes as he peered down at Karl.

'A very particular book. A book that may have been brought to you, or may be about to be brought to you. A large handwritten volume, with an unusual binding. I will pay very well for such a book.'

'You would have to speak to my master,' Karl managed to say. He was thinking furiously. If the wizard wanted the book, then it was even more valuable than it looked, and he would certainly get a better price at Neugierde's than from this itinerant hedge-wizard.

'Your master, eh?' The wizard drew himself up. He was so tall that his head almost brushed the cobwebby rafters of the ceiling. 'Very well. You give no choice but that I come back. I hope your master will be more helpful. I will call again tomorrow. And remember this, young man.'

The cloak flew up and Karl jumped back, but the wizard was too quick. His cold hand fastened around Karl's wrist, pulled. Then Karl was leaning half across the table, his face only inches away from the wizard's.

'Remember this,' the wizard said, softly.

'I don't forget anything,' Karl managed to say. He met the wizard's gaze, trying not to be intimidated. But there was an odd tingling between his eyes, as if he was about to cry, and after a moment he had to look away.

'Things may be more than they seem, or less.' The wizard let go of Karl's wrist, drew his cloak around himself. 'Good day to you, young man, and good luck.'

Somehow, Karl managed to behave as if nothing out of the ordinary had happened when Otto von Stumpf came back in the evening, although the old man had drunk so much of the Wolf's Grip's vinegary ale that he probably wouldn't have noticed if Karl had grown another head. After a meagre supper of boiled barley flavoured with fatty scraps of mutton, von Stumpf had Karl help him up the winding stairs to the filthy garret where he slept. Then Karl curled up on the mattress in the stockroom behind the shop and gloated over the book and the map by the light of a tallow candle. But it had been a long day, and soon enough he fell asleep.

HE WOKE WITH a start to moonlight falling through the room's only window, thinking someone had touched him on the hand. But it was only a beetle clambering over the hollow of his palm, its antennae waving furiously. Karl flicked the insect away, and then realized with alarm that the book was gone.

He managed to get the candle lit, and saw that the book was lying in the curtained doorway between the shop and the stockroom. Shadows seemed to scatter from it as he went over and bent to pick it up. Nervous, and fully awake, Karl went into the shop and listened at the crooked stairs that led up to von Stumpf's garret, and grinned when he heard the old man's rasping snore. Still befuddled by sleep, Karl was about to go back to bed when he happened to glance out of the window and saw a black-cloaked figure moving past, towards the door. It was the wizard.

In an instant, Karl was through the back room, fumbling at the bolts of the door to the yard. He managed to get it open just as the lock of the shop's door sprang with a heart-stopping click. And then he was over the wall of the yard, almost falling on top of the figure that stood in the alley below.

For an instant, Karl thought that the wizard, who obviously had found out about the book, had somehow magicked himself from one side of the building to the other. But then the man pushed back his hood and said, 'Come with me – be quick now.'

Karl was about to ask who the stranger was and why he should follow him when an eerie blue light flared on the other side of the wall. Without a further thought he took to his heels, clutching the book to his chest.

The stranger ran as though his feet were skimming an inch above the cobbles, his cloak streaming behind him. After dodging through the alleys, they came out on the bustling Burgen Bahn, where bands of students roved noisily among crowds of ordinary citizens. By this time Karl was panting hard, but the stranger hardly seemed to be breathing at all. His eyes glittered as he looked about alertly, one hand on the hilt of a long sword; he was a young, smooth-skinned and handsome man wearing baggy corduroy trews and an embroidered leather vest under the cloak – curious, old-fashioned clothes. Seemingly satisfied that they weren't being pursued, he turned and looked down at Karl, who shrank a little under that glittering unforgiving gaze.

'You have what we came to take back,' the swordsman said. He had an odd, harshly buzzing accent, probably from some country district or other. That would explain the old-fashioned cut of his clothes, too.

'If you mean the book, I came by it fairly. I'm a bookseller, and I bought it,' Karl said, more defiantly than he felt. After all, he was telling the truth. More or less the truth.

'We pay,' the swordsman said, 'even though it was stolen from us.' He effortlessly plucked the book from Karl's grasp, then dropped a heavy drawstring purse to the ground. Karl pulled the purse open as the swordsman paged through the book, and gasped when he saw that it was crammed full of gold. Then his gasp turned to a frightened squeak as the swordsman grabbed the front of his shirt and lifted him clear off the ground. 'The map,' the swordsman said, his face inches from Karl's own. His breath was sharply acid, and his eyes glittered crazily in the light of a nearby streetlamp. 'We want the map.'

'Put me down and I'll tell you where it is,' Karl managed to gasp, and then his heels struck the pavement hard as the swordsman let go. Karl tugged at his dishevelled shirt, hotly aware of the group of students who had turned to snigger at this contretemps.

'Where?' the swordsman said.

'Back at the shop,' Karl lied, knowing it was in his pocket. He had seen an opportunity to make even more money, enough to set him up for life, maybe. A purse full of gold could be spent in a night, if you were foolish enough. But if the map led to buried treasure, and there were legends of all sorts of dwarfish hoards hidden in the catacombs and corridors of the city beneath the city, then anything was possible. And although Karl was clever, he was also inexperienced enough to harbour the belief that no matter what, he wasn't anywhere near to dying.

So he added quickly, 'But we don't have to go back there, and face that wizard. He was the one who stole the book from you, wasn't he?'

'His apprentice,' the swordsman admitted. 'We nearly caught him, but he jumped over the edge of the Cliff of Sighs, and when we got down amongst the trees and found his body, the book was gone.'

'But now you have the book, and fortunately for you, I am at your service. I found the map and looked at it long enough to memorize it.' This was the truth; Karl had an exceptional memory for things that might be useful to him. He said, with more confidence than he felt, 'I can take you past the traps, lead you to the treasure, once we are close enough.'

'Treasure,' the swordsman said. 'You wish to share this treasure.'

'Let's call it a finder's fee.'

The swordsman closed his eyes and began to mutter to himself – or more precisely, buzz and chatter in his odd dialect. Obviously he was thinking hard, and obviously thinking hard did not come easily. At last he said, 'We are agreed, then. You help, for a fee.'

'On your word that you will give me ten per cent of what we find, and not harm me in any way?' Karl said, as steadily as he could.

'We give our word,' the swordsman said, with an alacrity that made Karl wish he had asked for fifteen, or even twenty per cent. He added, 'Now you will lead us to the nearest entrance to the sewers, where we will begin our journey.'

Karl smiled. 'It's easy to see you're a stranger to the city. The main sewer entrances are guarded by the City Watch. Even a swordsman like yourself will not be able to outfight the Watch. Er, what is your name, anyhow?'

'You may call us Argo.'

'Well, I'm Karl. But don't worry, I know another way, although you may have to pay a kind of admission fee. There's a tavern down in the Ostwald district, the Drowned Rat, which has a way into the sewers in its cellar. You just have to pay the landlord, that's all.'

'You have all the money, now.'

'Do I? Oh, I see. Well, I suppose it is a kind of investment. Come on then, Argo. The place I'm thinking of is on the other side of the city.'

KARL WASN'T AS confident as he had sounded. He knew about the Drowned Rat and its secret passages into the sewer network only by rumour, and he had made up the story about the entrance fee on the spot. As he and the swordsman made their way deeper into the narrow streets of Ostwald, what little confidence Karl had soon evaporated.

There were no streetlights in the Ostwald district, and the mean, crowded streets were illuminated only by what light fell through heavily curtained windows, or the red flames of torches a few people carried. Karl kept as close to the swordsman as he could – not an easy task, because the man strode along at a rapid pace, the darkness and the ill-favoured crowds slowing him down not at all.

There were probably no more drunks here than along the Burgen Bahn, but while on that prosperous street drunkenness was merely the end result of too much high spirits, here it was due to a kind of savage desperation. Men far gone in their cups staggered along shouting curses at the world in general, and from more than one alley came the noises of fighting. Beggars with every kind of disfigurement and disease bawled out for alms, ignored by the poorly-dressed labourers and better-dressed thieves alike, their cries scarcely louder than the shrill cries of the whores who shouted down at potential clients from upper-storey windows of the close-packed timber-framed buildings.

Karl looked for the sign of the Drowned Rat with increasing desperation. For all his pretended knowledge of the city, he had rarely been in the Ostwald district, and didn't like it. He wanted nothing more than to find the tavern and get into the sewers beneath these dangerous streets, forgetting for the moment how much more dangerous the sewers could be. But when at last he did spy the sign, the last of his confidence seemed to ooze from the soles of his boots.

It was a tall, narrow, ramshackle building, set a little apart from its neighbours, its filthy windows glowing sullenly, its door in deep shadow.

Even as Karl and Argo approached it, a man staggered out, clutching the top of his head. Blood streamed down his face, suddenly bright as he staggered through the light of a nearby lamp set in the window of a whorehouse. He turned and bawled out, 'Cutthroats! Lousy thieves! Sons of diseased mutant whores!' Then he groaned and clutched his head again and staggered on.

Argo, hardly seeming to notice the man, strode through the shadows and ducked beneath the tilted lintel of the tavern. Karl had to hurry to catch him up, slipping through the door just as a couple of heavyset thugs pushed it closed.

The main room of the tavern was almost as dark as the street outside, and hazed with yellow-grey smoke which gathered in thick reefs just beneath the sagging ceiling. Wolfish looking men sat at half a dozen rough tables scattered along the walls, and all were staring at the swordsman in unnerving and hostile silence.

Argo crossed to the counter, his boots rattling the loose floorboards, and said softly to the large, bearded man behind it, 'We wish to enter the sewer system. We will pay whatever is necessary.'

One of the ruffians behind Karl chuckled and dropped a huge, scarred hand on Karl's shoulder. 'Your friend is a bold enough fellow, laddie. I always do like 'em bold.'

The landlord spat into a glass and smeared the spit around with a grey rag. 'We don't like strangers coming in here, friend. On your way now. I can't help you.'

'We'll just have a word with 'em,' the man holding Karl said. 'Straighten 'em out, like.'

'Whatever you want, lads,' the landlord said indifferently, turning away as the second ruffian, his head brushing the ceiling, stalked towards Argo, a weighted cosh dangling from one paw. Karl started to shout a warning, but a foul-smelling hand clamped over his mouth and nose. Argo turned, his cloak flaring, as the cosh swept towards his head… and then suddenly he was to one side of the man, his sword flashing through the smoke. Something hit the floor with a thump, blood pattering after: it was the ruffian's hand, still holding the cosh. The wounded ruffian shrieked, and then Argo's sword flashed again, and the ruffian fell to the floor, his throat spraying blood.

The thug holding Karl started to back towards the door, ignoring the apprentice's struggles. There was a tingling pressure between Karl's eyes, at the bridge of his nose. For some reason he remembered the wizard's humiliating stare, and when the ruffian let go of Karl's mouth to pull at the latch, Karl managed to shout out the spell of bafflement he'd seen in the book. It was the only thing he could think of, but to his amazement it worked.

The man let go of him and scratched at his head, his pig-like features twisted in confusion. He didn't seem to notice his companion, fallen on the floor in the centre of a widening pool of blood, or Karl, or Argo, who pushed Karl aside and ran the ruffian through with his already bloody blade, its steel scraping against ribs as he drew it out. For a moment, the man didn't seem to notice his mortal wound either, but then he gave a bubbling groan and toppled full-length, his fall rattling every flagon in the room.

Now the silence in the room had a different edge to it. Karl discovered that his nose was bleeding, and dabbed at it with his sleeve. He pulled the dead man's knife from his belt while everyone was watching Argo. The latter stepped around the body of the ruffian who had first attacked him, kicking aside the severed hand, and up to the counter. He pulled at the landlord's beard, lifting the big man half over the counter and repeating his request to be allowed into the sewers, as if nothing at all had happened.

The landlord's eyes crossed in disbelief. For a moment, the sound of his beard coming away at the roots was the only sound in the room. 'The cellar,' he managed to say at last. 'Of course. You just follow me.'

The cellar was reached by a steep winding stair, its stone steps slippery with water that dribbled down the walls. Things moved in the darkness beyond the light of the landlord's upheld lantern. Rats, the landlord said, but the thing Karl glimpsed was twice as big as any rat he'd ever seen, and seemed to scurry away on more than four legs. Argo, indifferent to any danger as usual, followed the landlord into the darkest recess of the vaulted cellar without hesitation, past rotting casks and heaps of rubbish and broken furniture.

There was a low door set deep in the wet stones of the wall, barred with iron and held shut by massive bolts, which the landlord threw back with some effort. A rush of hot malodorous air gushed out as the landlord pulled the door open. Argo started through, and Karl said loudly, 'We'll need light.' He didn't want to go down there, but he could hardly expect to be allowed out of the tavern alive any other way. If he was going, he wanted to be able to see.

Argo turned and plucked the lantern from the landlord, then ducked under the lintel. As Karl followed, the landlord swore and slammed the door shut on their backs, yelling through the wood that they'd never get out, he'd see that they didn't. There was a rattle as he threw the bolts home. And then there was only the drip-drip-drip of water from overhead, and the faint rush of more water somewhere below.

A winding stair led down to one of the sewer tributaries, a smelly brick-lined tunnel scarcely tall enough for Karl to stand up in, through which a stinking stream of brown liquid gurgled. In turn, this gave out onto one of the main channels, where high stone walks ran either side of a fast-running, filthy stream.

Argo raised the lantern, peered at Karl. He brushed a cold finger over the drying blood on the apprentice's upper lip, and put it in his mouth. 'The price of magic,' he said, after a moment.

'It was only a little spell, something I read in that book. I didn't even think it would work, but there was nothing else I could do.'

'You are modest. But do not try and use your Art against us, I warn you. We are not bound by it.'

Karl looked up at him, a shadow behind the lamplight, eyes glittering. 'I didn't even know the spell would work,' he said again. 'Really. Now, where do we go?'

'We will take you to the beginning of the maze,' Argo said. 'Then you must lead the way.'

Karl thought hard. 'The map showed that there was a kind of big round room from which the maze started. There were drawings of statues all around its walls.'

'I know it. That is where we must begin.'

Black rats scampered away from the light of the lantern Argo carried. Looking back, Karl could see a hundred pairs of little red eyes watching from the safety of the darkness. Sometimes, tantalizingly, he could hear the noises of the streets above, the cries of beggars or food sellers, or the rattle of wagon wheels over cobbles. But soon Argo led him away from the main channel, down a rubble-strewn slope that dropped steeply through the living rock, down into the necropolis beneath the living city.

Karl soon lost all track of time. He knew only that he was tired and hungry and frightened... and thirsty too, for the tunnels that wound ever deeper into the rock were surprisingly dry, their floors coated with dust as fine as flour. With every moment he was growing more and more afraid, and he was beginning to wish that he had never seen the book, or tried to cheat von Stumpf of its price.

Worst of all, he kept thinking that he heard footsteps in the darkness at his back, a steady even pace that always stopped a moment or two after he stopped to listen. Although dwarfs still lived in certain parts of the underground tunnels, most were rumoured to be inhabited by mutants and worse. Anything could be out there in the darkness, anything at all, and the knife he had taken from the dead thug in the tavern seemed little enough protection. But Argo ignored Karl's fears, and, rather than growing tired, the swordsman seemed to gain strength as they descended through the tunnels.

As if he were at home in them, as if the darkness and the weight of rock above – the weight of the whole city – were comfortably familiar. Certainly, he knew the way to go, although that was strange, too, now Karl thought about it. Hadn't Argo said that he was a stranger in the city? There was much more to the handsome young swordsman than met the eye.

Most of the tunnels were narrow and low-ceilinged, and once or twice they had to stop and backtrack when they came upon a cave-in that had blocked the way forward. On one occasion they disturbed a colony of bats which exploded around them in a fury of leather wings. Argo stood his ground, unperturbed, but Karl huddled on the floor until the creatures were gone. On another, they passed through a high ruined chamber, fungi of every description growing over the wreckage of a wooden floor. Some toadstools were taller even than Argo, and bracket fungi stepped up the rock walls, glowing with a virulent green light. On the way across, Karl stepped on a round growth which exploded in a cloud of spores that burned his nostrils like a dose of boiling hot pepper, making him sneeze uncontrollably. Argo, who didn't seem to be affected, had to wait until Karl could go on.

As they ducked through the narrow crack that led out of the chamber, Karl heard stealthy padding footsteps, many of them, all around in the darkness and coming closer and closer. Argo raised the lantern, and Karl saw a hundred or more small shadowy figures creeping along high ledges, stepping down slopes of rock scree. None was taller than three feet, and all were naked but for loincloths, their warty green skin smeared with dirt, their wide fanged mouths grinning, their pointed ears rising above bald pates. They were armed with pointed staves and crude hammers or axes. A tribe of goblins.

In the time it took Karl to realize what the creatures were, and to draw out the knife he had taken from the dead ruffian, the first of the goblins scuttled towards Argo, who drew out his sword while still holding up the lantern. The creatures hissed with fear and started back – even as Argo cut off their heads with a level sweep of his weapon. Others higher up began to pelt him with crude bombs stuffed with fungus spores. The poisonous dust fumed thickly around him, crackling in the flame of the lantern, but seemed not to affect him at all. He split one goblin almost in half, lopped off the arm of another. Two jumped on his back, and he ran backwards and crushed them against the rock wall.

Meanwhile, others were advancing on Karl. He managed to stick one with his knife, but it fell backwards, squealing in dismay, and pulled the haft of the knife from Karl's hand. Its companions grinned widely and raised their crude weapons higher, their slitted yellow eyes burning upon him. Karl backed away until stone hit his back, watching with dismay as the lead goblin, no bigger than a child but with the face of a psychotic toad, raised its notched axe. Karl felt the tickling pressure between his eyes again, and before he knew what he was doing he had thrown up his hands and gabbled out the spell of binding he had read in the book.

Instantly, every goblin in the chamber froze. One or two toppled off-balance and fell stiffly to the floor. The pressure between Karl's eyes became a knife blade prying at his brain. He fell to his knees and felt blood gush from his nostrils, as rich and hot as fresh gravy.

Argo calmly sheathed his sword and helped the apprentice to his feet. He ordered Karl to follow, and set off amongst the frozen goblins as if nothing had happened. Karl staggered after him, so weak that he could hardly stand, but frightened of being left in the dark with the goblins, who surely wouldn't remain bound by magic for long. The front of his jerkin was soaked in his blood, and he couldn't seem to stop the flow completely, although he pinched the wings of his nostrils shut. The price of magic. It was lucky there hadn't been any more goblins, and that they had been small, too. Otherwise the magic needed to bind them might have burst his body like an overripe tomato.

At last, they reached a huge round chamber, tall statues standing around its walls. In the centre was a kind of altar, a stone table ringed with skulls, its surface cut with channels and bearing the torn remnants of some obscene sacrifice. An animal, Karl hoped, and didn't look too closely in case his worst fears were realized. On the far side of the chamber a statue taller than all the rest was carved out of the living rock wall, half man, half beast, so tall that it was beheaded by darkness. Its right hand clutched a dozen snakes; its left held a staring human head by the hair. Between its hoofed feet was the narrow entrance to the maze.

'Now you will lead us,' Argo said, and handed Karl the lantern, his eyes glittering in the light.

Through the red veils of his exhaustion, Karl called up his memory of the map. It was still in his pocket, but he didn't dare draw it out. Argo could take it from him and leave him there, alone in the dark, prey to whatever was following them.

The passageways of the maze were high and narrow, carved roughly out of granite as dark as obsidian. The rock absorbed the light of the lantern rather than reflecting it, so that Karl had to find the way by only the feeblest of glows. Still, considering the circumstances, he thought that he was doing well enough, turning right and left and right again, avoiding passages that turned into steep slippery slopes dropping to waterfilled shafts, slabs set in the floor that would tip the unwary into deep pits, a dozen sorts of mechanical trap that couldn't be revealed by magic.

Perhaps he was overconfident; or perhaps he was simply tired. In any event, he didn't realize his mistake until one of the paving stones gave slightly with a fatal click under his foot, like a bone breaking. There was an ominous rumbling above, and then a steel grip snatched him back as the massive weight slammed down, fitting the passage precisely. The wind of its falling blew Karl's hair back; the noise of its impact half-deafened him. When Argo let go of his shoulder, he fell to his knees. 'You are a fool,' Argo hissed in his ear.

'You can bet I'll try and do better,' Karl said. The smooth stone of the deadweight was only inches from his tender, bloody nose. He was so shaken that he almost took out the map to make sure of the way, but he remembered that if he did Argo would take it and leave him here in the dark – with his head cut off too, as like as not.

Right and left, deeper into the bowels of Middenheim Rock. The crushing weight of it seemed to press all life out of the stale black air. Karl had no room in his head for his fears or what he would do when they reached the treasure, no room for anything but remembering the route. Right and left, deeper and deeper until they reached the heart of the maze.

It was a square chamber, with no way out but the passage which led into it. But dimly outlined by the glow of the lantern which Karl held, sketched in faded paint, was an ornate doorframe, the way to the treasure.

Argo threw back his head and opened his mouth amazingly wide, and let out a chattering, inhuman cry. Karl's heart froze. Striding out of one of the dark passageways behind them came three skeletons, yellow bones gleaming in the lantern-light, feet clicking on the stone floor, eye sockets holding fell red glows. Each carried a notched, rusty sword, and one wore a golden helmet that an age ago had been cleft by a fearsome blow.

'Our brothers,' Argo said, and whirled on Karl, his smooth, handsome face without expression. 'Now you will tell us the password.'

'P-p-password?'

'You know it. Either you speak it now, or we will kill you and have your corpse speak it for us, when it has rotted enough for the magic to take hold.' Argo's breath smelt like crushed ants; his eyes glittered more fiercely than ever. 'Now, boy?'

There was a flare of blue light. Argo collapsed and the three skeletons burst apart, bones crumbling to powder even before they hit the floor. Blinking, Karl saw the wizard step out of the shadows of the passageway, his white face grim.

'A strange place to find a bookseller's apprentice, and strange companions for him, too,' the wizard said. 'Do you have any idea of how deeply you have meddled, my boy?'

Karl could only shake his head. Blue spots still floated in his vision.

'My apprentice was killed by this creature of Undeath,' the wizard said, nudging Argo's body with the steel-shod toe of his boot. 'He was bringing to me a map which led to a certain ancient treasure, treasure that in the wrong hands could do untold harm. He had hidden the map in a book of simple spells, the kind of thing a wizard's apprentice would carry. But still, somehow, he was found out. He managed to gain entrance to the city, but before I could come to his rescue, he was cornered, at the Cliff of Sighs. He was a brave boy, and knew what would happen if the map were taken.

'So he threw himself from the cliff, and was torn to pieces by the trees far below. Before I could rescue the book, and before this creature could lay his hands upon it, one of the scavengers found it, and brought it to you.'

'You knew I had the book,' Karl said.

'Oh yes. Never lie to a wizard, boy. Let that be your first lesson in your new life. I lent a little of my power to you, and waited until the creature found you. When you used the spells in the book, I was able to follow you by the traces of magic you left. Luckily enough for you, I arrived here just in time to use a spell of my own to unbind the magic which held the skeletons together.'

'And Argo? Why was he—' And then Karl understood. 'He was a deathless one too! That's why the spell of binding that I used on the goblins didn't affect him. And why their spore bombs didn't affect him either.'

'Indeed. Some poor man whose corpse was revived through necromancy.' The wizard pulled at his long black beard. 'And now, you will want to see this treasure, no doubt. You may speak the password.'

'I've had enough nosebleeds, thank you.'

'The magic was laid down by the efforts of someone else, long ago. The word merely releases it.' The wizard held up the scrap of paper he'd somehow taken from Karl's pocket. 'If you won't say the word, then I will.'

So Karl said the word of unlocking, and a wooden door suddenly appeared in the sketched doorframe, and flew open with a thud that brought a cloud of dust from the ceiling.

'The first thing you've done right,' the wizard said, and stepped forward.

Karl followed – and then was struck from behind and thrown across the chamber. As he got to his hands and knees, he saw that Argo had thrown his cloak over the wizard's head, pinioning his arms and cutting off his breath at the same time. Without thinking, Karl picked up one of the rusty swords and swung at Argo's legs.

Blunt though the blade was, it cut through to the bone. But instead of blood, hundreds of small insects gushed out of the wound. Argo howled and let go of the wizard, tried to staunch the flow. Beetles were everywhere; some had even taken to the air and were battering at the lantern, maddened by its light. Their wings glittered just like Argo's eyes. Argo fell to his knees; he seemed to be shrinking inside his skin. And then the wizard managed to gasp a spell, and the swordsman's clothes and skin flew apart, revealing a seething mass of beetles still clinging to the skeleton within. The wizard said another spell, and there was a sudden acrid smell in the chamber, and the beetles all stopped moving. A thousand brittle little corpses rained from the air.

'My fumigation spell,' the wizard said, picking up his spectacles and examining them. 'Who would have thought I needed it against one of the undead? Those insects must have been acting as one organism, using the skeleton and a false skin to give them human form.'

'He always said "we",' Karl ventured, 'never "I".'

'Indeed. When I used the spell of unbinding, they must have been only temporarily discommoded, and soon knit the bones back together again. Undeath spawns more kinds of evil than we can ever imagine.' He set the spectacles on the end of his long nose. 'Now, let's get to the treasure. Bring the lantern.'

Together, they stepped into the room beyond the door. Karl held up the lantern eagerly... and then groaned aloud. All around, on shelves carved into the rock, covered in dust yet still giving off that familiar sweet musty smell, were hundreds, thousands, of leather-bound books.

'Not all treasure glitters,' the wizard said. 'This is the library of Fistoria Spratz, among the greatest scholars of the magical arts this city ever produced, preserved and hidden here by the last of his magic. You understand why the forces of evil should not gain hold of it. And now, my boy, I must prepare a teleportation spell that will take us and these marvellous books back to my rooms in the city above. It will take a little while, time for you to consider if you would become my apprentice.' He held up a beringed hand. 'Think carefully. I will say that you have what it takes. The door would not have opened if you did not have some trace of the power, nor would you have been able to channel the power I lent you so easily. You are a trifle vain and arrogant, it is true, but you are also brave, and more than a little lucky. Be quiet and think.'

But Karl did not have to think. He was ready with his answer long before the dark rock faded around him, and he found himself together with the wizard and stacks of dusty books in a bedroom overlooking the familiar dingy street where Otto von Stumpf's bookshop stood. Karl took a deep breath, and said the one word that would unlock a long life of adventure.

THE LIGHT
OF TRANSFIGURATION
by Brian Craig

OF ALL THE stories I know, said Orfeo, with an unaccustomed softness in his voice, the ones I love best are those set in the region where I lived as a child, which is the Loren Forest. I wish that all the tales which I could tell of Loren were as happy as my memories of it, but alas it is not so. You will know the forest by repute as the abode of the virtuous wood elves, and it was by those elves that I was found and raised when I was abandoned there, but the forest is vast and there are many others who have sought solace and shelter in its wilder parts, among them bad and dangerous men who have increased the burden of evil and suffering which lies upon the world we love.

Most of the men who live on the fringes of the forest are honest worshippers of Taal, and many of those who live closer to its heart still follow caring traditions of the old religion, but there are parts of the forest which are host to the worshippers of darker gods, and to those who make treaty with daemons. One such tainted area is to be found in the lower reaches of the steep mountains called the Vaults, which I was taught in my youth to avoid. Because the wood

elves do not teach without explanation, they told me all that
the wisdom of lore and legend had to say about the place,
and it is one tale from that legacy which I will tell you now.
It is one of that sad multitude of tales which warn us to
beware of the wiles of those daemons which are sent by
wicked gods to seduce and torment us.

ON ONE OF the lesser crags of this region, near a town called
Selindre, there once stood a fortified manse, which was a
centre of forbidden worship until the king who was great-
grandfather to our own beloved sovereign appointed his
favourite knight, Lanval de Valancourt, to lead a crusade
against the daemon-kin.

All good Bretonnians have heard the story of that great
adventure, and you will know already that Lanval's courage
prevailed at last against the evil magic of the sorcerer
Khemis Kezula – but the versions of the tale you have heard
from other tellers undoubtedly ended with the moment of
Lanval's victory, and with the implication that all has been
well in Selindre's demesnes since it was achieved. Alas, it is
a truth which we too often forget that the shadows of evil
cast by dark magic often linger long after the destruction of
the magicians themselves.

It was because he knew this that Lanval de Valancourt,
having acquired the estates of Khemis Kezula by right of
lawful conquest, caused the fortress to be razed to the
ground and its stones scattered about the mountainsides by
his men-at-arms. Lanval never set foot among the ruins
again, and when the time came for him to die – which he
did in his bed, as all heroes deserve to do, though few
achieve it – he advised his son Guillaume to leave it alone
also. Guillaume, being a wise man as well as a dutiful son,
did as he was instructed.

Guillaume lived ten years less than his father, departing
this life at the age of fifty-two, and was misfortunate enough
to die far from home, while fighting a campaign for his
liege-lord the king. In consequence of this, his own son and
heir, Jehan de Valancourt, acquired the lands around
Selindre without receiving any solemn warning in regard to
his use of them. All his knowledge of them, in fact, was

drawn from the tales of his grandfather's glorious victory, which many story-tellers less scrupulous than myself had altered somewhat for the purposes of prettification and flattery.

Jehan so loved to bask in the reflected glory of his ancestor's heroic exploits that he took an early opportunity to visit Selindre, and was somewhat surprised to discover that the people of the town were less than grateful for the privilege of receiving him. He was a young man still, and had not quite understood how happy men can be when their liege-lords live distantly and do not put them to the trouble of providing obligatory hospitality.

When Jehan proudly rode up the slope to Khemis Kezula's blasted fortress to inspect the scene of his grandfather's victory he was unlucky enough to be thrown from his horse. He fell awkwardly, splitting his head upon a square-edged stone. Though his skull was not broken the wound never healed, and for the remainder of his life Jehan was tormented by evil dreams and periodic bouts of madness, during which the ordinary light of day seemed to him to be eclipsed by a brighter and more colourful light whose constant changes made him dizzy with anxiety.

Jehan became convinced that the ruins of Khemis Kezula's citadel were accursed – though whether he was mad or sane at the moment when he was persuaded of it, none can tell. For this reason, he inserted a clause into his will which said that the hill on which the fallen fortress stood should be set aside from the demesnes of Selindre, and should not be handed down to his own eldest son, who was called Lanfranc. Instead, the hill was given to the Sisters of Shallya, the goddess of healing and mercy, in order that they should raise in that wild and tempestuous region a shrine of their own. By means of this device Jehan de Valancourt sought to employ the power of the best and kindest of the gods to erase the memory and the legacy of wicked Khemis Kezula, whose prayers had undoubtedly been offered to a very different deity.

THE SISTERS OF Shallya were not entirely delighted to receive Jehan de Valancourt's legacy after his death. It was not that they feared any curse which might lie upon the land, but simply that the region was remote, and was home to very few followers of the goddess. The Council of Couronne, after much deliberation, sent envoys to Lanfranc de Valancourt to say that the gift of land would not be useful unless he could also provide for the hire of a company of masons and carpenters to build a temple and a house upon the site.

Lanfranc, despite that he harboured some slight resentment that the Sisters should inherit land which might have been his, agreed to assemble such a crew from those in his service, provided that the Sisters would go to the hill with them, so that their prayers and their magic could provide protection against the effects of any curse which might lie upon the land. This was agreed.

In consequence of these decisions, a company of Sisters was dispatched from Quenelles, travelling up the River Brienne to the limit of its navigability, where they met the Valancourt builders whose task it would be to build the stones of Khemis Kezula's ruined manse into a residence and a temple.

The nine Sisters who were appointed to this mission accepted their lot, as they were bound by their vows to do, unquestioningly. Some, indeed, were pleased by the prospect. For Mother Thelinda, who was appointed Superior of the company, there was a welcome increase in authority to compensate for the disruption of her former life; and for the likes of Sister Penelope and Sister Myrica – neither of whom had ever taken to city life – there was the lure of the forest and the fresh mountain air. But there were also those whose uncomplaining acceptance masked a certain unease, and one of these was Sister Adalia.

Adalia was twenty-two years old, having served Shallya for eight years. She was the daughter of a craftsman glassworker in the service of the governor of Quenelles, who had attracted the attention of a priestess of Shallya by virtue of an unusual aptitude for spellcasting which she had shown as an adolescent.

Alas, her aptitude had failed to mature with her body, so that her cultivated skills proved to be nothing out of the ordinary.

This disappointment had not detracted from Adalia's loyalty towards the goddess while she remained in her native town, where she was close to her relatives and where all the best houses boasted at least one window made by her father. She was stern in her determination to avoid curiosity about what might have become of her had she taken a different path in life. She never asked herself whether it was right and fair that the dull woman she now was should inherit the consequences of decisions made by the over-eager and falsely-promising girl she once had been. When she was commanded to leave Quenelles, though, she soon became conscious of a certain emptiness in the secret chambers of her heart, which her prayers and acts of charity could not begin to fill.

The hardship of the early days on the slopes above Selindre could not help but magnify any unease which the Sisters felt. Although it was summer the weather was often chilly and damp, and though the builders worked as fast as they could to erect two big houses – one for themselves and one for the Sisters – their progress was slow. The huge black stones which had formed the walls of Khemis Kezula's citadel were very difficult to shift and raise, even with block-and-tackle; and the tall trees which had to be felled for timber had hard, dark wood which blunted the carpenters' drills and saws. In the meantime, the whole company shivered in their tents.

Adalia, though she was far from being the tallest or the strongest of the Sisters, was instructed to help the workmen in their lighter tasks, fetching and carrying for them or mixing mortar. The work was so hard that her back always ached and her hands often bled, and though her magic won her some relief from such sufferings there was always more work to renew them. Myrica, seeing her distress, told her gently that the sunlight and the fresh air would soon bring colour to her cheeks and more strength to her limbs, but Adalia could discover no such change in herself as the long days went by.

The Sisters and the workmen moved into the two houses as soon as the roofs were in place, though they were by no means entirely finished. Each of the Sisters was alotted a room, bare-floored and bare-walled, with a pallet on which to sleep and two candle-brackets set on either side of a slit-window. So black was the stone of which the walls were made, so narrow were the windows, and so poor were the candles manufactured in Selindre, that these rooms seemed at first to be dreadfully gloomy.

Adalia's room was in the second storey, beneath the eaves. It faced north, so that the sun never shone directly through the narrow window, and it overlooked a stand of uncommonly twisted trees whose tattered crowns seemed to mutter arcane imprecations when stirred by the wind. It was by no means as comfortable as the room which she had occupied in Quenelles, whose walls had been hung with tapestries depicting flocks of flying doves, and whose latticed window had faced the rising sun – but she was resolved that she must not hate it, and it was certainly a relief to possess some space that was all her own after weeks of sharing a tent.

Mother Thelinda instructed that each of the Sisters must make her room a fit place for prayer, first by staining the dark walls white and then by inscribing on their surface the sacred symbols of Shallya: a heart of gold, a white dove in flight, and a tear-shaped drop of blood. Though none complained, all found difficulty in executing this task, for the black stones which had once protected Khemis Kezula were resistant to the stain of purity, and whitewash had to be applied several times over before the walls would condescend to be lightened.

Adalia found the task particularly frustrating, but in the end achieved a shade of grey which did not seem intolerably grimy. By this time, the white habit which she wore seemed to have lost its crisp cleanness forever, and no matter how she scrubbed it she could only bring it to the same shade of grey which she had contrived to impart to the walls of her room. It was little comfort to her that all the other Sisters had the same difficulties to afflict them.

THE PEOPLE OF Selindre were not ungrateful for the Sisters' presence, for they had heard what power the devoted followers of Shallya had to cure the sick and ease pain. Mother Thelinda received a steady stream of pleas for aid, which never went unanswered. Though no price was asked for such assistance, the villagers began to send gifts of food and live-stock – and by this means the Sisters acquired a flock of chickens and a milking-goat. They also became inheritors of the rich tradition of cautionary tales and rumours which had been handed down to the people from the times when Khemis Kezula had been their oppressor.

Among these stories there were the usual horrific accounts of cannibalism and child-sacrifice which inevitably accumu-late about those of sorcerous inclination, and the usual flights of fancy regarding storm-riding daemons and mon-sters of the night. But there were other items too, more unusual and idiosyncratic, some of which were contained in sayings and warnings whose import was no longer properly understood. One apparently pointless tale alleged that Khemis Kezula had made alliance with a tribe of dwarfs which had forsaken the worship of Grungni in order that another god might teach them the secret arts of crystal mak-ing; and one mysterious instruction, known to every child in Selindre – though none knew what it meant – bade all who dared to walk upon the mountain slopes to Beware the Glorious Light which floods the hidden valleys of the soul.

The Sisters of Shallya were no ordinary women, but they shared the delight which all women have (and which men also share, if the truth be admitted) in fearful fancies and ominous whispers. They repeated these tales avidly to one another while they worked, and though they laughed to show what little fear they had of the daemons with which long-dead Khemis Kezula had once made pacts there was always a tiny thrill of anxiety in their laughter.

Although work still remained to be done on the houses when the Sisters had whitened their walls and inscribed the sacred symbols of their faith, plans had already been made for the erection of the temple. After careful consultation with the masons, Mother Thelinda had decided that this should be sited on a square platform overlooking a steep and densely-thicketed slope. Here the eastern tower of Khemis Kezula's fortress had stood, and the first task facing the temple-builders was clearing the rubble from the site. There were few huge stone blocks here, but there was a great accumulation of smaller debris, which had long been over-grown by mosses, lichens and ferns.

Once the obscuring cloak of vegetation had been stripped away, it quickly became clear that there might be useful things to be gleaned from the wreckage. No doubt the people of Selindre had made some effort over the years to search for weapons and items of commercial value, but they had not troubled to steal away such commonplace things as wooden bowls and clay goblets, or bronze cooking implements and copper sewing-needles, for which the thrifty Sisters of Shallya could easily find a use. Mother Thelinda therefore appointed Sisters Adalia and Columella to the task of sifting through the debris as it was exposed and cleared, to recover and repair anything which could be put to use.

This was a duty which Sister Adalia found at first to be much more to her taste than fetching and carrying. It was far less wearying, and the pleasurable possibility that a new discovery might at any time be made was ample compensation for the dullness of most of the work involved. The work had its less pleasant side, for the artefacts buried in the rubble were sometimes to be found in association with grisly reminders of the fierce conflict which had raged within the fortress when Lanval invaded it, but Adalia was not afraid of skulls and skeletons and parchment-like fragments of skin.

It was not Adalia herself who discovered the first pieces of coloured glass; they were brought to her by a workman who thought them odd, though he did not realize that they might be valuable. But the glassworker's daughter knew well enough how rare and precious stained glass is, and quickly realized that the fragments must have come from a window. She demanded to be taken to the place where the shards had been found, where she began to rummage about for others.

When she found several more shards, some the size of fin-gernails and others the size of copper coins, she immediately commanded the workman to set aside his spade and proceed more carefully. She asked him to collect all the pieces of glass which he could find, and any strips of lead which might have been used to bind them together. In the meantime, she hurried off to tell Mother Thelinda what she had found.

Mother Thelinda was less enthusiastic than Adalia expected. Though she was city-bred and had seen stained-glass windows in the houses of noblemen, she had never looked at the windows of Quenelles with the same proud and interested eyes as Adalia. In fact, she considered such decorations to be mere frippery.

'I suppose you had better collect all you can,' said the Superior dismissively, 'if it can be of use or value to somebody. Perhaps we can make a gift of it to Lanfranc de Valancourt, to appease him for the loss of his craftsmen. He seems to be the kind of man who might take pleasure in toys and baubles, and I dare say that he has a clever window-maker at his beck and call.'

Adalia was annoyed that her discovery should be so casually minimized – and, as it seemed to her, her father also. However, she took what had been said to her as permission to make an effort to recover as much of the window as she could. She therefore gave Columella and the workmen instructions to be very careful in working near the spot where the first fragments had been unearthed, and to save all the shards which they found, no matter how tiny. For the rest of that day and all of the next she waited fretfully nearby, ready to pounce on any glint of coloured light which showed as the rubble was scraped away from the rock beneath.

By the evening of the second day she had hundreds of pieces of glass and dozens of pieces of the lead which had once secured the pattern of the window. The idea was born in her mind that if she could recover a sufficient number of fragments she might eventually be able to reconstruct the pattern of the window – enough of it, at least, to know what had been depicted there. She had no delusions as to the difficulty of the project, but she felt compelled to make the effort, so she cleared a space on the floor of her room and began to lay out the pieces there, shuffling them around in the hope that she might begin to see some semblance of order amid the chaos.

After an hour's pondering – which somehow used up the time which she should have spent at her private prayers – Adalia was forced to admit to herself that the task seemed hopeless. Although she had collected a good many fragments, many of them quite large, it was obvious that they were only a small fraction of the number into which the window had been shattered. She readily guessed that the vast majority of the remaining fragments must be very tiny, and would be very difficult to recombine even if they could ever be found. Because she had no idea what the pattern had looked like, it was hard to know where to start in trying to rebuild it.

More fragments of coloured glass turned up on the next day, and a few more on the next, but by now the workmen had completed the preparatory work of clearing the site, and it was obvious that no more pieces would be thrown up by the appointed routines of labour. Adalia turned her attention to the heaps of earth which had been shifted from the great platform, and to the cluttered slope which descended from its rim. She knew that much of the original rubble from the felling of the tower would simply have been tipped over the edge, and she knew that some of the glass from the window must have gone with it – but the slope was very steep, and the workmen had no intention of clearing the undergrowth from it.

Mother Thelinda soon relieved Adalia and Columella of the task of sorting through the debris, on the grounds that everything useful had now been recovered, and gave Adalia – who still seemed too pale and frail for heavy work – a list of domestic duties to be carried out in the house. Adalia had no option but to accept them, but found that the duties were sufficiently lenient to allow her a few hours of spare time even during the hours of daylight. She began to use these hours in looking for more fragments of glass, wherever she thought they might be found – and she found enough, day by day, to make her feel that it was worth her while to persist in the task. Indeed, she came gradually to believe that she had a special instinct which guided her search, and might eventually bring it to a successful end.

As SUMMER GAVE way to autumn and autumn to winter the hours of daylight decreased and those of darkness expanded. This reduced the amount of time which Adalia could devote to her search for pieces of glass, but increased that which she could devote to the attempt to figure out how the pieces she already had might be connected with one another. This puzzle became very absorbing indeed – so much so that it routinely absorbed the time which should have been given to her devotions – but when Mother Thelinda once suggested to her that she might be neglecting her prayers, she denied the charge vehemently.

There were several occasions when she was brought to the brink of despair, and became convinced that the project was hopeless, but on each occasion her half-formed resolution to give it up was subverted by a sudden gleam of inspiration which showed her how a group of pieces might be slotted together, or where a junction in the lead could be reconstructed. Eight years as a servant of Shallya had taught her many things, including the value of patience, and an occasional happy discovery was enough to persuade her that the task should not be abandoned.

While the pieces remained scattered on the floor of her room she could never leave them alone for long, but was always drawn irresistibly back to the puzzle. Her moments of insight gradually accumulated into an emergent understanding of the form and organization of the original work of art. She discovered that the window had been circular, and that there had been several concentric circles within the outer one. She deduced that the paler-coloured glass belonged mostly to the outer circles, with more vivid blues and roseate shades closer to the centre. She realized that the innermost circle had contained a detailed image of some kind, perhaps a representation of a bird with bright plumage.

Each of these discoveries reinforced her resolution, and encouraged her to increase her efforts, which she began to do by denying herself sleep. It was soon noticed, however, that Adalia burned more candles than any three of her companions, and she was summoned to the Superior to explain why this was so.

She took Mother Thelinda to see her work, sure that the sight of the partially-reconstructed window would be sufficient explanation and excuse, but the Superior had no notion of it as an intriguing puzzle to be solved, and could not see the picture emerging within the confused array of lead and glass. Mother Thelinda saw the broken pattern only as a silly and trivial mess, and said so.

'You must see, Sister Adalia,' she said, in a gentle and kindly fashion, 'that the objective cannot be worth the effort. What could you possibly gain by completing a task whose achievement would bring no worthwhile reward? You must understand that it is not fitting for a priestess of Shallya to become obsessed with worldly things. A window of coloured glass, however beautiful, is only a window on the everyday world. Our concern is to bring the mercy of Shallya to those who suffer grief and pain, not to play with ornaments.'

Adalia accepted these rebukes very mildly, but her penitence was feigned, and she was glad that Mother Thelinda did not think to offer a specific instruction commanding her to abandon her work. Nevertheless, she did resolve to try harder to perform those observances which her faith required of her.

For some days she was unable to collect more than a handful of very tiny fragments of glass from the slopes beneath the burgeoning temple. Nor, in those few days, did she use more candles than any of the other sisters. But her enthusiasm for her task was not really lessened at all; almost every piece of glass which she found was now the cause of a tangible thrill, for she was very often seized by the conviction that she knew exactly where her new find would fit into the growing whole.

The outer circles of the window came steadily nearer to completion, and she soon redoubled her efforts once again in searching for the missing fragments.

When the outer circles had been restored, save for a mere handful of fugitive shards, a most astonishing thing happened.

There began to emerge from those outer rings of glass, during the hours of deepest darkness, an uncanny glow, which grew by degrees into a flickering silvery radiance. It was as though the window was no longer laid out on a solid floor at all, but had been set in place to transmit the effulgence of a dawnlit sky.

Had Sister Adalia been less absorbed in her project, she might have been made anxious by this mystery. She might have remembered that this window had not been an ornament in some nobleman's pretty palace, but a part of the fortress of Khemis Kezula, where it might conceivably have had some other purpose than mere decoration. She might even have recalled to mind that curious warning about 'glorious light' which had passed through the company as an item of idle gossip.

Had she been able to think in this way she would then have understood that her duty to Shallya demanded that she consult her Superior at once. But her mind was filled by now with other thoughts and desires, and she had already acquired the habit of secrecy. As things were, the thought which first sprang into her mind when she saw this radiance was that it would help her to save candles, and thus be freed from further pressure to abandon her self-appointed task.

Her stratagem worked well; Mother Thelinda was satisfied with what appeared to be a return to normal conduct – and Sister Adalia was trapped in the unfolding web of her deceit, unable now to seek advice about the significance of the eerie light which lit her room for a few hours on either side of midnight.

She did not feel as if she was imprisoned by her deceit. Indeed, she felt more contented than she had ever been before. It was as if that emptiness within her being, of which she had only been half-aware, had been filled as neatly and cosily as it could be. She was now possessed of a completeness which all her sincere and heartfelt prayers to Shallya had somehow never provided for her.

Most of the pieces of glass to which her instinct led her as she patrolled the slopes beneath the temple were rosy or blue in colour, and the reconstruction of the circles where they belonged soon progressed to the point where almost every piece could be put unhesitatingly into place. And as these inner circles neared completion, they began to add their own measure to the light which poured into Sister Adalia's room in such a magical fashion.

Adalia loved that light – which was certainly very beautiful – and delighted in studying its many changes. It was not in the least like true sunlight, for it had a ceaseless ebb and flow in it; what had earlier been a casual flickering was now a more tempestuous agitation. Whenever she knelt beside the window, bending over it in search of the place where a particularly problematic shard belonged, her many shadows would move on the whitened walls behind her like a troop of wild dancers capering about a magical fire.

The dingy walls of her room were quite transformed by the light of the window; their greyness was utterly banished by it and the sacred symbols of Shallya's worship were completely blotted out. So too was the dreary greyness of her habit redeemed, for the light made it blaze with brightness, as though it were not a priestess's robe at all but the coloured costume of some mighty wizard of the Colleges.

Of the figure in the centre of the picture, however, Adalia could as yet see almost nothing. There were only a few fugitive pieces of glass which seemed to belong there, which gave the merest impression of feathery form, without any proper indication of the configuration of the wings, nor the least sign of beak or eye. No light came, as yet, from the innermost circle of the window.

ADALIA'S QUEST WAS nearly brought to an abrupt conclusion when Sister Penelope and Sister Myrica, who chanced one night to be out and about at an unusual hour, reported seeing strange lights in her window. Adalia was summoned yet again to see the Superior. She became very anxious lest it be commanded that her work must cease, and she stoutly denied that anything unusual had occurred. She insisted that she had been asleep at the time the light was reported, and knew of no possible source from which it could have come.

Because Penelope and Myrica could offer no tentative explanation of their own, Adalia's word was accepted, but Mother Thelinda took the opportunity to question her further about the fate of the stained glass which she had collected. Adalia denied that she was any longer interested in the reconstruction of the window, and said that in any case, no sizeable pieces of glass had been found for some considerable time. Because the latter part of the statement was true, the whole was believed.

After this interview, Adalia took the precaution of hanging up a dark cloth to curtain the narrow window of her room while she worked, and always left the greater window on the floor covered by a rug when she went out.

That Mother Thelinda believed Adalia's story was due in part to the conviction with which she told it, but also to the fact that she seemed so healthy and cheerful nowadays that it was impossible for any of her fellows to believe that she was going without sleep. When the Sisters had come to Selindre, and for some time after, Adalia had been pinched of feature and pasty of face, and far from being the strongest of the company – but now her skin was tanned and lustrous, and her laughing eyes were as bright as a bird's.

Her companions could only think that it was the sunlight and the air, and the hard but willing labour, which were at long last changing her for the better.

Adalia no longer fell eagerly upon the few tiny slivers of glass which were occasionally found while work on the temple proceeded; indeed, she professed indifference to them. One way or another, though, the fragments disappeared into her sleeves and pockets, and were carried anxiously at the end of each evening's communal rituals to the privacy of her room. There, the periphery of the innermost circle was slowly filled in, and she waited with rapt anticipation for the vital moment when the light which streamed through the outer circles would spread to the centre – when that enigmatic image would, as she thought of it, 'catch fire.'

She lived for that day; nothing else seemed to matter at all.

Unfortunately, the central motif remained irritatingly absent; there were a few fragments of glass which seemed to represent feathers, and enough lead to imply that the figure was the head of a bird, but of the beak and eyes there was still no trace. By now she had searched every inch of the slope beneath the burgeoning temple most assiduously, and she knew that there was little hope of finding anything but tiny fragments there.

Without the vital pieces, there was little more of the puzzle to be done, and nothing to occupy her hands and mind in those hours when the light of another world filled her room with its gorgeous colours. Her old habits reasserted themselves, but when she prayed – without taking care to specify which deity it was to whom she addressed her prayers – she prayed only for a gift and a revelation; her prayers expressed the yearning of her obsessive heart, which had no other object of affection than the face in the centre of the window.

For seven times seven nights the light waxed and waned, and each time it died Adalia went meekly to her bed. But on the next night, she was so filled with the glory of the light that she was utterly entranced, and was driven out by the fierceness of her hunger – out of her room and out of the house.

Winter had come by now and the night was bitter. Snow was falling on the slopes, its whiteness all but invisible in the cloudy night. But she did not feel cold at all, and made her way unerringly to the site of the temple, which was nearly complete.

In the courtyard of the temple, someone was waiting for her. He carried no lantern and she could not see his face, but she knew by his stature and his voice that he must be a dwarf.

'I have something which you want,' he said, 'and you have something which my master desires. Will you make a contract of exchange, so that your heart's desire might be answered?'

'I will,' she said. She felt as though she was lost in a dream, and in dreams one does not ask too many questions.

'Here is what you need,' said the dwarf, and she felt a rough and hairy hand as he gave her a parcel of rags which had something hard and sharp-edged within it.

As the other turned to go, Adalia said: 'Take whatever I have to give, in return.'

And he replied: 'It is already taken.'

Then she took the parcel back to her room and carefully hid it away before she went to sleep.

ON THE NEXT night, when all had become quiet, she uncovered the window to let free its turbulent light and took out her prize. She carefully unwrapped the bundle, exposing half a hundred pieces of coloured glass and a few twisted slugs of lead.

The fragments of glass were mostly small and mis-shapen, and it was clear that it would be no easy task to fit them together in the correct order. It had been a long time since she had had so many new shards to work with and she was delighted by the challenge. Her nimble fingers began the work of turning and sorting, flying as though impelled by an intelligence other than her own, and she felt meanwhile as though she was laughing inside. She was very quick in slotting the pieces into place, for each one seemed to know exactly where it belonged.

The eyes she placed last, and when she placed them, she knew that her work was finished – that although a hundred tiny cracks and crannies remained in the grand design, she had done enough.

Incandescent light sprang from the heart of the window, and the figure detailed there was suddenly present in all its resplendent glory.

For a few fleeting seconds she still thought that the figure was the head of a bird – perhaps that legendary firebird which was still occasionally glimpsed above the cliffs of Parravon. Then, she thought that it might be the head of a griffon, like the one displayed as a trophy in the Great Hall of the Governor's Palace in Quenelles. While its colours were still limned by curves of clotted lead it might have been either of those things. But then, as the cataract of light poured through the window between the worlds, the lead which held the pieces of coloured glass seemed to melt and shrivel, so that the image ceased to be an image, and became reality.

Then she saw that the central figure was neither bird nor griffon, nor any other mere animal intelligence. Plumed and crested with gorgeous feathers he might be, but this was a person, whose gaze was brighter with wisdom and knowledge than the eyes of any human or elven being she had ever seen.

There was a tiny voice of warning within her, which tried to cry 'Daemon!' in such a way as to make her afraid, but the voice seemed to Adalia to be no more than a tiny echo, feeble and forlorn – and if, as she supposed, it was the last vestige of that love and adoration which she had once given freely to Shallya, then its insignificance now was clear testimony of the transfer of her loyalty to another power.

The face which looked at her, out of that other world which was so wondrously filled with ecstatic light, was incapable of smiling – for the beaked mouth was set as hard as if it was carved from jet – and yet she was in no doubt that he was glad to see her. She was perfectly certain that he longed to enfold her in his feathery embrace, to cover her tenderly with the splendour of his fiery plumage.

The sheer beauty of the prospect overwhelmed her, and she threw wide her arms to welcome that transcendent embrace.

Behind her, crowded upon the cold and narrow walls of that space which had been given to her for her allotted share of the world of mortal men, a hundred coloured shadows strutted and jostled, utterly unaware of their own thinness and insubstantiality, uncomprehending of the fact that they were mere whimsies of a light from beyond the limits of the earth.

Adalia, who had once been a Sister of Shallya, gave voice to a liquid trill of pure pleasure – and those eyes which she had so recently restored to their proper place focused upon her an astonishing, appalling look of love, which was full of laughter and the joy of life…

WHEN SISTER ADALIA did not appear for morning prayer Sister Columella and Sister Penelope were sent to inquire whether she was ill.

They discovered her naked and supine upon the floor of her room, with her arms thrown wide and her legs apart.

It was, they said, as though she had been seared from top to toe by some incredible fire, which had burned her black. The walls of her room, and her discarded robe, were similarly black and ashen. And embedded in Adalia's vitrified flesh, sparing not a single inch of it, were thousands upon thousands of tiny pieces of glass.

These coloured fragments, as Mother Thelinda was able to observe when she was summoned by her horror-stricken messengers, gave Adalia's corpse the appearance of being encrusted with an extraordinary quantity of precious gems.

Had they not known that it could not possibly be another, Columella and Penelope told their friends, they might never have guessed that it was poor Adalia. She had been so utterly transfigured by her mysterious death that she might have been anyone at all.

THE SPELLS BELOW
by Neil Jones

KATARINA KRAEBER STROLLED through the streets of Waldenhof. Early morning sunlight slanted in over the close-crowded rooftops; the air was full of the smell of freshly baked bread. Around her, townsfolk were already going about their business, calling out the occasional greeting to one another. Katarina felt relaxed and happy: she was on her way to her lessons in wizardry.

Above her, mounted on a high gable, she saw a gilded weathervane clearly outlined against the blue summer sky. The spells that Anton Freiwald – and her father before him – had taught her came whispering into her mind.

A glance up and down the street showed her that no one was looking in her direction. Lifting one slim hand, her brown eyes intent on the weathervane, she began to murmur the words of a spell.

Very slowly, the weathervane began to turn, moving counter to the breeze that was stirring the morning air. It completed one full turn, and then began to pick up speed, creaking as it did so.

161

A plump merchant stopped directly across the street from Katarina. He looked upwards, frowning, then peered suspiciously at Katarina. Her blue tunic, hose and cap clearly marked her out as an apprentice of the Wizards' Guild.

Katarina broke the spell at once and continued on down the street, her easy mood gone, replaced now by a sense of unease. Wizardry was legal in Waldenhof, but both Anton and her father had warned her about the need to be circumspect. Ordinary folk feared magic, often with good reason.

As she hurried on through the streets, she sensed that the mood of the townsfolk around her had begun to change, too. Some of them were exchanging words and glances, as if there were something going on that she was not aware of.

She turned the corner into Ostgardstrasse and, looking down it to where it opened onto the expanse of Sigmarplatz, she saw the steel helms of soldiers. A feeling of alarm went through her as sharp and as sudden as a knife-blade.

She pushed her way through the crowd that was beginning to gather and found herself behind two burly soldiers. Beyond them, there were hundreds more already in the square. Sunlight glittered off their weapons and armour. The banner of Waldenhof's graf, Jurgen von Stolzing, fluttered in the breeze.

The soldiers were drawn up into an arc that went around three sides of the square and stretched into Zoffstrasse on her left and Merzbahn on her right. The row of elegant four-storey mansions directly opposite her was surrounded. And in the centre of that row, its red-lacquered door and shuttered windows gleaming against grey stone, was the residence of Anton Freiwald.

Anton, Katarina thought, remembering. When her father had died in debt and there had been no one she could turn to, it had been Anton who had come to offer her his help. Recognizing her talent, he had made her his apprentice. And then later, when her respect and gratitude had been joined by other, stronger feelings – of attraction, affection – they had become lovers.

Now Anton was the one in trouble and it was her turn to help him.

Taking a chance that everyone's attention would be focused on the square, Katarina cast a simple garrulity spell upon the two soldiers immediately in front of her. One promptly leaned towards the other and muttered: 'Remember, the graf said to take him alive. There's a reward in it for us if we do.'

'It's secrets they're after,' the second man whispered back. 'Dark magic secrets. They want to put him to the question. But it's a waste of time. Everyone knows you can't torture anything out of a dark magician.'

'What's it matter so long as we get paid?'

The squat bulk of a siege engine came into view, rumbling slowly forward across the cobbles. Following behind it were people that she recognized – all members of the Wizards' Guild. With alarm, she saw that there were dozens of them, wizards of every level, from all of the various colleges. Hastily, Katarina allowed her spell to fade, hoping it had not been detected.

As the wizards gathered together in the square immediately in front of her, a brazier was set up beside the siege engine. Strange odours began to rise from it, spicing the morning air.

The house seemed a hundred miles away but she knew she had to get across Sigmarplatz to it and quickly. Her only chance was to slip past the soldiers and then make a run for it. The thought of it terrified her – but there was no alternative, not if she was going to help Anton. And she would have to do it now, before the graf began his assault.

She took a slow, deep breath. Then another, searching for calm. She took a step forward – and a hand closed on her arm. 'Now,' a cold voice said, 'what sort of wizardling have we here?'

HELD BY AN iron-hard grip, she looked up into a dark-bearded face she recognized: Gerhard Lehner, Magister of the Wizards' Guild – and Anton Freiwald's bitterest rival.

Two soldiers moved in to take hold of her arms. They marched her forward and a moment later she was standing before a tall, richly dressed figure: Graf Jurgen von Stolzing himself.

'What's going on?' he demanded, his gaze moving from Lehner to Katarina.

'A little surreptitious spell-casting, my lord graf,' replied Lehner. He raised his hand in a deprecatory gesture. 'Fortunately, very little indeed.'

The graf stared at Katarina, suspicion gleaming in his pale blue eyes. 'Who are you?'

'Allow me to introduce you,' said Lehner. He reached out to knock Katarina's blue apprentice's cap to the ground. Her hair shook free. 'This is Fraulein Katarina Kraeber, apprentice...' he lingered faintly over the word, '...to Anton Freiwald.'

The graf inspected her coldly, took in the brown hair, cut neatly at the jawline, the high-cheekboned face, the green eyes. 'So,' he said. 'Another acolyte of Chaos?'

'Quite likely, graf,' replied Lehner.

Chaos. The full extent of the charges against Anton came home to her. No wonder they had come for him with such overwhelming force.

Then her name finally registered with the graf. 'Kraeber?'

'Yes, my lord. Her late father was Joachim Kraeber, of my own guild. Her grandfather–'

'Yes, yes,' said the graf. 'I remember the family.'

'They gave you loyal service my lord,' said Katarina, seizing her chance to speak. 'As I–'

'What were you trying to do?' demanded the graf, his thin face drawn into tight lines. 'Tell me, or you'll be made to.'

Katarina's eyes went to the mansion, impossibly distant across the square. 'My duty. Only that.'

'Your duty? As a citizen of Waldenhof – or as a servant of the dark magician, Anton Freiwald?'

'My lord,' protested Katarina, 'don't believe Magister Lehner. He's jealous of Anton's talent, his spells, his–'

'Spells?' said the graf sharply. 'What do you know of them?'

Immediately, Katarina became guarded; Anton had warned her to say nothing of his research. 'Only the ones he has taught me,' she answered after a moment. 'Those proper to an apprentice.'

'I think she knows much more than she's telling us, my lord,' put in Lehner. 'Best she be put to the question.'

'Yes,' agreed the graf. 'Alongside her master.' He swung around to face the house. 'It's time we flushed that corrupt devil out.' He gestured to Lehner. 'Begin.'

Lehner stepped confidently forward until he was standing before the brazier. He lifted both arms into the air, his lips began to move – and then a voice was booming out over the cobbled expanse of the square. A human voice, the voice of Gerhard Lehner, but magically amplified. It echoed across the tiled roofs around them, out across the whole city of Waldenhof. 'Anton Freiwald. You are charged with practising dark magic. Surrender! In the name of Jurgen von Stolzing, Graf of Waldenhof.'

An expectant hush fell over the crowd. Moments passed. There was no response from the house. The graf looked towards the siege engine, and brought his hand down in a decisive gesture. The command to fire rang out across the square. Wood and leather creaked, and then a massive stone was whistling through the air.

The stone arced across the square, towards the house. Abruptly, there was a sound like water being poured onto white-hot coals – and rainbow light exploded around it.

A massed gasp of astonishment went up from everyone in the square, hands were raised against the glare. The light began to dim and the stone became visible once again. It was absolutely still, hanging suspended in mid-air.

For a few seconds longer it remained there. Then it dropped to the ground and shattered against the cobbles. The shield, Katarina thought with sudden hope. The shield of spell-power that Anton had talked of. Somehow he had managed to get it operating in time.

'Gerhard,' said the graf in a hushed voice. 'Have we come too late?'

'Perhaps, my lord,' replied Lehner in a whisper. He looked shaken. 'Or perhaps only just in time.'

The grip on Katarina's arms had slackened. The two soldiers who held her had given all their attention to the stone, and were still staring at the shards scattered across the cobbles.

With a sudden effort, Katarina wrenched herself free of them. As she ran forward, hands grabbed at her. She struck out at them, dodged from side to side.

Then she was out onto the open square, running towards the house.

FROM BEHIND THERE were shouts to halt. She ignored them. An arrow flew past her on the left. It sparked against the invisible wall across the square and fell to the ground, all its energy spent.

Katarina ran on, calling out the words of a warding spell, praying that she had remembered it correctly. Then the air around her was bristling with arrows. Her boots thudded on the cobbles. Sigmarplatz had never seemed so vast.

She sensed magic stirring behind her, knew that Lehner and the others were spell-casting at her back. Then rainbow light was shimmering around her. She had reached the safety of the shield.

Her movements slowed; it felt as if she were moving underwater. Safe now, she told herself. Almost home. All you have to do is keep moving.

She could feel Anton's magic flowing through her, protecting her.

Then her eyes snapped shut as the light around her brightened to a blinding intensity. It sounded as if a host of daemons were screeching at her. She tried to put her hands to her ears but they moved with dreamlike slowness.

Something had struck the shield. Not a rock this time – something magical, she realized. A spell. Lehner and the rest of the Guild. All those wizards, of every level, acting together. Creating a combined spell of tremendous force, designed to tear the shield apart.

Magical energy surged through her body as the two spells – shield-wall and shield-breaker – clashed. Too much raw magic, coming at her much too quickly. Anton could have weathered it easily, she knew. But despite his coaching, she was still so very inexperienced, barely out of the apprentice stage.

For a moment, she stood there, twitching like a fly freshly caught in a spiderweb, her feet rooted to the ground. Then she remembered Anton's strength spell, brought his voice into her mind, heard him reciting it to her once again.

She took a single step forward – and stepped fully into the sanctuary of the shield. As she stumbled across the remaining distance, she looked back over her shoulder. Light licked at the shield: gold, blue, crimson, jade. But the shield was holding.

The red-lacquered door opened and two men wearing leather and chain mail darted out: Anton's hired Kislevite guards. As they pulled her roughly inside, she saw the other three Kislevites waiting in the hallway, their braided yellow hair hanging down across their shoulders. They had their weapons drawn. Katarina was surprised that they had all remained loyal.

The door to Anton's study opened and then the wizard was standing in front of her. His dark hair hung loose to his shoulders, framing his broad, surprisingly youthful face. He was wearing an elaborately decorated robe; inscribed upon the chest was his personal symbol, based on the great wheel of magic itself. Each of its eight spokes was a different colour, representing the eight colours of the magical flux. The wheel's rim was comprised of bands of the same colours, each in their proper station.

'Katarina,' the wizard called out angrily. 'What in Taal's name did you think you were doing?'

Still trying to catch her breath, she said, 'I came to warn you, Anton. You can't surrender. They mean to torture you.'

'I already knew that,' he said, but his voice had softened.

A diminutive figure, even smaller than a halfling, appeared behind Anton, one bony hand clutching at the wizard's robe: Anton's familiar. Despite its physical approximation to humanity, the look of its pale coarse-grained flesh gave it a rough, unfinished appearance. It glared up at Katarina with its red-rimmed eyes, its lips parting in a snarl.

Katarina looked quickly away from the creature, feeling the instinctive revulsion she had never been able to rid herself of.

'Anton,' she said. 'They think you've turned to Chaos.'

'What?' he responded, clearly astonished. 'They think that – and still they want to steal my knowledge?'

The captain of the Kislevites called to them. Peering through the shutters, they could see that the graf's troops had begun to move out across the square, were advancing on the house. Spell-light sheened their weapons.

'Will the shield stop them?' asked Katarina.

'Not for long. Not with the whole of the Guild out there to help them. But it should slow them down.'

Katarina shuddered, remembering her own struggle to pass through it.

Anton was looking around at his handful of mercenaries. 'Men,' he called out, his voice vibrant. 'The graf is sending his soldiers against me. But I can stop them. All I need is a little time to charge my spell to its fullest strength.'

'You can stop them?' echoed Katarina in wonder.

'Yes,' Anton said levelly, his eyes on the mercenaries. 'But I will need time.'

'My lord,' the Kislevite captain protested, in heavily-accented Reikspiel, 'there are hundreds of them.'

'When they try to pass through the shield they'll be vulnerable,' said Anton.

The man's seamed face was full of doubt. 'We'll try, of course, but–'

Anton raised his hands, murmured something Katarina could not catch. The air around his fingertips quivered with the force of his spell. The mercenaries straightened, as if sudden new resolve had come into them. 'My lord,' the captain said. 'We'll hold them.' His eyes were shining.

A loyalty spell, Katarina realized. Anton had placed a loyalty spell upon his Kislevites and now he had raised its strength to the limit. That Anton had used such a spell disturbed her. It seemed… wrong. But then she recalled the forces arrayed against him and knew that he had simply had no choice.

Anton turned away, went down the hall to an oaken door, and slid a key into the lock. The door opened soundlessly, revealing a stone stairway that spiraled downwards into darkness. It led to the lowest level of the house, the level that held Anton's laboratory.

'Let me come with you,' Katarina called out. 'Perhaps I can help.' In all the time she had known him he had never allowed her – or anyone else – to enter his laboratory.

Anton stared at her, as if he were trying to reach some sort of decision. The familiar gave an impatient tug at his robe, staring balefully at Katarina. 'No,' the wizard said finally. 'It's best you stay here.'

When she started to protest, he lifted her hand to his lips, kissed it briefly. 'This once, Katarina, obey me.'

She touched the back of her other hand to his shaven cheek; the slight roughness – and the sharp male scent of him – felt reassuring. 'Of course. Good luck.'

A glowing ball of light rose from his hand and preceded him down the stairway. The familiar scuttled after him. The door swung shut behind them and the lock snicked into place.

THERE WAS A noise from above, as if one of the shutters in one of the upstairs rooms had opened. Katarina looked up to see a shadow detach itself from a darkened side-door on the landing. It glided soundlessly towards the balustrade, a movement that was so swift and silent that it was as if the shadow was drifting through her mind rather than the house, as if she was dreaming its brief prescence.

Instinctively, she turned to block the door Anton had taken.

The shadow-shape leapt from the balustrade and landed lightly in front of her. It stood there for a moment, regarding her; a tall muscular man-shape, clothed in black, eyes gleaming at her out of a dark mask. And on one sleeve the scorpion symbol of Khaine, god of murder.

An assassin. If Anton Freiwald could not be taken alive then the graf wanted to be very sure of his death.

On the man's waist Katarina saw an amulet that bore the Guild's insignia. To one with her training, it practically writhed with spell-charge. Already it had brought the assassin this far – through the shield and past Anton's other warding spells. If enough of the wizards had poured enough of their power into it then perhaps it might be strong enough to take him safely down to the laboratory itself.

'Stand aside,' the assassin said. 'My contract is for your master's life, not yours.'

'You mean Anton Freiwald, the wizard?' Katarina said quickly. 'But he's outside. With the guards.'

The assassin's eyes shifted to the side for a fraction of a second and, taking her chance, Katarina sprang at him, both hands clenched, aiming low.

The assassin twisted aside easily and, tripping Katarina as she went past him, sent her toppling to the floor. Shaken but unhurt, Katarina got quickly back to her feet but the assassin was gone – and the door to the lower level hung open.

She shouted down into the spiral stairway, but her voice was lost in the gloom. She tried again, calling out as loudly as she could, but again the darkness absorbed her words, like a sponge soaking up drops of water.

There was no torch to light her way and she was afraid. Afraid of the spells that guarded the place, afraid of what was down there. But Anton Freiwald – her protector, her lover – was in danger. She stepped forward.

WITH HER FOOT poised above the first step, she heard a voice – Anton's. 'Back,' the voice said sternly. 'This level is forbidden to all.'

For a moment, she thought he was coming back up the stairs. But then she realized it was merely the taboo spell speaking in her mind. The first of Anton's barriers. She could feel its magical pressure in her head.

'Anton, I'm trying to help you,' she protested. She tried to move her foot. But the muscles in her legs had locked. No matter how hard she tried, they wouldn't move.

Katarina strained again and again to take that first step, to break through the spell, but it was as if the lower half of her body was paralyzed. The harder she tried, the louder the voice in her head became, commanding, threatening, until it was a shout echoing inside her skull. She lifted her hands to her ears, trying to shut it out. It rose in volume, became a thunderous roar, blotting out thought.

Swaying on her feet, eyes tightly closed, she summoned her own image of Anton. The lean, muscular body; the grey eyes, the long silken hair. His lips were on hers, his arms around her. She could feel the warmth of him against her.

The love she felt for him was as bright and sharp in her mind as a knife-blade. It brought her the strength she needed to break through the spell, the strength to disobey him.

The cold chilled through the sole of her boot as she placed it on the first step. The wizard's voice dropped, until it was only a shout once again. Then, a second step, a third. All she could hear now was a shrill whisper.

She continued downwards. As she passed the first turn in the stairs, the voice faded completely.

Below her, the darkness stirred. From out of it, a small questing head appeared, attached to a long serpentine neck. Its teeth were bared and its yellow eyes glowed like tiny amber coals. The head regarded her for a moment. Then it began moving steadily up towards her.

Katarina halted, but did not retreat. The stairs were the only way down to Anton's laboratory. She had to get past this creature. She knew what it was; Anton had talked to her of his defences. It was not a living creature, but a reflection of her own inner fears, given shape – but not substance – by Anton's spell. It could kill her, but only through terror of her own making.

Knowing what it was, she told herself firmly, would be enough. She could pass it. Shutting her eyes, she put her foot onto the next step.

There was a hiss of rage and the scrabbling of claws on stone. An acrid stench drifted up to her nostrils. The sound of laboured breathing was amplified by the narrowness of the stairway.

Down the stairs she went, not stopping, knowing that if she did she was lost, feeling her way, her hands on the cold, clammy stone. At any moment she kept expecting to feel that small mouth on her body. But the creature was only her own fear given form. She held that knowledge in her mind like a talisman as she descended.

The air grew chill. She had lost count of the turns now. Her feet and hands were becoming numb from cold. The stairway seemed to go on forever.

Abruptly, one foot jarred on stone that was well above where the next step should have been. She stepped forward, knowing she had reached the bottom.

There was a scraping sound and something brushed against her leg. Then she felt a sudden sharp pain as teeth closed on her ankle. Her heart seemed to stop and her eyes came open.

A little light seeped down the stairway behind her, enough to dimly illuminate the narrow corridor that led to the single door: the entrance to Anton's laboratory.

She saw the mind-monster staring at her. But it was far away at the end of the long corridor, coiled in front of the door. Its outline had lost definition, and the colour had leached out of its yellow eyes. As she watched, it finally faded out altogether, blending back into the darkness it had come from.

Katarina's mouth was dust-dry. Her breathing was coming in short, shallow gasps. That bite had felt so real that her ankle still throbbed. Looking down, she saw something small and pallid moving at her feet; its eyes glittered in the dim light.

The familiar. She kicked at the creature and it scuttled away on hands and feet, finally halting at the far end of the corridor, beyond the door to the laboratory, well out of her reach.

In the gloom it was barely visible, but the faint reflections from its eyes told her that it was staring back at her. Faintly, in the quiet, she could hear its breathing.

Drops of blood smeared her hand as she bent and massaged her ankle. The creature repelled her. Even the thought of its touch filled her with disgust. It was a homunculus, created by Anton in his laboratory to serve as his familiar. Despite its vaguely human form, it was little more intelligent than an animal. It must have attacked her simply because she had descended to this forbidden level. Normally it never left its master's side. Had it been driven outside the laboratory when the assassin attacked?

Moving cautiously, trying to keep one eye on the door and the other on the familiar, Katarina made her way down the corridor. Additional light seeped out from around the door frame – but the room beyond the thick wooden door seemed silent. All Katarina could hear was her own laboured breathing and an occasional muted sound from the familiar.

The stillness was shattered abruptly: a scream rang out, coming from within the laboratory. Katarina stood there, held rigid by the sound. It was the wizard's voice. And full of such rage and pain.

Images of Anton injured, even dead or dying, filled her mind. For an instant longer, she remained motionless. Then, as the scream ended, she sprang to the door. Anton might be fighting for his life. She had to get inside.

She put one hand on the massive bronze door knob; it was icy cold to the touch. She tried to turn it, first one way and then the other. It would not move. And the knob felt as if it were slightly warmer now, almost the same temperature as her body.

Using both hands this time, she tried again. Still the knob would not turn. Katarina could sense that it was resisting her pressure and its temperature was definitely increasing now: already it was unpleasantly hot. Her palms and fingers were beginning to hurt.

Calling out the words of an opening spell, she exerted all her strength. Still the knob was immovable. The heat rose, the pain in her hands was much greater now, it felt as if the skin were burning. Somehow she forced herself to hold onto the knob, straining to turn it, knowing that the only important thing was to get inside the laboratory, to help Anton.

The pain continued to worsen. But when she looked down at her hands, half expecting to see the skin burnt, and saw to her astonishment that they were unmarked. Once again, she brought Anton's image back into her mind and held it there. The pain wasn't real, she told herself. Only the door was real.

Anton's spell held for a moment longer, then the knob gave an almost human groan and slowly, reluctantly, the door swung open.

THE ROOM BEYOND gleamed with light. A ring of skulls was revolving slowly in the centre of the chamber. Each one floated in the air, suspended only by magic, its jaws opening and closing at intervals as if chanting a spell, but no sound emerged. The eye sockets were giving out a soft, bone-white radiance.

Katarina stared at the turning skulls for a moment, both horrified and fascinated. As they slowly swung past her, she found herself counting them: there were five.

Once Anton had spoken to her of the source of his great magic – he had talked of a mechanism, a reservoir – that allowed him to accumulate magical energy, to use whenever he needed. Was this grisly assemblage of skulls Anton's secret? Could this be what powered his spells?

Chaos magic? No, she decided. Not Anton Freiwald. He was of the Rainbow College and was willing to use any and all of the colours of the magical spectrum. But not the undivided black of Chaos.

Then the memory of the scream finally returned to her and she called out, 'Anton?'

There was no answer. Neither the wizard nor the assassin was in sight. Nothing moved except the skulls. The whole room was silent. The shifting light from the eye-sockets reflected off the contents of jars and vials that lined the left-hand wall, producing shafts of rainbow light. A faint sulphurous odour hung in the air.

Across the room from her, half hidden behind a curtain, a door stood ajar. Beyond, she could see cold stone. A tunnel, leading out of the chamber, perhaps to the city above. Had Anton taken it, perhaps pursued by the assassin?

She stepped forward and almost immediately saw a face. It was staring towards her from the opposite side of the room.

Again, she called out. She recognized the features now; they were Anton's. But another step closer and she realized it was only a portrait of the wizard hanging on the far wall. Then, further to her right, half-hidden by shadow, she saw a dark shape sprawled in front of a wall lined with bookshelves. A human shape.

Katarina took a step towards the body. Anton? No, it was a man, but dressed completely in black: the assassin.

His eyes stared up at her through a fine grey mesh that covered his face. The lines were drawn so tightly that they had cut into the skin beneath. The man's hands were clutching at the mesh in what must have been a last desperate attempt to rip it off.

When she heard the noise behind her she whirled around but it was only the familiar. It stood in the doorway for a moment, sniffing the air, its eyes searching. Then it ran forward on its thin legs and disappeared behind the large oaken desk on the other side of the room.

Katarina approached cautiously and peered over the desk at the creature. The familiar was squatting on a body. Anton's body. Katarina knew the face immediately, even though the features were contorted by rage and pain. He was dead; a slim black-hilted dagger was buried in his heart. His robe and the brocaded carpet beneath it were soaked in blood.

But Katarina's grief was buried by disgust for what the familiar was doing. The creature was bent over the body, its thin hands clutching at Anton's tunic, its tiny mouth at the wizard's throat.

Filled with loathing, Katarina reached for something – anything – to throw at it. As her fingers closed on a flask that stood on the wizard's desk, the familiar raised its head, flicked a glance at her, and bared its teeth in a snarl. Its lips were smeared with blood.

She hurled the flask with all her strength, and it struck the familiar on the side of its head. The creature toppled off Anton's body to sprawl, limp and bleeding, beside its master.

Breathing hard, tears streaming down her face, Katarina stared down at Anton then, and waited for her grief to overwhelm her. Nothing mattered any more. He was dead. How could she go on living without him?

The feeling that finally came was a ghost of the grief she had expected. Its lack of intensity astonished her. Anton Freiwald, the man she loved, the man who had meant more than her own life to her, was dead. Why did she only feel – regret?

Shocked, she turned to her memories, in search of something that would inspire some deeper feeling. Trying to remember the gratitude she had felt for him, the respect, the loyalty, the love.

Memories came, but they were blurred, wavering, as if reflected off moving water. Her father's death, the debts she could not pay. And then Anton offering her his protection. Gratitude. She knew she should feel gratitude. And yet...

As she struggled to make everything come clear, something broke in her mind – rainbow light shimmered in the corners of her vision for a second and then was gone.

A spell, she realized. Someone had used a spell on her. Someone – Anton! He had clamped a magic shackle around her mind.

Her memories came into focus – to be seen from a stark new perspective. Her talent for magic was great, as her father had told her often enough. Anton had seen an opportunity to harness that talent for himself. He had come to her when she was vulnerable and put the shackle in place. All the lessons with him, the magic he had taught her, had been simply so that he might use her more effectively.

Feelings burst up from deep within her and churned through her mind. There was rage and hate and bitterness – and a sense of violation.

She had been his slave. Only that. Love him? How could she ever have believed that she had loved him? What she had felt in his arms had been a forgery. The memory of his hands on her body brought the taste of bile to her mouth.

'All the gods damn you, Anton!' she cried out. Her hands clenched, she stood above Anton Freiwald's body, not touching it – unwilling to – but wanting to strike it, to hurt the wizard as he had hurt her.

Tears slid down her cheeks. She almost wanted him to live again so that she could kill him, and this time watch him die. Almost.

Then, a new thought came: free. She was free. Her mind was her own again, her body hers and hers alone. A feeling of joy went through her, grew until it was almost dizzying in its intensity. Free, she told herself again. And she was going to stay that way.

A glance at the ring of skulls and her new exhilaration faded. It was slowing, its light fading. Anton was dead, and his spells were dying with him. When the skulls stopped completely, the spell-shield above would fail – and Gerhard

Lehner would lead the graf's soldiers down to the laboratory. All she could expect from them was torture and –
eventually, death.

Swinging around, she found the tunnel that led away into
darkness. The air that wafted out of it was dank and icy cold.
It looked very old – perhaps it had been carved by dwarf
engineers in the days of Waldenhof's founding.

Anton had never intended to fight, Katarina knew then,
only to escape. This tunnel was his secret escape route. Now
it would be hers.

She started towards the tunnel – and then halted. Anton
had told her of his grimoire, a listing of all the spells he had
mastered, from every branch of the art, and drawing upon
all the magic colours. It was somewhere here, Katarina was
sure. If she could find it and take it with her, then she could
continue her studies and slowly, patiently master the spells
Anton had never intended to teach her.

The bookshelves that lined the right-hand wall from top
to bottom and wall to wall caught her eye. Once she would
have been fascinated by the wealth of knowledge the wizard
had accumulated here, could have spent hours raptly studying them.

Now she thought only of the grimoire.

Books tumbled to the floor as she hunted for it. The grimoire was not among them.

The drawers of the desk came open easily. Inside were
papers bearing magical signs and script in Anton's precise
hand. But again no sign of the grimoire.

The skulls were barely moving now, their light a dim glow.
At any moment they would stop completely. Anton had hidden the grimoire too well. Perhaps she should run while she
still had the chance.

No. She had suffered too much. It had to be somewhere
down here and she would find it. Then her eyes chanced to
return to the portrait on the wall and she felt a sudden sharp
certainty.

'Come no further!' a voice called out as she took a step
towards it.

The voice froze her, her fear returning in a sudden rush.
She wanted to turn, to look at the wizard's dead body. But

her eyes were still on the portrait. Its thin lips were moving, its dark eyes flashing. 'Come no closer, intruder. Or you die.'

The words were coming from the portrait. Another spell. But the face was expressionless, the voice flat, as if the effort of animation was now too great for it.

'All the gods damn you, wizard,' she said again, hating him, and reached for the portrait.

Dust rose from the thick, patterned carpet to sting her face and arms. She screwed her eyes shut and brushed at it furiously. Something drifted down onto her head and shoulders from the ceiling. Her eyes flicked open again. A spider's web. It settled on her and began to tighten. She put both hands up to it to pull it away. Its silken strands had the strength of steel. They tightened further, biting into her flesh. She couldn't breathe!

An image of the assassin's masked face came into her mind, the mesh that had killed him tight around it. Choking, she pulled again at the web, this time in desperation. One of its strands parted, with a sharp twang. Then, one by one, others followed. Katarina sucked in air through her mouth and, a moment later, she ripped the thing from her face and flung it onto the carpet. It writhed there for a time, like some dying grey insect, the dust drifting back down to the ground around it.

Katarina massaged her face and neck for a moment, knowing that if Anton's power had not almost completely drained from his spell, if only a little more of his strength had remained in it, she would be dead now.

Stepping up to the portrait, she took it carefully in both hands. 'Beware...' the wizard's voice intoned as she lifted it away from the wall. Behind it was a small round hatch, bearing Anton's rainbow wheel symbol.

'Intruder,' the portrait was droning at her. She smashed it against the wall, heard the frame splinter, the canvas rip. She broke off a piece of the frame, letting the rest drop onto the floor, and began trying to prize the hatch open. At the same time, she called out spell-words, commanding it to unseal. When it wouldn't move, she beat at it with the wood, hitting it again and again, as hard as she could, imagining it was Anton she was striking.

Abruptly, the hatch flew open with the same groan of despair that the door to the laboratory had made. Inside, an arm's length away, was a book. It was bound in leather and embossed with the rainbow-wheel: the grimoire.

Transferring the piece of the frame to her left hand, she reached into the vault with her right. Her fingers found the book.

The vault grew teeth along its rim, then closed on her arm with a snap. She screamed. As the vault gnashed at her, her vision blurred and she felt as if she would pass out from the pain. A shard of canvas was whispering from the carpet, 'Beware. Come no further.'

She beat at the vault with the bar of wood in her hand, then stabbed at it with the splintered end. Finally, when she felt as if she had no more strength left, the vault opened fractionally and, with an agonized cry, she managed to wrench her arm free.

As she stared at the blood, expecting to find her limb half-severed, she saw with surprise that the cuts the teeth had made were only superficial. Then that spell, too, had been almost exhausted.

But, most of all, she was amazed to find that in her hand she held the grimoire of Anton Freiwald.

THE BOOK WAS hers, and so was its knowledge. Nothing would stop her now. Laughing, feeling much as she did when Anton had made her drink too much wine, she clutched the grimoire to her as if she had already mastered its many secrets, had already become a wizard of the highest level.

The canvas fragment on the carpet whispered: 'Beware.' Again she laughed, but her eyes moved to the ring of skulls.

Stories had been whispered of Anton Freiwald in the taverns and the market-place, stories she had shut her mind to. Now they came back to her. Stories of him moving from city to city across the Old World, through the years. How many cities? How many years? And darker rumours of a death in each of those places: Anton's death.

The skulls swung around in their stately decaying orbit, their jaws moving in unison, as if they were telling her the

answers to her questions in a language she could not understand. The skulls – there were five of them.

As Katarina watched, the ring of skulls began to spin
faster and faster, its light brightening. A silken shivering
went up and down her spine. Slowly, drawn by a fear that
she could not have put a name to, her eyes dropped to
Anton's body.

It was still lying in the same position, the knife buried in
its chest. But it was shrivelled, fleshless. The skin was intact,
but now it was only a parchment-thin covering hanging
loosely over the wizard's bones, like the abandoned skin of
a snake. The familiar was gone from beside the body.

At that moment, a pale hand appeared from the other side
of the oaken desk and clutched at its edge. It flexed there a
moment, trying to secure its grip. Then, a second hand followed. After a moment, a head came into view, and then the
rest of the body was rising on the other side of the desk,
swaying unsteadily. It was the familiar – Katarina knew it by
the chalky complexion of the skin, the coarse features of the
face – but its body was now man-size.

Its flesh was moving, rippling and twitching, as if still trying to settle itself into its new shape. The mouth opened but
no sound came out. The grey eyes glistened, not quite
focused.

As she stared at it, the face began to change, moulding
itself into a new image. The lips thinned, the cheekbones
came into prominence, eyebrows bristled into view.

Katarina took a step backwards, towards the tunnel, and
her booted foot brushed against the husk of Anton's body.
Bones scraped together, but she did not look down.

The creature's eyes were shifting, searching for the source
of the noise. They slid past her, then swung back to focus on
her.

'Katarina,' the half-formed thing said, in a slow, slurred
whisper. 'What are you doing here?' The eyes regarded her
with vague surprise at first. Then, as they moved to the book
in her hand, understanding came into them, understanding
and a cold anger. 'So.'

The creature reached out with one pale hand. 'My grimoire. Give it to me.'

Staring into those grey eyes, Katarina found herself start-ing to obey out of sheer force of habit. Then the hate for the wizard that she had discovered inside herself returned with almost sickening force. She shook her head. 'No, Morr damn you.'

The creature's jaw slid down in surprise. 'My slave spell. You've broken it!' The protean features shifted; the expres-sion was unrecognizable. Then, an almost affectionate malevolence came into its eyes: they were wholly Anton's now. 'But it will only take me a moment to replace it.'

The creature gestured at her. A nimbus of rainbow light left its fingertips and drifted through the air towards her. Her eyes followed it, hypnotized, unable to pull away. The light blossomed as it neared her, its colours opening out like the petals of some iridescent flower: gold, jade, blue, grey, amethyst, crimson, amber, white. The eight colours of magic.

They splashed onto her eyeballs, soaked softly through them and into her mind. They shimmered and sparkled there, and then began to crystallize into a familiar pattern: an eight-spoked wheel.

'No!' She remembered it now, had lived with it inside her head. 'Not again!'

Her reaction was instinctive. As the wheel began to spin within her, to grip her mind in its familiar embrace, she visualized her hands clenched inside her own mind, and hit out at it with all her strength.

The colours pulsed.

Sigmar give me strength, she thought, and struck again. This time a crack appeared. Another blow. More cracks. She hit the wheel again and again, until there was a webwork of fractures patterning the rainbow form. She smashed at it a final time, imagining the hammer of Sigmar in her hands. The wheel shattered into a thousand pieces.

'Katarina!' the creature said in surprise. 'My little Katarina. But so strong now. It's hard to believe. To break my slave spell a second time.' The voice dropped. 'That's dangerous.'

It stumbled forward, its movements still not fully coordi-nated. Before she could draw back, it reached out with surprising speed and grasped her right wrist.

The contact sent a wave of disgust through her body; its skin was clammy, the smell that came off it not quite human. She tried to wrench her arm free, but the grip was too strong.

With its free hand it reached out for the spell-book. Half-turning, she flung the book behind her. The creature made a barely articulate cry of rage and struck her in the face. Then, wrapping its free arm around her, it used its strength and weight to force her to the ground. As she went down onto the carpet, she felt her head bump against the wizard's skin-draped skeleton.

The man-thing put its rubbery lips to her ear. 'Pain, Katarina,' it commanded. 'Pain.' The words sank into her mind as if they had been arrows. Her nerves were suddenly alight. Every part of her body had been put to the torch. She screamed.

'A sample, Katarina, of what I could teach you if only we had a little time to ourselves again.' The voice in her ear was a hoarse murmur, unmistakably Anton's. 'All the magic you could ever wish to learn about.'

In desperation, the pain threatening to wipe out all rational thought, her eyes rolled upwards, towards the city above.

'No,' the creature whispered as it shifted on top of her. 'There's no help there. My Kislevites will fight on until they die.'

It reached for something behind her, tugged at it, grunting with the effort, until it came free, then brought it forward so that she could see it. It was the skull from Anton's body.

The creature's head came back into her field of vision; its eyes were glossy. 'Death.' It shuddered. Then, slowly, its features contorted into a caricature of a smile. 'The graf and those Guild bumpkins thought that it would stop me. Instead, it has given me one more component to add to my ring of power.'

The skull rose from the creature's hand, beginning to glow as it did so, and floated across the room towards the ghostly chandelier of skulls, its jaw already moving in the same soundless chant.

Through the agony that was burning its way through her body she heard the creature continue. 'With six skulls I can charge it to a new level of strength, an order of magnitude greater than was possible before.'

Surely, Katarina thought in desperation, this new addition would disturb the delicate balance of the structure. If it would only distract Anton, for as much as a second, then she might have a chance.

The skull joined the ring, the others shifting smoothly to make a place for it. At once the glow from the eye-sockets sharpened, and the jaws began to move with even greater vigour.

'Not Chaos, Katarina,' the creature whispered. 'That is a snare – the fool's road to destruction. No, my path is slower, spread across many lifetimes. My magic is merely a little darker-hued than most.' It leaned closer again, whispered confidentially into her ear. 'The skulls will come with me, of course. To a new city, a new life. I wish I could take you too, Katarina. But your talent makes that too dangerous. No, I'll have to kill you. But quickly. I promise you that. First, though – my grimoire.'

The creature reached out for the book. As its attention left her, the pain diminished fractionally. Her right hand was trapped, still held in the creature's grasp. With her left, she fumbled for something, anything, to strike at it with.

Her fingers found the body behind her head and felt along the soft fabric of the wizard's robe; the outline of the skeleton stood out plainly beneath it. Then they touched something sharp-edged: the assassin's blade.

Her hand reached for the hilt. Too far. She stretched her arm as much as she could. Still could not grasp it.

As the creature's pale hand closed on the book, Katarina closed her eyes, murmured the words of a fetch spell. The knife slid free with a scrape of steel against bone, rose into the air, spun slowly around. Then drifted towards her extended hand.

The creature had the grimoire now, was grunting in satisfaction.

Katarina's hand closed around the hilt. She brought the knife up above the man-thing on top of her and, jerking her right hand free with a sudden effort, clasped the knife in both hands.

As the creature swivelled its head back towards her, she brought the blade down with all her strength, driving it into the creature's back.

'No!' the man-thing called out, furious, as the blade pierced it. Its eyes glittered, brimming with anger but empty of pain, as if the half-formed body still lacked the capacity to feel any. It swung the grimoire at her like a club, and its empty hand came around to fend off the knife. The lips moved again, chanting the pain spell.

Katarina shut her mind to the pain. It was not real, she would not allow herself to feel it. Nothing was real to her but her rage and her hate. Those feelings – and the knife she held in her hand.

Katarina wrenched it free, raised it, brought it down again, sensing it sink into the body above her. Then another time, and another, repeating the cycle over and over, ignoring the pain burning at the edges of her personal universe, the hands clutching at her arms.

'No.' Suddenly there was fear in the voice. And Katarina knew why: this time there was no homunculus prepared and waiting to take up the wizard's life. This time there would be no resurrection.

'Die, Sigmar damn you! Die!' Again and again she struck, until she had lost count of the number of times she had driven the blade into the creature's body, until her hands were sticky with its blood. Its arms thrashed feebly; the mouth opened and closed, but no further sound came out.

FINALLY, LONG AFTER the creature had stopped moving, Katarina pushed its body off her and got to her feet. The ring of skulls was slowing once again, its light dwindling. Breathing hard, her tunic ripped, and streaked with blood and dust, she stared down at the body on the floor.

It was quite dead. And this death, she thought with grim satisfaction, was the wizard's final one.

With the grimoire in one hand and the dagger in the other, Katarina Kraeber ran towards the tunnel that led upwards to freedom.

CRY OF THE BEAST
by Ralph Castle

TOMAS WOKE SUDDENLY, with his senses alert and his heart pounding. For a moment there was nothing but the hiss and roar of the surf on the beach outside his bedroom window. But then, once again, he heard the noise that had roused him. It was a high-pitched wail – an inhuman cry rising and falling on the wind.

He slid silently off the straw mattress, struggled into his boots, breeches and leather jerkin, and crept to the window. He cupped his hands around his eyes and peered through the tiny panes of hand-blown glass. It was still night outside, but the foam on the waves glowed white, catching the first faint light of dawn.

Again, the strange cry echoed around the bay. Tomas's skin tingled. He shivered.

He crept across the rough-hewn boards and opened the door into the other room of the little cabin. He paused and listened. Brodie was lying quietly on his cot beside the hearth. The fire in the grate still smouldered and the room smelled of wood smoke. In one corner were shelves of dishes and pots and pans above a simple wooden table. In another corner was a washtub. Everything was neat and clean and stowed in its place.

Tomas crept across the room. Carefully, silently, he lifted the stout oak bar that secured the front door.

'Tom?' There was a rustle of blankets as Brodie sat up. 'What are you doing, there?'

'I was just – going for a walk.'

'A walk?' Brodie's voice rose in disbelief.

Tomas hesitated. 'It's almost dawn.'

'But not quite.' Brodie lit the oil lamp and struggled out of bed. He was a halfling, a tubby figure less than four feet tall, with a round, friendly face and a tousled head of hair bleached white by the sun.

Muttering to himself, he set about dressing in his usual clothes – a faded blue sailor's jacket, leather breeches and boots that looked one size too large. A red silk handkerchief was stuffed into his breast pocket, a rusty sword was sheathed at his hip and an ornamental flint knife hung on a thong around his neck.

He ambled over to Tomas. 'What's your hurry? After breakfast, it'll be light enough to venture out.'

Reluctantly, Tomas let go of the wooden bar. Having just passed his eighteenth birthday, he didn't like being told what to do. 'I heard something,' he said.

Brodie put fresh wood on the fire and used leather bellows to fan the flames. He broke eggs into a cast-iron pan, set the pan over the fire, then picked up an old cutlass and sliced a fresh loaf of heavy, dark bread. 'I know what you heard.' His voice sounded gruff. 'I heard it too.' He put the bread on a plate, then pointed at Tomas with the cutlass. 'I'll wager you don't have the slightest notion what kind of creature would make a sound like that.'

Tomas shrugged. 'That's why I wanted to find out.' He sat down at the table. 'Do you know what it was?'

Brodie shook his head. 'I'd rather not talk about it.' He glanced toward the window, then looked quickly away. He slid the eggs out of the frying pan, onto a plate. 'Eat your breakfast.'

* * *

WHEN TOMAS STEPPED out of the cabin half an hour later, the sun had risen into a clear, pale blue sky. A breeze from the west was raising spray from the white caps of the waves. It was a brisk, bright spring morning.

Brodie's cabin stood on a wide ledge of rock just twenty feet above high tide, beneath chalk cliffs that formed a shadowy white wall around the bay. The cabin had been built before Tomas was born, using planks salvaged from a shipwreck. He had shared this tiny refuge with Brodie for as long as he could remember.

Brodie's fishing boat was anchored out in the bay, and a small rowing boat lay on the sand.

Tomas started picking his way down the familiar path from the cabin to the beach. It was his job, on most mornings, to take the tarpaulin off the rowing boat and push it out into the surf. Together, he and Brodie would row to the fishing boat, tether the smaller boat to the bigger one, then set sail for the open sea.

Today, however, the routine was interrupted. Something was lying on the beach where it had washed ashore during the night. At first, as Tomas started toward it, it looked like a sodden bundle of rags. But as he drew closer, he realized that it was far more than that.

'Brodie!' he shouted. 'Come quick!' And he started running, his feet spraying sand.

It was a body – thin, pale and frail – wrapped in a cloak soaked with seawater. The arms were stretched out, as if trying to cling to the sand beneath, and the face was turned to one side.

As Tomas circled to get a better look, he saw that the features were not human.

'By Ulric, it's an elf woman!' he shouted, as Brodie came hurrying down from the cabin.

The halfling reached the prostrate figure, kneeled, and gingerly touched his finger to the side of her throat. 'Seems she's still alive. Help me turn her on her stomach. Quickly, now.'

Methodically, he started moving her arms and massaging her back, forcing seawater out of her lungs. For a long while, there was no sound other than the roar of the surf, the occasional cry of a gull and Brodie's breathing as he worked hard on the unconscious figure. Finally, after Tomas would have been ready to give up, the elf woman stirred. She made feeble choking noises, coughed some water onto the sand, and tried to turn over.

With gentle strength, Brodie sat her up. 'Easy,' he said. 'You'll be all right, now. Easy.'

She coughed again, then turned toward him, blinking in the sun. 'Thank you,' she gasped. Her thin, delicate face widened in an attempt at a smile. Tomas saw that she seemed to be just a year or two older than himself. She was deathly pale, her hair was plastered flat to her head and there were dark circles under her eyes. Even so, she had an exquisite, fragile beauty.

'Back to the cabin,' Brodie said. 'You hold her under the arms, Tom, and I'll lift her knees.'

Together, they carried her across the sand. As they started up the path, she looked out at the ocean. 'My brother,' she said weakly. 'Still out there.'

'One thing at a time,' said Brodie. He kicked open the door and laid her in front of the hearth. He threw two new logs on the fire, then turned back to her. 'We'll wait outside while you get your wet clothes off. Here, dry yourself with this,' he gave her a towel, 'and then put this on.' He handed her a blanket.

'Where do you think she came from?' Tomas asked, as he and Brodie left the cabin and pulled the door closed behind them.

The halfling scanned the ocean. 'Shipwreck. See the timbers there, just off the point?' He pulled out his spyglass and peered through it.

'Two-masted brigantine. Must have run aground just before dawn. Smashed to pieces; there's little of it left. The crew must have drowned.'

'Maybe the wailing sound I heard,' said Tomas, 'was the elf girl crying for help.'

'No.' Brodie's voice was a curt denial. He stowed the spyglass back inside his jacket and massaged his fleshy face. 'Look, if you give that girl some hot food, I'll take the rowboat out there for a look around, just in case.'

'Won't you need help?'

'I can manage well enough. You take care of her for me. Will you do that?' His voice sounded unsure, almost plaintive. For some reason, he seemed to have lost his usual bustling confidence.

Tom looked into the halfling's eyes, and saw a trace of fear.

THE FIRE HISSED and crackled. The elf maiden sat huddled in her blanket, sipping a mug of soup, while Tomas hung her clothes up to dry. 'If your brother's still alive, Brodie will find him,' he said. 'He's an expert seaman.'

She stared into the embers of the fire. 'If I am to face the truth, I have to admit my brother must be dead.' She sighed deeply. 'He gambled, last night in Remas. Lost most of the money we'd made from trading our silks and yarns, then drowned his sorrows in wine before he set sail. And now, he's drowned himself, as well.'

There was a long, uneasy silence. 'What's your name?' Tomas asked.

'Linna.' She turned her pale grey eyes toward him. 'And you?'

'Tomas Fenman.' As their eyes met, he felt strangely drawn toward her.

He had never seen a human woman so delicately beautiful.

'You live with a halfling,' she said. 'How is that so?'

'I never knew my parents. Brodie found me wrapped in a blanket when I was just a few months old. He took me in and cared for me.'

'The halflings are well known for their hospitality.' She smiled faintly. 'A generous people.'

'Yes,' said Tomas.

'And he makes a living as a fisherman?'

'Yes.'

'And you help him?'

'Yes,' he said again. He felt annoyed, as if he ought to be able to think of more to say. But there was something unsettling about her steady stare and her questions.

'It must be a dull life here for a strong, independent young man like you,' she said, looking frankly at his broad chest and muscled arms.

'It isn't dull at all,' he answered defensively. 'I've studied to be a mariner–'

'On your fishing boat, yes.' She shrugged. 'I saw it anchored in the bay.'

'When we trade our catch in the town,' he went on, 'I earn money as an entertainer. I do backflips, and I juggle anything the crowd gives me. Stones, coins, even swords and daggers with bare blades.'

She nodded thoughtfully, as if picturing it.

'Some time, I hope to join a travelling carnival.'

'But that would mean leaving your friend Brodie. He must be getting old, now. Nearing his hundredth birthday? I'm sure he needs your help here. And you seem a kind person. I think you're too kind to abandon him. So if you dream of adventure, you must know, really, it can be no more than a dream.'

Tomas felt suddenly angry – all the more because what she said was uncomfortably accurate. 'I don't think that's any of your business.'

'Oh.' She looked down into her lap, and then nodded to herself. 'You're right, I spoke without thinking. I am upset about what has happened. My brother is gone; our ship and crew are gone; I have nothing left. I apologize for offending you.'

Tomas's anger left him abruptly. 'It doesn't matter.' He shifted uncomfortably. 'If there's something I can do?'

'You could sit here beside me,' she said. 'Your presence might be a comfort.'

He joined her on the cot. He felt himself grow tense, reacting to the nearness of her beauty. He didn't quite trust himself to look at her.

'Thank you,' she said. She rested her head on his shoulder, as if it were the most natural thing in the world, and closed her eyes.

Minutes passed. From her breathing, Tomas realized she had gradually fallen asleep. After a while, he carefully moved her so that she lay stretched out on her back. She muttered something, but didn't wake up. He laid another blanket over her, then paused and looked at her. Her face was serene in sleep. The curve of her neck lay revealed beneath her tangled blonde hair. How could someone who battled storms in the Great Western Ocean seem so fine and frail?

WHEN THE HALFLING came back to the cabin he was weary and dejected. 'No sign of her brother.' He eyed the elf girl, still sleeping soundly. 'There's a few things worth salvaging, but I'll need your help, Tom.'

'Shall we wake her?'

'No, best not.' Brodie glanced around. 'We'll keep an eye on the place from outside.'

Tomas frowned. 'What are you afraid of?'

Brodie slapped his belly. 'Afraid? Me? Hah.' He took Tomas's arm. 'Come on. She'll be fine.' But his eyes still moved quickly, checking every shadow.

By late afternoon they had recovered the ship's log – which was in an elven script that neither of them could read – and some food supplies in small wooden crates. They returned to the cabin, woke Linna, and Brodie cooked a meal.

The food seemed to revive her. She told them something of her home life on an island she said was called Ulthuan, where she had lived in one of the elven kingdoms. Her parents had been traders who had died unexpectedly in a typhoon that sank their ship. She and her brother had tried to continue the trade alone, and had scraped by for a couple of years. The two of them had made the hard voyage from Ulthuan to the Tilean Sea half a dozen times or more.

As the sun set over the ocean, turning the sky gold, Brodie broke out a keg of rum. He started telling some of his old sea stories, of lost treasure, piracy and giant serpents that could swallow a ship and all the crew besides. 'But that's not the half of it,' he went on, happy as only a halfling could be when his belly was full with ample quantities of food and drink. 'Why, there are creatures to the north, in the Sea of Claws, that would eat such a serpent for breakfast.' He bent toward Linna, as if sharing a deep, dark secret. 'Did you ever hear of a mariner by name of Richard Crowell?'

'I know little of human legends,' Linna said.

'This man was no legend. Fifteen years ago – maybe a little more – it was a bad summer. Day after day the skies were dark with storm clouds, the land was wet and cold, and the nights seemed longer than they had any right to be. There was talk that the creatures from the underworld were rising up against us. Babes were carried off by griffons, even hereabouts in the Tilean cities, and beastmen were seen roaming the hillsides. People were scared to go out even by light of day.'

Tomas had heard this story too many times before. He stifled a yawn.

'Well, Richard Crowell gathered together the best swordsmen, the bravest fighters. He routed the creatures of darkness from their caves and tunnels underground, and he found sorcerers who would use their magic to strip the monsters of their spells. He made Remas safe for honest folk to live in once again. And then, not content with that, he led an expedition up the coast, across the Middle Sea, to the Sea of Claws. He'd heard that this was where the evil beasts were coming from, and he wanted to stop them at their source.'

There was a short silence. 'And what happened?' Linna asked politely.

'Oh, there were battles the like of which you cannot imagine. All manner of flying things, creatures with tentacles instead of heads, humans that were half man, half woman – there was a screaming and a wailing, a gnashing of fangs and a beating of wings.' Brodie paused. 'Well, that's what I was told. I wasn't there myself, you understand.'

Linna smiled. 'No, I suppose not.'

Brodie finished his rum. 'We halflings are simple folk. A warm home and a full belly, that's all the excitement we need.'

'And what of Richard Crowell?' she asked.

Brodie's mood became more sombre. 'Some say he succumbed to the evil forces he pitted himself against, after he made landfall and ventured into Norsca. But no one really knows.'

'Norsca?' Linna's eyes narrowed. 'I've never been there. It's a faraway place.'

Brodie set his glass down abruptly. 'Indeed it is. So far away, I wonder why we're wasting our time talking about it.'

'How do you–'

'Just stories I've heard, that's all.' He stood up. 'I declare, it's past my bedtime.' He belched and steadied himself against the table, then yawned loudly. 'You should bed down for the night in Tomas's room, my dear. He and I can sleep in here.'

She rose gracefully to her feet. 'Thank you.' She smiled at Brodie, then turned to Tomas and took his hand. 'It was a special pleasure to meet you, Master Tomas.'

Her touch was cool and light, yet he felt a wave of warmth spread from her hand to his. 'Good night,' she said, looking into his eyes.

'Good night,' he answered dumbly. Neither he nor Brodie said anything more until she had left the room and closed the door behind her.

'I don't know, Tomas,' the halfling said finally. He threw a thick overcoat onto the floor in front of the fire, then stretched out on it on his back. 'Hard to tell, whether things are what they seem.'

Tomas knew from the halfling's slurred speech, but this was no time to pay much attention to his ramblings. 'Will you be all right sleeping down there?' he asked.

'Right as rain.' Brodie yawned again.

Tomas lay down in Brodie's cot and pulled a blanket over himself. He stared at the wooden ceiling, watching it flicker in the light from the fire. He imagined Linna in the other room, in his bed. Had it been an invitation, the way she'd looked at him when she said good night? No, she must still be grieving over the loss of her brother. If he went creeping in to see her now, he'd just be making a fool of himself.

He tossed and turned in the narrow bed, while Brodie snored where he lay on the floor in front of the fire. Tomas kept seeing Linna's face. Even when he finally fell asleep, she was in his dreams.

TOMAS FELT A hand on his shoulder. He woke with a start, looked up, and saw a shadowy figure bending over him. It was Linna, he realized, and she was fully dressed. 'There's someone outside,' she whispered. 'Quickly. Come and look.'

The fire had died down until it lit the room with a dim red glow. Brodie still lay in front of it, snoring, his hands clasped across his stomach. Tomas considered waking him – but the halfling was in a stupor, sated with food and drink.

Linna went quickly to the window beside the door of the cabin. Tomas lit the oil lamp and carried it over to her. 'Someone knocked on the window of my room,' she explained. 'It was so dark outside, I couldn't be sure.'

Tomas held the lamp up high and peered through the rippled glass. He saw a ragged figure standing in the night, his clothes soaked with seawater. He raised his hand imploringly, and his mouth opened as though he was trying to speak.

Linna pressed her face to the glass. 'It is my brother!' She ran to the door, her eyes wide with excitement. She lifted the oak bar and dropped it with a thump on the floor.

Brodie muttered something and rolled over. He opened his eyes and squinted in the light. 'What?'

Linna was already tugging the door open. A gust of icy air wafted in, making the flame in Tomas's oil lamp flutter. 'Corma!' she called. 'It's really you!'

'Wait,' said Tomas, as she started out of the cabin. There was a strange odour in the cold night air. He sensed that something, somehow, was wrong.

'Wha's going on?' Brodie sat up. He saw the open door, and Linna stepping into the night. 'Hey!' he shouted. 'Stop there!'

But it was too late. In the flickering light from the oil lamp, Tomas saw the elf girl throw herself into her brother's arms. But her moment of joy turned instantly to horror. As Tomas watched, the figure of her brother changed hideously. Linna screamed in panic and started struggling to free herself from the tight embrace.

One of the arms that clutched her had turned into a huge purple crab's claw. The other was a brown tentacle, coiling around Linna's waist. A lumpy, fur-covered body literally burst out of the sodden clothes, and a razor-edged reptilian tail thumped onto the ground and started lashing from side to side. The creature's feet were hooves, and its face contorted until it looked like the head of a bear, with bulbous,

bulging eyes and black horns that sprouted from its forehead.

It growled, revealing long, curved, yellow fangs. Its breath
steamed in the cold air.

'Vile thing!' Brodie shouted. 'Let her go!'

Tomas turned and saw that the halfling had struggled up
onto his feet. He was clutching the flint dagger that he normally wore on a thong around his neck.

The creature picked Linna up with its tentacle and tossed
her across its shoulders. It tilted its head back, uttered a
long, wailing cry, then strode away into the blackness.

Tomas was trembling. The wailing cry was the very same
sound that he'd heard the previous night.

'Tomas! Help!' Linna cried. Her voice was almost lost on
the wind.

Clouds were covering the moon, and the light from his
lamp reached no more than a dozen feet. Summoning all
his courage, Tomas stepped into the darkness.

Something ran in front of him: a deformed near-human
shape with green, leathery skin. Another joined it. Goblins,
he realized. They stood barring his path, hissing menacingly.

'Tomas!' Linna called again, and he saw her briefly silhouetted against the stormy sky as the beast carried her
down the path to the beach.

In despair, Tomas hurled the oil lamp. His aim was true:
the lamp hit the creature in the back of its legs and smashed,
scattering droplets of fire. The thing cried in pain, and for a
moment seemed about to drop the elf girl. But then it continued on its way, disappearing into the night.

Brodie appeared beside Tomas. He drew his rusty sword
from its cracked leather sheath and brandished it at the goblins. 'Begone!' he shouted.

They hissed again and started forward.

Brodie raised his sword above his head. Tomas saw that
the halfling's hands were shaking. 'I'm warning you!'

The goblins continued toward him with their teeth bared
and their claw-like fingers extended. And then, without
warning, they stopped still, as if there had been a noise that
only they could hear. Suddenly they turned and ran off into
the darkness, leaving Brodie and Tomas alone in the night.

Brodie sheathed his sword. He shook his head as if to clear it, then grabbed Tomas's arm. 'Quickly. Back inside.'

Dazed, Tomas allowed himself to be led toward the door. 'But we have to save her,' he protested.

'No.' Brodie hauled him bodily into the cabin.

Tomas pried at the halfling's fingers. 'Let me go!'

'That thing has powers you've never dreamed of. And you don't even have a weapon to defend yourself.'

'You mean we're just going to do nothing? You want us to hide like cowards?'

Brodie slammed and barred the door. He glowered at Tomas. 'You'd see the sense of it, if you knew what I know.'

Tomas was barely listening. 'It took her, Brodie. It just took her away.'

Brodie stumbled to the bed and sat down heavily. With hands that still shook, he lit a candle. 'The beast you just saw was once a man. It got deformed when it chose to serve the... Dark Powers.'

Tomas frowned. 'It looked just like an elf, at first.'

'That was magic. It disguised itself, see, with a spell of illusion, to tempt the elf girl out. But my dawnstone, here, showed it for what it was.' He patted the wedge of flint that hung around his neck.

'Dawnstone?'

'It's enchanted. Has the power to undo the effects of magic.'

He shook his head grimly. 'I only wish I'd used it sooner, to reveal the beast before she went to it.'

Tomas reached out and touched the dawnstone. It was cold and smooth. His fingers slid over its polished surface. 'I always thought it was just a flint dagger. Where did you get it?'

Brodie chewed for a moment on his lower lip. He gave Tomas a sidelong glance. 'Well, we don't need to talk about that now. You had a nasty shock out there. A terrible tragedy. Let's brew some tea, and–'

'I want to know the truth,' Tomas said firmly. 'What happened out there? How did you get the dawnstone? How do you know all these things about creatures and dark forces?'

The halfling fidgeted uneasily. 'I was there, see,' he said in a low voice. 'With Crowell and his crew.'

'In the Sea of Claws?' Tomas stared at him with disbelief.

The halfling shrugged. 'I was only the ship's cook. Never was a fighter. But the fact is, Tomas, you were there too.'

For a moment, they stared at each other. Then Tomas laughed uncertainly. 'I don't understand.'

'You were a babe, so you don't remember. But Richard Crowell, he was your father. Your mother was killed only a week after you were born – killed by a beastman. That was the real reason for Richard's quest: he wanted revenge against the things that had taken his young wife away. Oh, but it was much harder than he'd thought it would be. He anchored his fleet off the coast of Norsca, told me to stay on board ship and take good care of you, and went ashore with his army. He promised to come back if he could. But he never did. Only one of his men survived long enough to get back to the ship, and he told us terrible stories about the creatures they'd seen on land, with terrible magical powers. He died from his wounds just a few hours later, and the crew were so scared they set sail right away, heading back south.'

Tomas felt stunned by what he heard. At the same time, he felt a growing sense of excitement after so many years spent wondering about his parents. 'This is really true?'

The halfling nodded. He grasped the dawnstone and lifted it over his head on its leather thong. 'Richard knew I wasn't a fighter, so he gave me this stone for protection. His wife had worn it, back before – before she was taken. Richard had another one just like it, which he kept himself. A matched pair, very rare indeed.'

'This one used to belong to my mother?'

'Indeed it did. Here, you need it now more than I do.'

Tomas held the stone in both hands. 'I wish you'd told me all this before, Brodie.'

'It was best you didn't know.' The halfling gave Tomas another quick, guilty look. 'If you'd known the truth, you might have done something rash, maybe even got it into your head to run away looking for your dad.'

Tomas nodded slowly, saying nothing.

'I wanted the best for you, Tomas. I cared for you as if you were my own.'

'I – I know that.' Tomas stared at the stone, expecting to see his reflection in the shiny black surface; yet somehow it seemed to absorb all the light that fell on it.

'If you ever think there's magic being used against you,' the halfling said, 'you take hold of that stone. You have to grasp it in your fist. Yes, like that. Just hold it, so.'

'All right. I'll remember.'

'Now put it on for safe keeping.' He watched closely while Tomas looped the leather thong around his neck and dropped the stone inside his jerkin. 'You see, it's you they really wanted, tonight.'

Tomas looked up in surprise. 'Me?'

Brodie stood up and paced across the room. He poked nervously at the fire, sending sparks flying up the chimney, then paced back again, the floorboards creaking under him. 'All these years I've been watching and waiting, expecting them to come for you. Your father must have hurt them badly, before they killed him, and they'll not forget it. Revenge; that's what they're after.'

'Then why did they take Linna instead of me?' Even as he spoke, he saw again the awful spectacle of the elf girl being dragged away into the darkness.

'I reckon they found her brother, last night. Maybe took him off the wreck. They would have got her too, but she swam for safety and didn't reach the shore until it was almost light. They don't like the light of day. So they bided their time until it was dark again, then lured her out, hoping you'd follow.'

Once again, he started pacing to and fro. 'We're not safe here, Tomas. That dawnstone protects against magic, but it's no use against brute force, and I'm not much of a fighter, and you've never learned swordplay.'

He shook his head ruefully. 'First thing tomorrow, we'll pack everything into the boat and set sail. Find us a quiet little haven – maybe in the Estalian kingdoms, on the Southern Sea. The winters are warm down there, and there's nary a creature of darkness to be seen. What do you say, eh?'

Tomas looked at the halfling in confusion. 'You mean – you'll let them drive us out of our home here?'

Brodie laughed bitterly. 'You think we have any choice? Look at us, what's a pair like us going to do against the forces of darkness?'

Tomas stood up slowly. His face was grim and brooding. He walked to the window and stared out into the night.

'Come away from there.' Brodie spoke sharply, but at the same time, there was a fearful, pleading sound to his voice.

Tomas remained where he was. 'She might still be alive.'

'Her? Alive?' The halfling laughed without any humour. 'They'll have drunk her blood by now. That's the terrible fact of it, Tomas. They make that wailing noise when they're hungry. The man who was with Crowell's army, he told us these things before he died, don't you see?' He went over and tugged at Tomas's shirt. 'Let's get our rest. We'll need it for tomorrow. We've got to pack our belongings, and there's a long voyage ahead of us.'

Tomas shook his head. 'It's not right.'

Brodie ran his hand nervously through his tousled hair. 'Now you listen to me. See sense, Tom. You saw that thing?'

'I can't run away and abandon her.'

Brodie swore. 'Do you think you're like your father, is that it? You'll be as dead as your father, too, before this is done.'

Tomas seized the hilt of Brodie's sword and jerked it out of its sheath.

Brodie's eyes widened with disbelief.

'I have to go out there.' Tomas shook off the halfling's plaintive, grasping hands, and opened the door.

THE NIGHT WAS as black as before. Heavy clouds moved swiftly across the sky, obscuring all but a faint trace of moonlight. The sea hissed and roared, and Tomas flinched as a cold gust of wind hit him in the face. He strained his eyes, trying to see into the darkness. Fear clutched his stomach as he imagined the creatures that might be lurking there.

'Tomas! Please, please come back!'

He looked at the little halfling standing in the doorway of the cabin, and for a moment he weakened. He loved Brodie as he would have loved his father, had he known him.

But then the wailing cry started again, and Tomas felt his fear give way to righteous anger. He strode forward, raising the sword high.

Behind him, he heard Brodie come out after him. 'I can't let you go, Tomas. I can't!'

Tomas leaped down onto the beach and crossed the sand in long, loping strides. Within a few moments, he had disappeared into the darkness, leaving the halfling far behind.

Tomas paused when he reached the cliffs at the opposite side of the bay. His heart was beating fast and his chest was so tight it was difficult to breathe. He paused, gasping for air, and tried to listen. This was where the wailing had originally seemed to come from.

Briefly, the large moon, Mannslieb, appeared between two clouds. In its faint light, Tomas saw tracks in the sand. There were large, deep hoof marks, and two sets of smaller subhuman footprints.

The tracks led around the point. He ran quickly, scaled a heap of boulders, and found himself in the next bay. He had played here often, in his childhood. There was a cave, up in the cliffs. The tracks ended immediately beneath it.

The moon disappeared behind the clouds again, but there were easy footholds in the rock. Tomas slid the sword into his belt and started climbing. He moved swiftly; his muscles were strong from the juggling and acrobatics he had practised. It only took him a few moments to reach the cave mouth.

He grasped the sword again and paused, hearing faint scuffling noises. 'Linna!' he shouted. 'Linna, are you here?'

There were chittering sounds, like distant daemonic laughter. A foul, sweaty stench wafted out. He tightened his grip on his sword and took a cautious step forward.

Something grabbed his leg. Sharp horny fingernails ripped through his breeches. Pointed teeth sank into his flesh.

Tomas shouted in fear and pain. He groped in the darkness and managed to close his free hand around the goblin's neck. He tore the thing from him, wincing as its teeth pulled free. It made a terrible screeching sound and writhed in his grip.

'Give her back!' he shouted.

The goblin hissed and spat into his face.

Tomas slammed the goblin down onto the floor of the cave, stamped on its neck, and stabbed his sword into its body.

The goblin's screams turned to a gargling sound as it choked on its own blood. The great moon reappeared in the sky outside, shedding just enough light for Tomas to see the creature impaled on his sword, squirming in its last death throes. Tomas jerked the blade free – then stopped in dismay. The tip of the blade had snapped off where it had plunged through the goblin and struck the rock beneath.

There was a scuffling sound. Tomas whirled around. Two more greenskins were running toward him with their teeth bared.

He leaped quickly to one side, avoiding the first. He swung the sword, using the sense of timing he'd learned from juggling in the village square. The blade caught the second goblin in the side of its neck.

It was a heavy blow, but the sword's edge was dull. The creature screamed and fell, but it was still alive.

Tomas spun around just in time to grapple with the first goblin as it returned and threw itself at him. He stumbled backward.

It screeched and tried to claw his face. Tomas turned as he fell, so that he landed on top of the creature, squashing it against the rocky floor. Momentarily, it was stunned. He picked it up by one leg, turned, and swung it. His aim was true: its head smacked into the head of its companion. Their skulls smashed together with a terrible wet crunching sound.

For a moment, the only noise in the cave was that of Tomas's laboured breathing and the gushing of goblin blood. Some of the hot, wet stuff was on his hands. He wiped it on his breeches and picked up his broken sword. Cautiously, then, with his pulse thudding in his ears, he crept further into the cave.

The moonlight faded into blackness with each step that he took. At the same time, he began to see a flickering orange glow ahead. He reached a bend in the passageway. Beyond this point, he knew, there was a large cavern.

He sidled around the bend with his back to the wall and his sword raised. Up ahead, two torches had been wedged in fissures in the rock, illuminating a ceiling festooned with stalagtites and a floor cluttered with huge boulders. Near the centre of the chamber was a frail, pale figure, tied to a column of rock. 'Linna!' he shouted.

The figure struggled and made smothered sounds. Tomas tried to suppress the surge of hope that he felt. He glanced nervously around. Where was the monster?

He saw movement from the corner of his eye – but when he turned his head, he found that the shape had just been a shadow. The whole chamber was alive with dancing shapes created by the flickering light.

He leaped up onto a slab of rock and circled around the edge of the cavern, coming gradually closer to the elf girl. She seemed to be unharmed. But caution held him back from running to her.

He reached for the dawnstone and closed his fingers around it as Brodie had shown him.

The figure of the elf girl shimmered as if he were seeing it through a heat haze. Suddenly, it dissolved. In its place was the beast, lashing its tail. Its bulging eyes were fixed on Tomas, and its fangs were bared.

'Where is she?' Tomas shouted. His voice echoed around the chamber.

The beast made a coughing, gargling sound that almost sounded like laughter.

'What are you?' Tomas demanded, fighting to suppress his overwhelming fear.

The beast's mouth widened in a ghastly grin. 'I am he who seeks revenge, in the name of my beloved master, the Lord Slaanesh.' Its words were slurred; its voice was guttural and inhuman. It screamed and hurled itself forward.

The wall of the cavern was behind Tomas's shoulders. He gasped in terror and swung his broken blade in a hopeless attempt to slash the creature's body. It seized the sword deftly in its crab-claw, twisted it out of Tomas's hand, and hurled it contemptuously aside. Almost in the same motion, it swept its razor-edged tail in a wide arc, aiming to cut Tomas in two.

Tomas dodged to one side and the tip of the tail grazed his chest, ripping his shirt. He found himself off-balance and falling. Flailing his arms, he toppled from the edge of the slab where he stood.

His reflexes saved him. He somersaulted as he fell, and landed hard on his heels. But as he looked up he saw that the beast was already coming for him.

Tomas ran. He scrambled up a series of ledges, then jumped up from one boulder to another. The creature was too cumbersome to match this kind of agility and its hooves slipped on smooth stone. It roared with anger and lashed its tentacle-arm like a whip, reaching for Tomas's face.

He ducked under it, then jumped higher, until he reached the top of a tall heap of boulders. The last one moved under his weight, and he realized it was precariously balanced. He looked back at the creature and saw what he should do. He turned his back to the wall, braced his feet, and pushed with all his strength.

The boulder teetered ponderously under him, then started tumbling. It dislodged other rocks beneath it, creating an avalanche. There was a rumbling sound, and the whole cave seemed to shake.

The monster vented an inarticulate cry. It stumbled backward as the rocks rolled down toward it. It had fierce strength but seemed to lack intelligence, Tomas thought. Perhaps all it knew was how to inflict pain and death.

The first boulder hit its legs, and the creature fell. With inhuman strength, it pulled itself out from under the rock – but its legs had been crushed, and it could no longer stand. It screeched in pain and tottered helplessly, raising its claw-arm in a futile effort to protect itself as two more boulders tumbled down. One hit the claw and smashed it into fragments. The other landed squarely in the creature's hairy chest.

It bellowed in agony as it fell beneath the rock. Blood spurted out and it writhed, lashing its tail. It vomited up a foul mixture of foaming, steaming, pink-and-brown sludge, and shouted again. Its struggles were gradually diminishing.

Tomas was shaking so badly he had to crawl down the tumbled pile of rocks on his hands and knees. When he reached the bottom he stood for a long moment, trying to regain his equilibrium as he stared at the creature. It glared back at him through eyes that were growing dull and dim. Its tentacle twitched in little spasms. It made a guttural, croaking noise, then gasped, coughed, shat convulsively, and finally died.

TOMAS RESTED AGAINST a nearby rock, taking slow, deep breaths. He checked the gash on his chest and found that it was bleeding, but was not deep. His leg throbbed with pain where the goblin had bitten him, but that too was not a major wound. He wiped sweat out of his eyes, blinked, and looked around.

He saw the stone column where the beast had disguised itself as the elf girl. 'Linna,' he exclaimed in a whisper. A pile of tattered clothing was lying there, and the rocks were slick with blood. Further back, where the creature had made its lair, there was an ugly heap of bloody bones and chunks of pale flesh.

Tomas clenched his fists. He willed himself to be strong. With a sense of hollow dread, he forced himself to go and take a closer look.

Some of the shredded clothes were Linna's. He remembered hanging them up to dry in the heat from the fire in Brodie's cabin. Other garments were also elfin in style, but seemed cut for a man. She and her brother had died here, there was no possible doubt. Tomas cursed himself for having come too late to save her.

He turned away, feeling sick with guilt. His father had been right: it did no good to hide. So long as people gave in to their fear, more innocent victims would die, and the creatures of the dark would multiply and grow stronger. The only way was to match their strength with greater strength.

Tomas turned and walked shakily back past the creature lying with its chest crushed beneath the boulder. The bulging eyes stared up blindly, and the mouth gaped in an ugly, silent scream.

Tomas paused. He saw something that gleamed in the flickering light. Trying to suppress his revulsion, he squatted down beside the corpse. Almost lost in the beast's thick fur was a shiny black object. He reached out, took hold of it, and dragged it into view. It was a dawnstone, just like the one that Brodie had given him.

With a trembling hand, he took the stone from around his own neck and held it beside the one that the creature wore. There was no doubt: they were identical. A matched pair.

He stood up suddenly, and felt himself swaying. What had Brodie said about Richard Crowell? *Some say he succumbed to the evil forces.* And: *The beast you just saw was once a man.* And: *He promised to come back if he could.*

Tomas clutched his stomach, nauseated by the idea that the corpse in front of him had once been his father. He took slow, deep breaths, trying to regain control. Part of him simply could not believe it; and so, again, he kneeled and compared the dawnstones.

They were identical in every detail.

In a sudden spasm of anger, he ripped the creature's dawnstone loose and thrust it into his pocket. Nothing but revenge, he realized, could take away the outrage that he felt. Whatever person or entity had concocted this travesty should surely be made to pay in some way.

He turned and started toward the exit from the cave, feeling a fierce new determination. Maybe he was being foolish; he was, after all, at the beginning of his manhood, and he had survived his first battle more by luck than skill. Nevertheless, he would go back and find Brodie, and ask the halfling for his help.

To search for vengeance in the Sea of Claws would be an enormous undertaking. It would require courage, resources, trained warriors, and expert seamen... not to mention the services of a good ship's cook.

A GARDENER IN PARRAVON
by Brian Craig

THIS TALE, SAID the story-teller, was told to me by a man of Parravon in far Bretonnia. He said he had no wish to add to the evil reputation which the city of his birth already had, but that he did not care to bear alone the burden of speculation as to whether his late friend, Armand Carriere, was as utterly and completely mad as everyone chose to believe.

You have heard of Parravon, and know of it what everyone knows. You know that it lies beside the great river Grismarie in the foothills of the Grey Mountains. You know that it is a prosperous city, whose wealthy folk are numerous and much devoted to the arts, as all men are when they need not work for their living and must find some idler way to spend their time. You also know that the beautiful face which it presents in the daylight wears an ugly mask when darkness descends, and that strange and evil things are said to stalk its streets.

The man who told this tale, whose name was Philippe Lebel, recommended that those who might have occasion to listen to it should also bear in mind certain other features of the town, which do not figure so large in its reputation, but which have some relevance to his story.

207

Firstly, he asked that hearers of the tale should remember that the crags and crannies of the chalky cliffs which rise around the city provide nesting-sites for very many birds, including some which are seen nowhere else in the Old World. Eagles can often be seen about the taller peaks, and it is said that both firebirds and phoenixes have nested there. It is also said that some of the creatures which fly by night about these rookeries are neither birds nor bats, but other things with wings.

Secondly, he asked that hearers of the tale should remember that among the arts of which the leisured classes of Parravon are fond, the construction of beautiful and exotic gardens has a special place, and that it is by no means extraordinary for men to devote their lives to the cultivation of rare and special flowers.

Thirdly, he asked that hearers of the tale should remember that although the people of the town are apparently orthodox in their religion, following the familiar gods, other kinds of worship are conducted there in secret. There are druids in the neighbouring hills, whose mysterious ceremonies are attended by some of the humble folk of Parravon – and there are other gods, perhaps older still, whose veneration is forbidden throughout the Old World, whose true nature none know and few care to contemplate, but whose influence on the affairs of men is sometimes felt in incidents of a specially horrible nature, which may befall the incautious and the unlucky alike.

PHILIPPE LEBEL HAD known Armand Carriere since boyhood, and yet had never really known him. Although their fathers were both respectable corn-chandlers, like enough in their habits and beliefs to pass for brothers, Philippe and Armand were very different.

Where the former strove always to follow convention and to fit in with the society of his peers, the latter set himself apart, finding anything ordinary dull. He came to fancy himself an artist of sorts, though he was equally unskilled as painter, poet and gardener, and Philippe often thought that his friend's 'art' was simply an ability to see the world from a strange angle, from which it seemed more magical and more malign. He was certainly attracted by all matters unusual and arcane.

With the aid of this tilted perception Armand might have become a spellcaster's apprentice, but his parents would not hear of such a thing, and he excused himself from going against their wishes – and hence excising himself from his father's will – by declaring that the wizards of Parravon were in any case a poor and shabby lot, far less powerful than they claimed.

(Those of you who have travelled will know that this is a common opinion; familiar spellcasters, if measured by their accomplishments, always seem less able than they claim to be, and less fascinating than more distant wizards whose abilities can only be measured by rumour and reputation.)

Young Carriere's affectations offended his family, but he saved himself from total disgrace by working hard to master the arts of reading and writing, which his illiterate father commended on the grounds that they might prove very useful to a man in trade. Armand, alas, had no intention of employing these arts in such a vulgar manner; his aim was to entertain himself with books of a questionable character, and seek therein the secrets of arcane knowledge.

The Carriere house was tall, and set upon the ridge of a small hill. Armand's room was considered a poor one, set just beneath the eaves on the side of the house which never caught the sun. He liked it, though, because his was the only window which faced that way, looking upon the wilder part of the hill, which was thick with thorn-bushes.

The only other building which overlooked that part of the ridge was a tower-house situated at its further edge, nested among dark trees alongside a high-hedged garden. Ever since boyhood Armand had believed that there was a mystery about that lonely house and its garden – whose hedges were so unnaturally high as to exclude the sun's direct rays, save for a brief period around the hour of noon.

While Armand studied his books and practised his script he would often sit by the window of his room, looking up occasionally to stare at the hedge. He knew that the plants which grew in the garden must be curious, partly because it was lighted for such a short time each day – and presumably contained only those flowers which could adapt to such a strange regime – but partly because the hedge was so clearly designed to keep prying eyes at bay. Once or twice when he had been a child he and Philippe had run the gauntlet of the thorn-bushes to reach the bounds of the garden (for there was no path between the two houses), but they had never been able to see what was within.

What Armand could see, however, was a certain strange traffic between the garden and the cliffs where the birds of Parravon made their nests.

Most of the gardeners of Paravon considered the birds their enemies, for they would come to peck the new-laid seeds, to spoil the pretty flowers with their droppings, and to devour the fruits which grew upon the bushes. The gardener of the tower-house seemed to be an exception, for there was never any indication of birds being shooed away, though they seemed to come in considerable numbers, especially in the hours when the garden was shadowed from the sun. At dusk, when the birds of Parravon were wont to wheel about the roofs, calling to one another stridently as they assembled in flocks before returning to their roosts, the birds which visited this particular garden would rise more sedately, one at a time, and drift away into the gathering gloom.

The more Armand watched, the more he became convinced that far more birds flew down to the garden than ever flew up again.

Armand called the attention of Philippe Lebel to this phenomenon on more than one occasion, but Philippe believed that his friend was trying to make a mystery out of nothing, and paid no attention. This disinterest served only to make Armand more determined to find a mystery, and he began to seek through the pages in his books for records of carnivorous plants which could trap birds. He found various travellers' tales containing believable accounts of plants which trapped insects, and rather unbelievable accounts of plants which devoured men, but no trace of any rumour about plants which fed on birds.

* * *

INVESTIGATION OF THE hillside beyond the tower-house revealed that there was no proper road to its gate, but only a path. Armand began to linger at the bottom of that path, waiting to catch a glimpse of the owner of the house – whose name, his father had gruffly told him, was Gaspard Gruiller. When Armand had asked further questions his father had simply disclaimed any further knowledge, and had stated that honest men did not pry into their neighbours' affairs.

Armand soon ascertained that Gruiller emerged from his solitary lair only two or three times a week, carrying two large bags which he took to the marketplace and filled up with food. He began to study the man, from a distance, and twice followed him into the town to watch him go about this humdrum business. Gruiller was tall and bald, with eyes which were very dark yet seemed unnaturally keen and bright – but if he noticed that he was under observation by Armand he gave no sign of it.

Armand asked several of the tradesmen who dealt with Gruiller what they knew of him, but none of them could tell what manner of man he was, or how he earned his coin, or to what gods he addressed his prayers. None of the tradesmen had a word to say against their customer, but on one occasion Armand saw a gypsy woman make a sign as he passed, which was supposed to ward off the evil eye.

This might have meant nothing at all, for gypsy women are ever so anxious to ward off spells that they frequently make such signs without any reason or provocation, but Armand was nevertheless encouraged to believe that she might have a reason. He knew that gypsies were usually followers of the Old Faith, and wondered whether this Gaspard Gruiller might be known to the druids as a bad man – and perhaps a cleverer one than any of those who went about the city boasting of their prowess as spellcasters.

On two or three occasions when he knew that Gruiller was not at home, Armand approached the lonely house, and peered through its windows. He tried to peer through the hedge, too, as he had done when he was a boy, but it was very thick as well as very tall, and he could see no more now than he ever had. He could hear something from the other side, though, and what he heard was a low rustling sound, which might have been the sound of birds fluttering their wings as they moved among the branches of bushes, or even the murmur of their voices as they clucked and chattered to one another. These sounds fed his curiosity so temptingly that he hungered to find out more, and this hunger grew in him by degrees, until he became determined that he would one day find a way to look into that garden, to see what went on there in the shady hours of the morning and the afternoon.

It was unfortunately typical of his frame of mind that he never once considered taking a straightforward course, seeking to make the acquaintance of Gaspard Gruiller so that he might quite legitimately ask what plants the garden contained.

ARMAND KNEW THAT he must get higher up if he was to see over the hedge of the enigmatic garden, and there was only one way to do this that was immediately obvious to him. There was no other room above his, but the house had a steeply-sloped roof of red tile, and a chimney-stack, which could offer him an extra twelve or thirteen feet of elevation if only he could scale it.

Because this seemed a hazardous project, he called upon the help of his friend Philippe, asking him to secure a rope within his room and pay it out yard by yard while he climbed, so that if he fell the rope would save him from serious injury. Philippe agreed, reluctantly, and waited impatiently when Armand had clambered out, wondering what possible account he could give to the Carriere family should the escapade go wrong. But he need not have worried, because Armand soon came back through the window unharmed, in a state of some excitement.

'What did you see?' asked Philippe, caught up for once in the tangled threads of the mystery.

'I could not see so very much,' replied Armand, 'but more than I have seen before. There is a trellis-work erection – perhaps a kind of summer-house, though I could only see the top of it – which is longer than it is broad, having the house at one end and an open space at the other. The trellis-work looks like the sort which is sometimes placed against the wall of a building to assist climbing roses and honeysuckle, but I could not tell whether there was a wall within. The roof of the trellis bears flowers of several different hues – huge flowers, with heads like trumpets. There are birds there, wandering about.'

'And did you see these flowers seizing and devouring the unfortunate birds?' asked Philippe.

'No, I did not,' admitted Armand. 'But I have not seen the like of those flowers before, and I feel sure that there is something strange about them.'

'Oh Armand,' said his friend, 'are you not satisfied? Must you still insist that although what you have seen is by your own account most ordinary, what remains hidden from you must be something unparalleled in its strangeness?'

'The birds are ordinary,' replied Armand, insistently. 'But their situation is not. I have never seen the flowers before, nor have I seen such a structure to mount them. What pleasure could it give a gardener to place his best blossoms on the roof of a structure, where he could not see them?'

'Ah,' said Philippe, 'but he can see them, can he not, from the upper windows of his own house? And you have said yourself that the garden gets too little sun – is it not probable that the entire purpose of this structure is to lift the flowers up, so that they receive more?'

If this speech was intended to set Armand's mind at rest it failed, for Armand was no longer listening. Instead, he was standing by his window looking out in the direction of Gaspard Gruiller's house.

Philippe went to stand by him, to see what he was looking at, and saw that the shutters of the one window which faced this way – which had been closed only a few minutes before – had now been thrown back. There was a man standing at the window, just as Armand was standing at his, and he was staring at the Carriere house. Philippe drew back reflexively, but could not resist peeping around the angle of the window to see what would happen.

After standing there for little more than a minute, Gruiller went away, leaving the shutters undone.

'He must have seen you on the roof!' said Philippe.

'I suppose he must,' replied Armand. 'But what of it? A man may climb upon the roof of his own house, if he wants to!' Despite the bravado of his words, however, Armand's face was pale, and frightened; it was as though all his excitement had been turned by that cool stare into anxiety.

'And yet,' muttered Armand, hardly loud enough for his friend to hear the words. 'There is some secret about that garden, and I would dearly love to know what it is. I feel an attraction to it, as though it had placed a spell on me.'

'It is only a garden,' said Philippe, soothingly, 'and by no means the only one in Parravon to contain special blooms whose owner strives to hide them from potential thieves.'

THAT NIGHT, ARMAND closed the shutters of his window tightly, as he always did – as all men do in Parravon, if they have any sense. But in his sleep he had a very curious dream, in which there was a tapping at those shutters, and a fluttering sound of wings in hectic motion, and a sharp scraping sound as though a claw was dragged momentarily across the outer face of each shutter.

Had he been really awake Armand would have clapped his hands to his ears and prayed for the morning to come, for he knew well enough that monsters were reputed to haunt the night in that city. But he was not awake, and in his dream he rose from his bed to go to the window, and threw back the shutters, so that he looked out boldly into the star-lit night, as he had never dared to do before.

He was startled by the eerie brightness of the light which the stars gave, and as he peered out into that imperfect gloom he saw black shadows moving within it – sinister night-flyers larger by far than those birds which filled the sky by day.

Though he could not follow these shadows as they wheeled and soared in the starry sky, he became convinced that it was around the roof of the tower-house that they gathered. And when he looked at the tower-house he saw that the window from which Gaspard Gruiller had looked out in the daytime was unshuttered, with a red light burning within it, and that someone stood there looking out, just as Armand was – perhaps Gruiller, perhaps another. And there was a strange scent in the air, like exotic perfume, which made him intoxicated as he breathed it in, and made him almost ready to believe that he could fly.

THE NEXT DAY, when he tried to recall this dream, he could remember it up to that point, but not beyond – he did not know what had happened next, if anything further had happened at all. He told what he could remember to Philippe Lebel, and found himself quite carried away when he told it, so that he argued very fiercely that the night-flyers he had seen were too huge to be ordinary birds. They might, as he assured Philippe with rapt insistence, have been anything.

'Well,' said Philippe, 'what of it? In our dreams, we may see whatever we will. We meet more daemons there than we ever could in everyday life.'

Armand did not take offence at this remark, but simply took his friend to the window, where the shutters had been thrown back to let in the daylight. He pulled one of them back until it was closed, and invited Philippe to crane his neck and inspect its outer surface. Then he opened that one and pulled the other back in order to allow a similar inspection.

Philippe saw that there were three long scratches in the wood, extending across both shutters, and when he measured their span with his hand he shuddered to think what manner of claw it might have been which had made them.

'But after all,' said Philippe, 'even if the scratching sound was real, the rest was only a dream – for you did not actually rise from your bed and open the shutters, did you?'

'Did I not?' said Armand, quizzically. But then, after a moment's hesitation, he threw the shutters wide again. 'You are right,' he said. 'I did not – and I surely never will.'

Armand attempted to put Gaspard Gruiller out of his thoughts for the remainder of that day, and returned with a new will to the study of a book he had found which had much to say about the tenets of the Old Faith. He tried not to dwell on the matter of the garden, but could not help pausing whenever he found a reference to flowers, lest he find some clue regarding the nature of the unknown blooms which he had seen upon the trellis in the hidden garden. But there were far too many flowers mentioned in connection with the worship of the Old Faith, with far too little in the way of description to allow them to be easily identified.

The next night, and the next, he slept very fitfully. Once or twice he was convinced that he heard the nearby flutter of wings, but nothing tapped at his shutters and nothing scratched the wood. He did not dream – indeed, it seemed that whenever he was about to escape from anxious wakefulness into the comfort of a dream he was snatched back from its brink so that he might continue to toss and turn upon his pallet.

By day he tried to tell himself that he had done everything he could to fathom the mystery, and must be content to let it alone. Indeed, he came close to convincing himself that he had had enough of Gruiller's garden, and did not care about it any more. But this was a mere sham, which could not stand the test of temptation.

Three days after his expedition onto the roof Armand and Philippe were walking in the street, intent on their conversation, when they suddenly found their way blocked. When they looked up to see who had accosted them, they were most surprised to discover that it was Gruiller.

'You are Carriere's son, are you not?' he said, addressing Armand, after directing a brief but polite smile at Philippe. 'You are my nearest neighbour, I believe. You are interested in my garden.'

All the colour had drained from Armand's cheeks, and he was too surprised to reply.

'I would like to show it to you, now that the proper season has come,' Gruiller continued, amiably. 'The birds love to visit it, as you must have observed.'

Armand still did not seem disposed to reply, so Philippe intervened, saying, rather uncertainly: 'You are kind, sir. Armand and I would be pleased to see your flowers.'

Gruiller responded with a litle bow. 'The time is not exactly right just yet,' he said. 'I think you will see the blooms at their very best in three days' time. I would like you to see them at their very best.'

'Shall we come at noon?' asked Philippe.

'That would be perfect,' replied the other, bowing again and walking on.

'Well,' said Philippe proudly to his silent friend, 'here is something to set your mind at rest for once and for all. We will see his garden, and the mystery will be extinguished. But I do think you might have spoken to him yourself – he seems a pleasant enough fellow, after all.'

Armand seemed to be about to disagree, but in the end he simply nodded, and said: 'Perhaps it is all for the best. We will go together, and see what there is to be seen.'

AT THE APPOINTED hour, Philippe and Armand made their way up the path to Gaspard Gruiller's door. Armand had told his father about the invitation, and had asked again what he knew about his neighbour, but the elder Carriere had simply shrugged his shoulders and said that tradesmen had no right to pry into the affairs of others unless their credit was suspect, and that as far as he knew, Gaspard Gruiller had no significant debts.

When Armand knocked he was promptly answered, and Gruiller took them through his house to the side door which was the entrance to the garden. The rooms through which they passed were well-furnished, the quality of the rugs and wall-hangings suggesting that Gruiller was not a poor man, but there was no clue to his occupation. They did not linger in the house, passing rapidly into the garden.

As they came through the garden door such a sight met their eyes that Philippe drew in his breath very sharply, and Armand released a gasp of surprise.

As they had already discovered, the centre-piece of the garden was a rectangular trellis-work erection, which formed a kind of tunnel, arching over a path which led from the doorway of the house to the open space at the garden's further end. This tunnel now extended before them, so that they saw it from the inside. It had many open spaces like small windows in the top and the sides, and because the sun was high in the sky the ones set in the roof were admitting distinct shafts of sunlight slanted from the south, which made a pattern on the paving stones beneath the bower, as if to mark out a series of stepping stones.

There were no green leaves or coloured flowers inside the tunnel. Its walls were matted with dangling tendrils, which were white or pale pink in colour. The great majority of these tendrils lay limp and still, though some trembled even though they were not busy. The minority, however, had a most curious occupation, for they were wrapped tightly around the still corpses of birds, writhing ceaselessly as they played with their prey and passed the shrivelling bodies slowly along the wall.

While they watched, Philippe and Armand saw a tiny bird come from without to perch upon the rim of one of the windows, peering into the tunnel with evident curiosity, as though wondering whether it had somehow stumbled upon a paradise of edible worms. But then it began fluttering its wings in panic, trying to launch itself back into the air, as it became aware that its tiny feet had been caught and held. Within thirty seconds the tendrils had pulled their victim inside, away from the window, and were dragging it across the inner face of the tunnel.

Its struggles were short-lived, though Philippe could not tell precisely how it had been killed.

Gruiller said nothing at first, but simply watched his guests, smiling at their confusion. Eventually, he said: 'I know that you have not seen their like before, my friends. There is nothing like this in any other garden in Parravon. But this is not a pretty sight, and I am sure that you would prefer to look at the lovely flowers.'

He led the two youths to the outside of the bower, where they could see the woody trunks of the climbing plants embedded in the soil, and the pale green leaves which surrounded the huge blossoms. The nearest flowers grew just above head height, and there was little foliage close to the ground because that part of the bower never caught the sun at all. The growth was lush, but the pattern of the trellis-work could clearly be seen from without, whereas it had been masked within by the sheer profusion of the clinging tendrils.

There were many birds fluttering about the garden. They were all – as Armand had lately observed from the roof of his house – perfectly ordinary. They wandered aimlessly about, as though they too were visitors invited for a leisurely inspection, come to enjoy the beauty of the blooms. They went unmolested as they perched on the outer stems and branches; only when they alighted by the windows, within reach of the pale tentacles, were they seized and pulled inside, without so much as a cry of alarm.

The flowers, as Armand had reported, were of many different colours, but all of one shape. Each flower was the size of a man's head, shaped like a bell, with a bright waxen style which rather resembled (Philippe could not help but notice) a male sex organ – but there were no stamens gathered around the styles, unless they were confined to the most secret recesses of the bells.

'These flowers are very rare,' Gaspard Gruiller assured them. 'You will not find their like anywhere in Bretonnia, save perhaps for the deepest parts of the wild forests. Nowhere in the world, I think, are so many gathered in any one place, for these plants are usually solitary. The bower is my own design, and I am proud of it – I knew that unusual steps would have to be taken if these beautiful things were to be persuaded to grow in such profusion as this. Perhaps Parravon is the only place in the world where it could be done – where else could one find so very many silly birds?'

Neither of his guests knew how to reply, but this time it was Armand and not Philippe who found his tongue. 'They are very beautiful,' he admitted. He reached up to touch one, and ran his finger around the rim of the bell. Then he touched the tip of the style – which Philippe would have been embarrassed to do, given its shape – but took his hand away suddenly, with a slight start of surprise. He looked at the tip of his finger, where there was a tiny droplet of liquid, red as blood.

'Do not worry,' said Gaspard Gruiller. 'When the flowers are at their best, they produce wonderful nectar.' He reached upwards to another blossom, so that his sleeve fell away from his unusually thin arm, and Philippe was surprised to see that his hand was slightly deformed, and that the fingers were like the claws of a bird. Gruiller did as Armand had done, and brought his finger away from the flower-head with a drop of red liquid on its horny tip. He put the finger to his mouth, licking away the drop with the tip of his tongue.

'It is sweet,' he said. 'Please try it. It will do you no harm.'

Armand hesitated, but then put out his tongue and touched the liquid to it.

'Oh yes,' he said, with evident surprise. 'Very sweet indeed.'

They both looked at Philippe, inviting him to try the experiment for himself, but he looked away and pretended not to notice.

While this occurred they had been walking along beside the flowered wall, and now they came to the further end of the bower, to the open space which separated the trellis from the hedge. Here there grew in a ragged circle five remarkable things which looked like giant toadstools, each one with a thick chitinous pedestal and a wide cap coloured black and silver. This colour was so odd that Philippe thought at first they might be carved from stone, but when he came closer he saw that they had the proper texture of fungal flesh.

He did not want to touch one merely to make sure, but Armand was not so shy, and placed his hand upon the nearest one.

'It is warm!' he said, in surprise.

'An ugly thing,' said Gruiller, apologetically. 'But not everything rare and precious is beautiful, and these are no more common than my lovely blossoms. They are not so attractive to birds, but they have their own place in the scheme of Nature, as all things have.'

This little speech reminded Philippe of Armand's earlier conviction that Gruiller was known to the followers of the Old Faith, and he wondered if the man might be a druid spellcaster, who cultivated these strange things because of some virtue which they had, but it was not the sort of matter which could be raised in polite conversation, and so he held his tongue.

As Gruiller led them back to the house he said: 'I am sure that you will think my garden odd, and so it is. Perhaps you will think it cruel to raise flowers which feed on birds, but they are very beautiful flowers, are they not? And Parravon has no shortage of birds, as you must certainly agree. There is room in the great wide world for many different gardens, and many different kinds of beauty.'

Afterwards, he watched them as they walked down the path towards the town, but he had gone inside by the time they turned the corner to walk around the foot of the ridge, returning to the house where Armand lived.

PHILIPPE WAS EAGER to discuss what they had seen in Gaspard Gruiller's garden, but Armand was disinclined to accommodate him. It had surprised Philippe to learn that Armand's wild surmise about the fate of the birds which visited the garden was actually correct, and it seemed to him an item of gossip worth spreading (for Gruiller had not asked them to keep silent about what they had seen). Armand, on the other hand, seemed only to desire solitude and the company of his books, so Philippe soon left him alone.

When night fell, Armand closed and locked the shutters of his window as usual, and went to his bed in a state of some exhaustion, having slept so badly of late. This time, however, sleep came very quickly to claim him, and he did not toss and turn at all. He was later to tell Philippe that he believed he had slept dreamlessly for a long while before he was visited by a very dreadful nightmare.

The nightmare began, as had his peculiar dream of some days earlier, with the sound of something attempting to gain admission at his window – first by rapping as though to demand that he open the shutters, and then by tearing at the edge of the wood with clawed fingers.

In the end, Armand explained, his dream-self had risen from the bed and gone to the window, unlocking the shutters and throwing them open. There, hanging upside-down from the eaves like a great bat, was a monstrous creature with brightly-coloured feathered wings and a manlike face with thick, rubbery lips. Its body resembled a plucked bird, the skin all puckered and dappled, and its limbs (of which there were four in addition to the wings) were like the limbs of eagles, scaly and taloned.

This creature snatched at Armand's dream-self, and lifted him as though he weighed hardly anything at all – but this action was not hostile, and almost seemed protective, for as the daemon launched itself into flight it hugged Armand to its bosom as a mother might clutch a child. Fearful of falling, Armand wrapped his arms about the waist of the peculiar creature, as though accepting and returning its embrace. He reported that as they flew he could feel the beating of the great muscles in the daemon's breast, where his face was pressed against the wrinkled skin.

There were, he said, no teats upon that breast at which an infant could suck.

The flight was but a short one, for it took him only to the further end of the ridge, where Gaspard Gruiller's house stood, with the facing window wide open and brightly-lit, as though the tower were a lighthouse for the insidious things which haunted Parravon at night.

Armand was delivered by his carrier into the garden beside the house, and found himself in the space between the end of the bower and the five great toadstools, which did not form a circle – as Armand now perceived them – but a pentacle.

Inside the pentacle stood a creature like the one which had brought him, but bigger by far, standing almost as tall as that strange high hedge. Its vast wings were feathered like the legendary firebird, glowing from within, all glorious in red and gold. Its capacious arms were stretched aloft, with the claws widespread as though to catch the silver light of the bountiful stars. Its slender legs had flattened feet like those of a fowl, so that it could stand upon the ground instead of searching for a perch, as its smaller companions must.

The expression on its face, as it looked at Armand, was paradoxical, for the face – so Armand said – was uglier than he could ever have imagined, with horrid bloodshot eyes and a nose like a huge serrated beak, mounted above a mouth crowded with sharpened teeth.

And yet, said Armand, the gaze of those foul eyes was not predatory but fond; and the black tongue which crawled in serpentine fashion between the cluttered teeth was not licking the outer lips as though in anticipation of a meal, but teasing him with its little motions as a mother might tease her child with friendly grimaces.

When his dream-self had borne this inspection for a few long minutes, Armand felt himself taken up again, and lifted to the roof of the bower where the brightest and the best flowers grew, and he was tenderly placed among them, in the middle of a crowd of perching daemons.

He already knew what to do, and bowed his head immediately to a succulent bloom, taking the central style into his mouth as all the others were doing, sucking greedily at the milk which was within, carefully prepared by the wondrous flowers from the tender flesh of captured birds.

The taste, so Armand said, was sweeter than he ever could have imagined – though his father's table, at which he had feasted throughout his life, had been as well-supplied with sugary delicacies as that of any tradesman in the city of Parravon.

WHEN ARMAND RELATED this dream to Philippe he told him that there had been more, and that his wild adventure must have continued for several hours, but that the rest of it evaded his waking memory, and could not be recalled.

Philippe was more impressed by this dream than he had been by the first which Armand had related. He was almost ready to believe that there was something truly awful about the garden which they had seen, and that Gaspard Gruiller might actually have signed some dire pact with the daemons of Parravon. And yet, he told himself as he listened to Armand's feverish recital, a dream is only a dream, and the shutters at the window had never in fact been opened – nor were there any additional scratches to be seen upon their outer face.

With these doubts in mind, Philippe told Armand that his nightmare, however frightening it may have been, could not be taken seriously as a revelation.

Perhaps, he suggested, the dream had been a kind of release, by which all the anxiety Armand had been storing up had at last been discharged.

Armand dismissed this explanation out of hand.

'There is more,' he said, excitedly, 'for when I woke this morning, and went to my book, I discovered at last the passage for which I have been searching – the passage which helps to explain what manner of things these monstrous flowers are, and what dreadful harm they can do.'

So saying, Armand placed the open book before his friend. But Philippe could not read, and Armand was forced to say aloud what was written there.

'The followers of the Old Faith,' he quoted, 'believe that every living element of the natural world is properly destined for the nourishment of others.

'As the flower feeds the bee which will make honey for the bear, so the leaf feeds the worm which will later take flight as a brightly coloured thing, which will feed the bird which feeds the hawk, which will fall in time to earth, as the bear falls also, to feed the tiny things which crowd the fertile soil, where the roots draw nourishment to feed the flower and the leaf.

'So it is that everything which lives is born from the soil and the sea and the air, and must return in time to soil and sea and air, so that all may be renewed, forever and ever without pause or end.

'But the followers of the Old Faith say also that there is an evil in the world, which seeks to pervert the weave of destiny. There is an evil which alters the flower or the leaf to become the nourishment of daemons, so to spread the seed of Chaos within the world.

'Those who believe this have the following warning to give to the unwary: beware the treasonous beauty of that which is food for daemons, for though it harbours the milk of ecstasy, it promises destruction.'

When he heard this, Philippe Lebel felt a chill in his heart, and for just one moment he saw the world as Armand Carriere saw it: as a peculiar and magical place full of threats and confusions, in which no man could live in comfort and safety.

It was not the kind of world in which he desired to spend the remainder of his days.

'Can you not see,' said Armand, 'that Gruiller keeps his garden for the nourishment of daemons, who fly there by night? I cannot tell whether he is their servant or their master, or what he may have to do with the other horrid things which happen in Parravon by night, but this I know: that

man's soul is not his own, and his garden is a thing so vile
as to terrify the mind of any honest man!'

But Philippe would have none of this. 'Armand,' he said,
truly believing that he was reaching out a helping hand to
save his friend from unworthy fears, 'this is nonsense. The
Old Faith is for gypsies and the ragged men of the forests.
We are of the town, and have better gods to guide us. The
excellent gardeners of Parravon have shown us that the flowers of the wild are there to be tamed, arranged and
regimented to our pleasure. Gaspard Gruiller is but a gardener, after all. He does not seek to make a secret of his
garden, but willingly took us into it to show off his pride in
his achievement. Lay down that book, I beg you, and take up
another, which will teach you the ways of the merchant in
the market and the arts of civilized men.'

Philippe said that his friend looked long and hard at him
then, but said nothing, and finally laid the book aside. They
both went to the window, to stare across the ridge at the
tower-house and the tall dark hedge which surrounded its
garden.

'Did we really play along that ridge when we were children?' asked Philippe, with a small laugh. 'The thorn-bushes
must have been sparser then, for I am sure that we could not
find a way among them now.'

'It was a long time ago,' Armand replied. 'And we were
children then, very different from what we have become.'

EARLY THE NEXT day, Armand's mother came to his room to
search for him, because he had not come to breakfast. She
found the room empty, with the bed in disarray and the
shutters wide open.

She went to the window and looked out, and immediately
saw her son's body, some little distance from the wall, deep
in the bosom of a thorn-bush.

It was not easy to reach the body, and the elder Carriere
had to call upon the assistance of his neighbours to hack a
way through to it. Philippe was one of those who helped
with this dire work, and thus was able to see the corpse of
his friend before it was taken – with great difficulty – from
the bush.

It was plain that Armand had fallen into the bush from a height, and the only sensible hypothesis which could be offered in explanation was that he had undone the shutters of his window during the hours of darkness, climbed up on to the sill, and launched himself from it in a prodigious leap, which had delivered him inevitably to his fate.

The thorns had punctured him in very many places, hard-driven by the force of his fall, and when they had finally pulled him free of the bush they saw that there was hardly an inch of his flesh unmolested.

It was as though he had been ripped and rent by many wicked claws.

When the company returned to the Carriere house Philippe told them all about the dreams which Armand had suffered, and about their visit to Gaspard Gruiller's strange garden.

Because it was the first time he had told the story it was far more confused in the telling than the version which you have just heard, but it would probably have made no difference if every detail had been in its proper place, for these were townsmen and tradespeople, and though they bolted their doors most carefully at night, they were inclined to believe that whatever the dark might hide was no concern of theirs. Nightmares, they agreed, were a sign of madness and folly, and if any more proof were needed that poor Armand had been utterly deranged, one only had to look at the peculiar books which he had chosen to read.

As for Gaspard Gruiller, the elder Carriere and all his friends were unanimous in declaring him a good neighbour. If the plants in his garden captured and devoured birds, that was certainly peculiar, but Parravon had no shortage of birds, and the great majority were a nuisance to other gardeners, so Gruiller's activities must be counted to the public good.

And if any further proof were needed that the gardener was worthy to live among honest tradespeople, there was the universally acknowledged fact that he was a man with no significant debts.

THE TILEAN RAT
by Sandy Mitchell

IT WAS ONE of those Marienburg fogs, the kind you get when the year isn't sure if it's time to be winter yet, and alternates sunshine and drizzle with sharp, dagger frosts. Then at dusk, when the freeze comes, hardening the puddles until they crack underfoot, the mist starts rising from the waterways that flow through the city like blood through its veins.

It always starts slowly, a smooth, even layer above the water, so the ships and the riverboats choking the channels look as if they're floating on clouds, and the hundreds of bridges stitching the isles of the Reikmouth together seem to rise unsupported between them. Then the breeze starts to form ripples in the vapour, sculpting strange shapes that slip away when you look at them. As it rises the turbulence grows, lapping around the pilings of the wharves, then higher still, until it begins to flow gently through the streets like the ghost of the river itself.

Once that happens, the city changes. If you walk the streets then you move like a ghost yourself, wrapped in your own shroud. Torches flare, their light swallowed by the smothering grey, and the voices of the people around you become hushed, huddled close to their speakers for comfort.

None of which mattered to Buttermere Warble. He was comfortably settled in his favourite corner of Esmeralda's Apron, a halfling dive on the edge of the Elven Quarter, working his way steadily through the menu. Right then his biggest problem in life was deciding between walnut soufflé and cherries Bretonnaise for dessert; so when the door banged open, to leave trouble hovering diffidently on the threshold, it took him a moment to notice her.

She didn't look like trouble then, of course, not to the casual eye, but Warble had a nose for it. So he glanced up as she pushed the door closed, snipping off a tendril of fog that had wandered in with her to see what all the noise was about.

There wasn't anything obvious about her he could put his finger on to account for the sudden sense of foreboding he felt then. Elves were a common enough sight in the Apron; it was close to their own part of town, and the food was well worth the detour. There were several in the tavern already, their knees jammed awkwardly under the halfling-sized tables, and at first he thought she was there to meet friends; she stayed close to the door, sweeping her eyes across the room, as though looking for someone.

But the pit of his stomach told him otherwise, so when their eyes met, and she started across the room towards him, he barely felt a flicker of surprise.

The Apron was always crowded at that time of night, so Warble had time for a good, long look at her before she made it to the table. Her clothes were well made, but nondescript: a black leather tabard over a woollen tunic and trews, both green; strong but muddy boots; and a black, heavy cloak. She had pointy ears, green eyes, all the usual features; the only thing that surprised him was her hair, which curled thickly down to her shoulders, and was the colour of a freshly-minted penny.

Redheads were almost unknown among elves; Warble had certainly never seen one before, and if something didn't exist in Marienburg, the saying went, it probably didn't exist anywhere.

'Mr Warble?' Her voice was a warm contralto, like melting syrup. He nodded, and motioned for her to sit. She still towered over him, but at least he could talk to her now without breaking his neck.

'Call me Sam,' he said. Nobody called him Buttermere, except his mother, whose fault it was.

'Sam.' The way she said it was like drowning in chocolate. 'I need help.'

'Everyone does,' he said, deciding on the soufflé. 'It's that kind of world.'

'It is if you come from Feiss Mabdon,' she said bitterly. Warble paused, his arm half raised to signal the waitress, and tilted his head back to look her straight in the eyes. He'd seen the handful of tattered refugees who'd made it to the Wasteland a few months before, picked up in mid-ocean by trading vessels; what news they'd brought had been garbled in the telling as it raced from street to street, but he was sure he was about to hear something that would put him off his meal if he let it.

'Go on,' he said finally, curiosity outweighing his more physical appetites. She paused for a moment, marshalling her thoughts.

Her name was Astra, and most of what she told him matched the story Warble had already pieced together for himself. It was common knowledge that the dark elves had overrun the northern isles of the elven kingdom, and that most of the population of Feiss Mabdon had drowned after taking to the sea, fleeing from the armies marching on their city. What he hadn't been prepared for were her tales of the atrocities committed by the invaders, which had made the near certainty of death in mid-ocean seem infinitely preferable to the wretched refugees. He'd been right, he did lose his appetite.

'So where do you fit into all this?' he asked eventually. 'You seem to have survived, at least.'

'I wasn't there.' Her eyes flashed, bright, cold emeralds boring into his own. 'I was on a trading voyage close to Lustria. When I returned…' She paused. 'You can still see the smoke where the city was. All I can hope is that my family drowned cleanly. Instead of…'

'I'm sorry.' Warble nodded. 'But I still don't see why you've come to me.'

'There's only one thing left, of all that my family once owned. A small statuette of a rat. It's almost worthless in itself, but it's very precious to me.' Her voice dropped. 'I took it with me, to Lustria. But just after we docked here, it was... it was stolen.' Her voice wavered a little, and Warble found himself patting her hand.

'That's tough,' he said. She sniffed, and forced a smile.

'I asked around. Everyone said go to Sam Warble. They said if anyone in Marienburg could find it, it was you.'

The halfling nodded slowly.

'I'll do my best,' he said. 'But I can't promise anything. It's a big city. And I don't come cheap.'

'I can pay.' Her smile became genuine, dazzling, like sunshine bouncing from the harbour on a midwinter morning.

'I charge thirty a day, plus expenses,' he said, expecting her to argue. Astra just nodded, took out a purse that would have choked a troll, and started to count. Warble's thirty crowns barely made a dent in it.

'Trade must be good,' he said.

'Good enough. When can you start?'

'I already have.' He pushed the empty plate aside. 'Where can I find you?'

'The Flying Swan. Do you know it?' Knowing every inn in Marienburg, Warble nodded. 'Ask for me there.'

'Is that where you lost the statue?'

'Yes. I'd spent the day in the market, trading. When I got back, the room had been ransacked.'

'Makes sense,' Warble said. 'Word gets around fast when someone's raking it in. Was anything else missing?'

'No.' Astra shook her head. 'Just the statue. Luckily I'd had my money with me.'

'Can you describe it?' Warble asked. She thought for a moment.

'It's a statuette of a rat, about eighteen inches high.' She held her hand above the tabletop, the palm downwards, to demonstrate. 'It's made of solid brass, so it weighs quite a bit. It's up on its hind legs, wearing armour, and carrying a sword. And it's standing on a piece of red quartz, with its talons clenched to hold it in place.' Her eyes lost their focus, and her voice became dreamy. 'My father bought it in Tilea, years ago, before I was born. I used to play with it as a child. I thought it looked silly.'

Warble nodded. He didn't rate his chances very highly, but he'd do his best.

HE STARTED LOOKING in earnest the next day, and, as he'd expected, he drew a blank. None of the regular fences had anything; he saw enough brass rodents to fill a sewer, but none of them were perched on a red quartz base. He came closest with Old Harald, a decrepit human of indeterminate age, who kept a curio shop down by the Fisherman's Steps. You had to know where it was; in that narrow tangle of streets it was easy to lose your way, and sometimes it seemed the place wasn't there at all when you set out to find it.

'Looking for it too, are you?' he said, once Warble had finished describing the creature for what felt like the two-thousandth time. Harald's eyes flashed blue in the musty-smelling shop, reflecting the light from the candles he'd scattered at random among the tumbled profusion of his stock, and for a moment it was easy to believe the street stories of strange, magical artifacts that sometimes fell into his hands. It was nearly noon outside, but the fog was as thick as ever; the only difference daylight had made was that Warble moved through the streets in a tiny bubble of milk-coloured air, instead of the bruise-purple gloom of the previous night. He tilted his head back to look at the man.

'Who else is asking?' he said. Harald shrugged, wiping a hank of greasy white hair from his eyes.

'You know me, Sam. I'm getting forgetful in my old age.' He sniffed, a droplet of moisture disappearing back up his nose just as Warble had expected it to make a bid for free-dom. 'Business is bad at the moment. Perhaps if I wasn't so worried about things…'

'Yeah, right.' The halfling took out a couple of crowns, spinning them idly on the lid of a nearby chest. Then he wandered over to look at a rust-pitted astrolabe that squeaked on its bearings, and showed constellations unmatched by any stars in the skies over Marienburg. Harald was standing in exactly the same place when he turned back, but the coins had disappeared.

'Bit of a gentleman, he was.' Harald nodded to himself. 'Well dressed, if you see what I mean.' He meant ostentatiously expensive, which was the only benchmark of quality he recognized.

'Can you describe him?' asked Warble. Harald nodded, stroking his chin, which rasped loudly under his fingertips.

'Fairly short. About a head under average, I'd say.' Short for a human was still tall for Warble; he corrected the picture mentally. 'And corpulent. There's a man fond of the good things in life, I remember thinking at the time. Maybe a bit too fond, if you know what I mean. Decidedly corpulent, to tell you the truth.'

Warble thought about it. A little of the unease he'd felt listening to Astra started worming its way to the surface again. Something about her story didn't add up. At the time he'd dismissed it, happy to take her money, but it still didn't taste right. If she'd really been tagged by the guild we don't talk about, why would they knock over her room while she was carrying all that gold around the streets? Besides which, the Swan paid good money to avoid that kind of inconvenience to its guests.

Of course that would explain who the fat man was; if someone was knocking over protected premises, the guild would want to administer a firm rebuke. But he couldn't have looked like a dagger, or Harald would have said, or, more likely, been too scared even to mention him, and anyhow they had better ways of tracking people down than trying to trace them back through their loot.

Stranger and stranger. He decided to let it simmer for a while, and see what boiled away.

'That's all you can tell me?' he asked. Harald nodded.

'He was the only one I spoke to. The little one never said a thing.'

'What little one?' For a moment the old shopkeeper hesitated, visibly debating with himself whether or not to hold out for more money, then he got a good long look at Warble's eyes and decided against it.

'I hardly even saw him, and that's the truth. They came in together, but the fat one did all the talking. The little one just stayed back among the shadows.' His voice took on overtones of desperate sincerity. 'You know my eyes aren't what they were.'

'I know.' Warble nodded sympathetically. 'But you said he was small. Like a halfling, maybe?'

'Could be. Or a child.'

'Or a dwarf?'

Harald shook his head.

'No. I'd have noticed a beard.'

'Fine.' Warble flicked him another coin anyway; it was all on expenses, and Astra could afford it. 'If they come back, you know where to find me.'

THE REST OF his regular contacts came up clean, although a couple of them had also had a visit from the fat man. No one had anything to add to Harald's description of him, except that he paid well for his information. No one else had seen his diminutive sidekick, but that didn't mean much; they could have split up to cover more ground, or he might have stayed outside to cover the door. With the fog still thick enough to burn, he would have been invisible a yard up the street.

Warble started glancing back over his shoulder, and keeping to the centre of the thoroughfares. By this time it was a more than even bet they'd have heard Sam Warble was after the rat too. That gave them an edge; he was a known face around town, while they were strangers. They wouldn't take long to find him, if they wanted to, while Warble didn't even have a name to go on.

No point worrying about it, then. He'd just have to wait for them to make the first move, and in the meantime he could check a couple of sources they didn't have access to.

Gil Roland was his favourite captain of the City Watch. Unusually honest for a man in his position, but not enough to compromise his efficiency, he liked to hang around with lowlifes like Warble who owed him favours and get his goodwill back in liquid form. The Blind Eye was almost opposite the watch headquarters, and attracted a large and faithful clientele of off-duty watchmen and petty hustlers in more or less equal proportions.

The taproom was dark and smoky, the way the customers liked it, and Warble began to relax in the convivial atmosphere. He wove his way through a forest of legs to Gil's usual table and hoisted a couple of tankards onto it. The watchman took the nearest one, and drank deeply, while Warble clambered laboriously onto the bench opposite.

'Thanks, Sam.' He belched. 'Long time no see. What have you been up to?'

'Nothing I want you to know about, captain.'

He laughed.

'Nothing changes. What are you after, then?'

'I just thought it was time to see my old friend, and express a bit of gratitude for the fine job you and your lads are doing in making the city safe for honest folk.'

'Yeah, right.' He drank again. 'Seriously, Sam, if you're in trouble...'

'Nothing I can't handle,' Warble said, remembering the fat man and his friend. 'At least I think so.' His hand went reflexively to the hilt of his dagger. Gil noticed the movement, but said nothing, faint lines appearing between his eyebrows. His florid face moved smoothly forward, his body, clad in the well worn leather jerkin of his trade, tilting with it across the tabletop. The hilt of his sword clanked quietly against the battered wood, and his voice dropped.

'What is it, then?'

'I just want a little information,' Warble said. 'Something's going on...'

'Something I should know about?'

'I don't know. Maybe you can tell me.' Gil began to relax. He knew he wasn't going to get the whole story, but he wasn't stupid. He'd work it out for himself, given the time and a reason to.

'I've been hired to find some stolen property,' Warble told him. 'But the story doesn't quite hang together. And someone else is after the... item.' Gil nodded, without interruption, and Warble began to see why he was so good at his job. 'I just need to know if there's been any trouble at the Flying Swan recently.'

'The Swan?' He shook his head. 'You'd have to be crazy to steal from there.'

'I know. Every latcher in Marienburg knows.' Warble paused. 'But the other interested parties in this are from out of town. Perhaps our putative thief was too.'

'We haven't found anyone floating in the harbour recently.' Gil looked reflective, having answered the obvious question without it needing to be asked.

'And no one's left town since the fog started.'

That went without saying. The watch had closed the gates as a matter of course, and there wasn't a skipper alive willing to put to sea or set off upriver in those conditions. Warble nodded.

'And you've heard nothing about any trouble at the Swan.'

'That's right. I've heard nothing.' The emphasis on the penultimate word was so faint it was almost lost, and all the more eloquent because of it. He finished his drink in a single swallow.

'What about a fat man? Well dressed, well off, might have a child or a halfling in tow.'

'Nothing springs to mind.' Gil shrugged. 'But it's a big city, Sam. We can't be everywhere.' He hesitated. 'Try to remember that.'

AFTER TALKING TO the official face of law and order, the obvious thing to do was spin the coin. So half an hour later Warble found himself standing in the back room of a leather merchant in the prosperous commercial district close to the southern docks. The smell of tanned hides was everywhere, permeating the brickwork, rising from piles of hides and the racks full of the finished products.

He picked up a jacket, soft as the fog, black as a goblin's soul.

'Try it on, Sam. It's your size.'

He put it down slowly and turned.

'Way too expensive,' he said.

Lisette smiled, her teeth a white crescent in the shadows, and slipped her stiletto back up her sleeve. She favoured black, matching her hair, and blending her into the corners of a room.

'What brings you here?' she asked. Her eyes flashed orange in the dim light, hard and predatory. There were stories about her on the streets too, but no one ever repeated them.

'Information,' Warble said. She stepped forward, eyes narrowed, looking down at him.

'Buying or selling?'

'Maybe trade,' he said. Lisette settled slowly onto a bale of cowhide, her right ankle resting on a leather-clad knee, and leaned forward, bringing her face level with his.

'I'm listening,' she said at last.

'There's something going on I don't like.'

'That's your problem.' Her voice was neutral, devoid of inflection. Talking to Lisette always gave Warble the shivers. He tried to match her tone, but halflings aren't really equipped for it.

'Maybe not. You know some people with an... interest in the Flying Swan, don't you?'

'I never discuss my business arrangements.' He knew that already. He didn't even know for sure if she was a member of the guild, let alone as high up in it as he suspected, but he did know from past experience that anything he told her would get back to them.

'I hear one of their guests was turned over the other day.' That scored a hit; her eyes narrowed, just a fraction.

'Who told you that?'

'The guest. I've been hired to recover the missing item.'

'I'll ask about it. What else?'

'A fat man. Also after the item. Hangs out with a child or a halfling, I'm told. One of your... contacts?'

'No.' A faint shake of the head left highlights rippling in her hair. Warble hadn't been expecting a straight answer, and was left floundering for a moment; he'd never seen her so agitated before. That alone was enough to convince him she was telling the truth, and that none of this had anything to do with the guild.

That should have made him feel better, but it didn't. He just kept wondering who could be stupid enough, or powerful enough, not to care about antagonizing them.

* * *

WARBLE HAD JUST turned the corner into Tanner's Alley when the fat man loomed up out of the fog, like a ship in full sail. The halfling spun on his heel, just in time to see a small figure with a big knife slip into the alley behind him. It wore a large floppy hat with a long feather, which effectively hid its face, and a velvet suit sprouting lace in strange directions. It took him a stunned moment to realize the hat was roughly level with his chest, before pulling his own weapon and backing against the nearest wall.

'All right,' he said. 'Who's first? The monkey or the organ grinder?'

To his astonishment the fat man laughed, in a loud, reverberating gurgle, like someone pouring a gallon of syrup into the harbour.

'By all the powers, Mr Warble, you are a fellow of mettle and no mistake. Your reputation seems less than exaggerated, indeed it does. Har har har.'

'Glad to hear it,' he said, keeping the blade up. The little figure to the right chimed in with a nervous, high-pitched giggle, and Warble shifted his weight ready for a kick to the chin. If he took him fast enough…

'Leppo, my dear fellow, please put that away.' The fat man har-hared again, and patted him on the head. 'You're quite spoiling Mr Warble's digestion, and we really can't have that.'

The little figure nodded vigorously, giggled to itself again, and sheathed the knife. Warble hesitated for a moment, then put his own away, sure he could take these clowns if he had to.

'That's much better, har har.' The fat man extended a hand wrapped in a velvet glove, and Warble shook it carefully. It felt like a small, furtive cushion. 'Allow me to introduce myself. Erasmus Ferrara, antiquarian of note, if not notoriety, har har har. My associate and I have been most keen to make your acquaintance.'

'Likewise,' he said. Ferrara nodded, and poured out more treacle.

'Of course, my dear fellow, of course. A man of your sagacity and resource must have become aware of our own interest in the rodent very early on. Almost from the moment of our arrival, perhaps.'

'Perhaps,' Warble said. He didn't like the man; an air of almost palpable decadence hung around him, from his elaborately coiffured hair to the exquisitely worked embroidery of his overstrained shirt. 'And perhaps you'd like to come to the point?'

That was a mistake. He had to ride out another paroxysm of gurgling laughter, echoed for the most part by the tittering of the fat man's tiny companion.

'By Sigmar's hammer, sir, you're a sharp one and no mistake. A man of business, sir, a man after my own heart. No beating about the bush for you, Mr Warble, but straight to the point, sir, straight to the point. Har har har.' Warble began to think about getting him to the point of his dagger. 'The point, Mr Warble, is that we'd like to engage your services.'

'I've already got a client,' he said. Ferrara nodded.

'Of course, my dear fellow, of course you have. The lovely Astra, no doubt. And no doubt she spun you a fine yarn.'

'I can't discuss my clients, or their business,' Warble said. Ferrara chortled for a while, like a pot preparing to boil over.

'Of course not, my dear sir. You're a fellow of principle, and I admire that in a man, indeed I do. But perhaps our interests coincide. Did she tell you what the rodent was worth?'

'A great deal to her,' Warble said. They must have known that much already. Ferrara nodded.

'And suppose I were to offer you an equal share, should the creature fall into your hands before dear Astra seeks you out again?'

'What would I want with half a brass statue?' he asked. The fat man shook his head, tears of laughter squeezing themselves from between his eyelids.

'Brass, my dear fellow. She really told you it was made of brass?' Then he choked on his own hilarity, and couldn't speak again for what seemed like forever.

'Perhaps you'd like to share the joke,' Warble snapped, feeling heartily sick of the pair of them. 'What do you think it's made of?'

The Tilean Rat

'Why, gold, my dear sir, solid gold.' Ferrara finally managed to get himself under control. 'The figure is worth an absolute fortune.'

Suddenly a lot of things started to make sense.

'Tell me about it.'

'Gladly, my dear sir. Gladly.' Ferrara paused for breath. 'But I can only offer you a third of the spoils. Poor Leppo would be most put out.'

The tiny figure bared its teeth and hissed its agreement. Warble nodded.

'Fair enough.'

'The statue was found in the Blighted Marshes of Tilea, close to the city of Miragliano, about four hunded years ago. Unfortunately, before its origins could be determined, the creature was stolen by unknown miscreants. Its whereabouts remained a mystery for centuries.'

'Until now.'

'Quite, my dear sir, quite. About fifteen years ago, in fact, when I stumbled across a reference to it in some old records in Tobaro. I won't bore you with the details, har har, but suffice it to say that I have been energetically pursuing it ever since, from city to city across the face of the known world. And now, it seems, the rat has gone to ground here, in Marienburg.'

'Fascinating,' Warble said. 'And where does Astra fit in to all this?'

'Why, my dear fellow, precisely where you would expect her to.' Ferrara chuckled again. 'My young friend and I are by no means the only ones searching for this reclusive rodent. By now the city would be crawling with our rivals, were it not for this fortuitous fog.'

'I see.' Warble nodded slowly.

'Indeed you do, my dear sir, indeed you do. It's apparent we've given you much to think about. Har har.' Ferrara turned, and took his tiny companion by the hand. 'We'll speak again, sir, when you've had time to consider where your best interests lie. Come, Leppo. Time, I think, to fortify the inner man.'

They vanished as quickly as they'd appeared, leaving a trail of turbulence in the muffling fog. A moment later a faint burst of oleagenous laughter erupted briefly, before fading away towards the Shoemaker's Square.

Warble turned slowly, and made his way thoughtfully back to the Apron.

ENTERING THE FAMILIAR taproom felt like coming home. In a way it was; he'd spent a lot of time there over the years, and knew every pattern of grain in the tabletops. Warble sank into his usual seat with a deep sigh of contentment; simply being able to sit down at a table with his feet still touching the floor, and see over it without asking for a cushion, were luxuries most folk could never fully appreciate. He waved a weary hand for the menu.

'You are looking I think for the rat statue, yah?'

Warble leapt to his feet, twisting aside, and sent the chair flying. The clatter seemed to fill the room in the sudden silence, and he had a brief, embarrassed glimpse of all the faces staring in his direction before his eyes reached the belt buckle of the blond giant standing behind him. After a moment the conversations resumed.

'Sorry. Did I startle you?'

'Just a bit,' Warble said, tucking his dagger away. It wasn't a giant at all, now he came to look at him properly, just a very big human. His build and accent marked him out as a Norse, probably from one of the merchant ships in the harbour. 'What do you know about the rat?'

'I know who has it.' He grinned. 'And who wants it. Tell the lady to meet me tonight, at the sandbar. She knows where.'

'I see.' Warble nodded slowly. 'And that's it? No demands? No threats?'

'What is the need for them?' The grin stretched. 'Either she buys, or the fat man does. An honest trade, yah?'

'Yah,' Warble said.

TO HIS IMMENSE lack of surprise, Astra's room at the Swan showed no signs at all of recent burglary. Like all of them, it was clean, spacious and well-furnished; Warble could have lived for a week on what they charged for a night's lodging. Astra greeted him with a show of fluttering nervousness that might have taken him in the night before, but which seemed to him now to be an obvious and shallow charade.

'Well,' she asked breathlessly. 'Have you got it?'

'Not yet.' Warble hesitated. 'But I may have a line on who does.'

'Who?' She grabbed his arm, her fingers digging painfully into the muscle fibres. Warble twisted free, and stepped back a pace.

'In a minute,' he said. 'First I want some answers.'

'About what?' She regained her self control with a visible effort, and sat down on the bed. Her eyes, level with Warble's now, were wide and ingenuous. 'Look, I'm sorry I got excited. But you know how important it is to me…'

'And to a lot of other people,' Warble said. 'I've been talking to the fat man.'

Her lips drew back from her teeth and she hissed like an angry cat. The halfling stepped back another pace, feeling his blood chill.

'What did he tell you?'

'That the statue's solid gold,' he said. He was in too deep to back out now. 'And that you never had your hands on it either.'

'He's lying. Surely you can see that.' She was forcing herself to remain calm. Her voice was conciliatory, but her fingers were twitching as though they were already embedded in his guts.

'That had crossed my mind,' he admitted. 'But so are you. This inn's protected; nobody steals from it. But you wouldn't have known that, would you?'

'No. You're right.' Astra hesitated. 'The truth is, the rat is valuable. Not as valuable as Ferrara said, but worth a lot to a collector. Both of us have contacts back in Tilea who'd pay through the nose to get their hands on it.'

'Go on,' Warble said. 'You still haven't explained why you came to me.'

'It turned up in Norsca, about six months ago. The owner agreed to meet both of us in Marienburg, and sell to the highest bidder.'

'Let me guess. He just happened to have a fatal accident on the way.' Astra nodded.

'A perfectly genuine one, believe it or not. But the statue disappeared; the ship's captain thought it was worthless and let one of the crew take it when he signed off.'

Warble considered the story. It made perfect sense and he still didn't believe a word of it. He nodded, slowly.

'Suppose I'd gone back to Ferrara?'

'Once he'd got his hands on it, you'd never have made it out of the door.'

That much he did believe. The only thing he was sure of by now was that he wanted nothing more to do with the whole business.

'I've got a message from your sailor,' he said at last. Astra tensed, her eyes fixed on his face.

'I'm listening.'

'Not so fast,' Warble said. 'I don't work for nothing, remember?'

'All right.' Her voice made the frost outside seem positively cosy. 'Let's negotiate. How much do you want?'

'Eight crowns. I told you, I charge for expenses.'

An interesting range of expressions flickered across her face, ending in what looked like genuine amusement.

'Eight crowns.' She excavated them from her purse, like an indulgent adult distributing sweets. 'You're an intriguing fellow, Sam. Why not try to cut yourself in?'

'We had an agreement,' he said.

AT LEAST HE thought they did. His sense of wellbeing, not unmixed with relief at the thought of never seeing any of these people again, lasted no longer than the walk back to the Apron.

He'd barely set foot in the place when Harald leapt up from a table by the door, intercepting him neatly on his way to the bar.

'Is this your idea of a joke? Cheating a poor, harmless old man?' He waved something under the halfling's nose, spluttering incoherently. Warble grabbed it on the third or fourth pass.

'What are you on about now?' he snapped, then got a good, long look at it. It was one of the coins he'd given the old man that morning, the crisp, yellow surface scarred by a deep, silver rut. Sudden understanding punched him in the gut. 'Holy Ranald, that's lead!'

'Absolutely. Counterfeit. And to think of all I've done for you, the times I've...'

'Shut up, Harald.' He spilled the contents of his purse across the nearest tabletop, and pulled his dagger, his hands trembling. An ominous foreboding tightened in the pit of his stomach as he drew the blade across the first coin.

'Lead! The bitch!' The coins rattled and rolled beneath the blade as he stabbed and slashed at them, scarring the wood beneath. Every single one of them was counterfeit. After a while Harald stopped whining, and patted him sorrowfully on the shoulder.

'We've been done, boy. Best just to face it.'

'Not yet we haven't.' By now Warble was riding on a wave of incandescent rage. 'I still know where to find her.' He paused, counting to ten like his mother used to tell him to do. It didn't help. 'And I want you to find someone else for me.'

TRAILING ASTRA FROM the Swan was a snap. The fog seemed denser than ever, and as night fell the thoroughfares faded into shadow-sketched phantoms. Warble felt he could almost have walked alongside her undetected, but an intimate knowledge of the local geography meant he didn't have to. Instead he hung back, doubling through gaps between buildings most folk didn't even know were there, getting close enough to make sure it was still Astra ahead of him once every minute or so. Before long he tasted salt in the air, cutting through the usual city odours of rotting waste and bad cooking.

The sandbar was one of the northernmost points of the city, facing the ocean; as Marienburg grew, commerce had shifted to the larger, more sheltered wharves further upstream, and the older, shallower basins had been allowed to silt up. Now hardly anyone used them, except for the deep-sea fishermen and a handful of smugglers.

As the ill-matched pair moved further into the region of mouldering dereliction and signs of habitation became scarcer, Warble began to move a little more cautiously. He lost sight of Astra several times, but the tapping of her boot-heels gave her position away as effectively as if she'd been blowing a foghorn.

The rustle of his own bare soles against the cobbles was almost inaudible, but he strained his ears anyway; the fog carried sound in strange directions, and the abandoned warehouses around them created peculiar echoes. Several times he stopped dead, listening, convinced he could hear other footsteps, until reason reasserted itself and allowed him to believe it was merely the sound of Astra's progress rebounding from the rotting timber walls.

A moment later, he froze. Astra was talking to someone, out of sight behind a crumbling wall, through the chinks of which a flicker of lamplight was visible. The voices were low, the words inaudible, but the cadence was familiar. After a moment he recognized the tones of the Norse sailor he'd met at the Apron.

Negotiations didn't seem to be going too well. The voices got louder for a moment, then the conversation ended in a single, choked-off scream.

Warble edged forward, his palms tingling, and felt something warm, wet and sticky underfoot.

The old wharf was deserted now, but he could hear the familiar rhythm of Astra's boot-heels receding in the night. The sailor was lying a few feet away, steaming gently, so the halfling picked up the lantern and trotted across to examine him.

One look was enough to make him wish he hadn't. The man was very dead indeed, most of his intestines straggling across the cobbles.

Warble dropped the lantern, which shattered on the ground, and spent an interesting minute or two trying to hold onto his lunch. Then he listened hard, locating the distant footsteps, and set out after the delinquent elf.

He closed on her rapidly, his footfalls padding almost silently, while Astra's grew louder with each successive step. Suddenly she stopped.

Warble froze, certain she'd heard him. But he was wrong. Her voice was raised and for a moment was drowned entirely by a familiar gurgling laugh.

The halfling edged forward again, keeping close to the shadows, feeling a peculiar sense of déjà vu. Gradually the scene ahead began to resolve itself.

The light appeared first, brighter than the sailor's lantern, seeping through the fog like oil in water. Gradually, as he moved closer, it sketched the outline of a derelict warehouse, leaking from the missing planks in the roof and walls. One of the gaps was about head height; Warble flattened himself against the rotting timbers, and peered through it.

The building was well lit, but filthy, hissing torches hanging from brackets in the walls. Strange designs had been daubed on the woodwork in brownish red paint, and an intricately carved wooden chest stood on a raised dais at the far end. At first he thought the stringy things hanging from the beams were ropes of some kind; then he got a good look at them, realized the paint wasn't paint, and this time his last meal won the race to escape before he could catch it. He was in deeper trouble than he'd ever thought possible.

Everyone on the streets had heard stories of a secret temple to Khaine hidden somewhere in the city and, like Warble, had laughed at the absurdity of the idea even as they eyed the shadows with sudden unease. Now he knew the ridiculous rumours were true; but whether he'd survive to tell anyone was in serious doubt. Gripped by a horrified fascination, unable to tear himself away, he watched the drama unfolding within.

Astra and Ferrara were arguing fiercely; encumbered by the statuette, she'd been unable to draw a weapon. Ferrara stood beyond her reach, a cocked crossbow in his hand, while his tiny companion sidled forward to take the rat. He'd discarded the hat, to reveal high, pointed ears embellished with gaudy ribbons.

Under any other circumstances the sight of a clean snotling, let alone one so fancifully dressed, would have astonished Warble; tonight it seemed perfectly reasonable.

'Believe me, dear lady, we've no wish to kill you. Certainly not here, har har, that would really go against the grain, would it not? But you must appreciate, we simply can't allow you to use the stone against us.'

'I'll bathe in your blood, Ferrara. I'll make your death seem an eternity of torment.' The words hissed from her hate-contorted visage, so strangled by rage they were barely coherent.

Ferrara laughed.

'Why, my dear Astra. I never knew you cared.' He blew her an exaggerated kiss. 'And they say the witch elves have no sense of fun.'

Screaming with a berserker's fury, Astra sprang forward, swinging the statuette like a club. It struck the little snotling on the side of the head. With a sickening crunch of shattered bone, the diminutive catamite flew across the floor of the temple.

'Leppo!' Ferrara fired as he screamed, the bolt catching Astra in mid-charge. She spun with the impact, the fletchings protruding from her chest, and staggered towards the altar. Ferrara flung the weapon after her and ran to the inert body of his companion. Large, greasy tears were running down his face as he cradled the tiny form. 'You've killed him!'

Astra said nothing, weaving from side to side as though drunk, intent only on reaching her goal. A few paces from it she began chanting, then swung the statue by the head to shatter the red stone against the surface of the altar.

Ferrara was chanting too by now, his face suffused with gleeful malice, and the thunderstorm tension of magic began to crackle in the air.

It was then that Warble became aware of the scuffling of footsteps around him in the fog, and rolled for cover into the shadows. Faint figures loomed in the mist, running for the building, their outlines distorted by the enveloping vapours. At least, that's what Warble preferred to think. From the direction of the main doors came the clash of weapons, and the incohate shrieking of damned souls locked in mortal combat. Of course, he thought numbly, neither antagonist would have gone to the temple alone.

Mrs Warble hadn't raised any stupid kids, apart from his brother Tinfang, who was dead; Warble was up and running as soon as the coast was clear. Propelled by blind panic, he never noticed what direction he was taking, just so long as it was away from the warehouse, and had only the vaguest idea of how long it was before he collided with something warm and yielding that swore at him.

'Sam! In here!' Lisette dragged him into a side alley, an instant before the night erupted around them. An eldritch glow suffused the darkness, punching through the muffling fog, and a demented howling rose to tear at the very roots of his sanity.

'What the hell's going on?' he demanded.

'I thought you might need some help.' Lisette held out a small flask. Warble gulped at it, finding a Bretonnian brandy that should really have been savoured under happier circumstances. 'I made some enquiries. Your lady friend was lying about a theft from the Swan.'

'I know,' he said. 'Thanks for the drink.'

'Pay me back later. So I had her followed, and asked some more questions. She's a dark elf.'

'I know that too. That's a temple of Khaine back there.'

'Really?' Her eyebrow twitched. 'That explains a lot.' Warble didn't ask what; if she wanted him to know, she'd have told him.

'The whole rat thing was a blind,' he said. 'Everyone was after the base it was mounted on. It's some kind of magic stone.'

'A bloodstone. Someone like your lady friend can use it to summon daemons.' Lisette nodded. 'Go on.'

'The fat man seemed to know what it was. He was trying to stop her from getting her hands on it.'

'He would. There's another cult active in the city. We don't know much about it, but they're just as bad for business. It seems they're in some sort of feud with the Khaine one.'

'They won't be active for much longer,' Warble said. 'They're tearing each other to pieces back there.'

'Good.' Gradually the magical light faded, to be replaced by the familiar red and yellow flicker of leaping flames. 'I think we'll let Captain Roland have the credit for mopping them up.'

'What?' Warble turned, listening to the clatter of approaching footsteps, and when he glanced back she was gone.

'Sam.' Gil appeared at the mouth of the alley a moment later, a squad of his watchmen behind him. Harald was somewhere in the middle of the group, clutching a battered pike from his shop, and puffing energetically. 'We missed you at the Swan. What's happening?'

'It's a long story.' Warble took another pull of Lisette's brandy, and sagged gratefully against the supporting wall. 'And I bet you thirty lead crowns you don't believe a word of it.'

More Warhammer from the Black Library

REALM OF CHAOS
An anthology of Warhammer stories edited by Marc Gascoigne & Andy Jones

'MARKUS WAS CONFUSED; the stranger's words were baffling his pain-numbed mind. "Just who are you, foul spawned deviant?"

'The warrior laughed again, slapping his hands on his knees. "I am called Estebar. My followers know me as the Master of Slaughter. And I have come for your soul."' – **The Faithful Servant**, *by Gav Thorpe*

'THE WOLVES ARE running again. I can haear them panting in the darkness. I race through the forest, trying to outpace them. Behind the wolves I sense another presence, something evil. I am in the place of blood again.' – **Dark Heart**, *by Jonathan Green*

IN THE DARK and gothic world of Warhammer, the ravaging armies of the Ruinous Powers sweep down from the savage north to assail the lands of men. REALM OF CHAOS is a searing collection of a dozen all-action fantasy short stories set in these desperate times.

More Warhammer from the Black Library

LORDS OF VALOUR
An anthology of Warhammer stories edited by Marc Gascoigne & Christian Dunn

'THE GOBLINS SHRIEKED their shrill war cries and charged, only to be met head-on by the vengeful dwarfs. In the confines of the tunnel, the grobi's weight of numbers counted for little. As they turned and fled, Grimli was all for going after them, but Dammaz laid a hand on his shoulder.

'"Our way lies down a different path," the Slayer said.' – *from* **Ancestral Honour** *by Gav Thorpe*

'MOLLENS SNARLED WITH surprise. The hulking Reiklander advanced towards him, his own glistening blade held downwards. With a speed and grace which belied his hefty frame, the Reiklander leapt with a savage howl. Mollens twisted and struck. For one terrible moment the two men gazed helplessly into each other's eyes, then the Reiklander collapsed into the cold mud.' – *from* **The Judas Goat** *by Robert Earl*

FROM THE PAGES of Inferno! magazine, LORDS OF VALOUR is a storming collection of all-action fantasy short stories that follows the never-ending war between the champions of darkness and light.

More Warhammer from the Black Library

The Gotrek & Felix novels
by William King

THE DWARF TROLLSLAYER Gotrek Gurnisson and his long-suffering human companion Felix Jaeger are arguably the most infamous heroes of the Warhammer World. Follow their exploits in these novels from the Black Library.

TROLLSLAYER

TROLLSLAYER IS THE first part of the death saga of Gotrek Gurnisson, as retold by his travelling companion Felix Jaeger. Set in the darkly gothic world of Warhammer, TROLLSLAYER is an episodic novel featuring some of the most extraordinary adventures of this deadly pair of heroes. Monsters, daemons, sorcerers, mutants, orcs, beastmen and worse are to be found as Gotrek strives to achieve a noble death in battle. Felix, of course, only has to survive to tell the tale.

SKAVENSLAYER

THE SECOND GOTREK and Felix adventure – SKAVENSLAYER – is set in the mighty city of Nuln. Seeking to undermine the very fabric of the Empire with their arcane warp-sorcery, the skaven, twisted Chaos rat-men, are at large in the reeking sewers beneath the ancient city. Led by Grey Seer Thanquol, the servants of the Horned Rat are determined to overthrow this bastion of humanity. Against such forces, what possible threat can just two hard-bitten adventurers pose?

DAEMONSLAYER

FOLLOWING THEIR adventures in Nuln, Gotrek and Felix join
an expedition northwards in search of the long-lost dwarf
hall of Karag Dum. Setting forth for the hideous Realms of
Chaos in an experimental dwarf airship, Gotrek and Felix are
sworn to succeed or die in the attempt. But greater and more
sinister energies are coming into play, as a daemonic power
is awoken to fulfil its ancient, deadly promise.

DRAGONSLAYER

IN THE FOURTH instalment in the death-seeking saga of
Gotrek and Felix, the fearless duo find themselves pursued
by the insidious and ruthless skaven-lord, Grey Seer
Thanquol. DRAGONSLAYER sees the fearless Slayer and his
sworn companion back aboard an arcane dwarf airship in a
search for a golden hoard – and its deadly guardian.

BEASTSLAYER

STORM CLOUDS GATHER around the icy city of Praag as the foul
hordes of Chaos lay ruinous siege to northern lands of
Kislev. Will the presence of Gotrek and Felix be enough to
prevent this ancient city from being overwhelmed by the
massed forces of Chaos and their fearsome leader, Arek
Daemonclaw?

VAMPIRESLAYER

AS THE FORCES of Chaos gather in the north to threaten the
Old World, the Slayer Gotrek and his companion Felix are
beset by a new, terrible foe. An evil is forming in darkest
Sylvania which threatens to reach out and tear the heart
from our band of intrepid heroes. The gripping saga of
Gotrek & Felix continues in this epic tale of deadly battle
and soul-rending tragedy.

More Warhammer from the Black Library

DRACHENFELS
A Genevieve novel
by Kim Newman writing as Jack Yeovil

NOW CONRADIN WAS dead. Sieur Jehan was dead. Heinroth was dead. Ueli was dead. And before the night was over, others – maybe all of the party – would be joining them. Genevieve hadn't thought about dying for a long time. Perhaps tonight Drachenfels would finish Chandagnac's Dark Kiss, and push her at last over the border between life and death.

DETLEF SIERCK, the self-proclaimed greatest playwright in the world, has declared that his next production will be a recreation of the end of the Great Enchanter Drachenfels – to be staged at the very site of his death, the Fortress of Drachenfels itself. But the castle's dark walls still hide a terrible and deadly secret which may make the first night of Detlef's masterpiece the last of his life.

Jack Yeovil is a pseudonym for popular sf and horror novelist Kim Newman.